DORM PORN 2

DORM PORN 2

More Steamy Tales
of Boys
on Campus

Edited by Sean Fisher

alyson books
NEW YORK

MANUFACTURED IN THE UNITED STATES OF AMERICA.

THIS TRADE PAPERBACK ORIGINAL IS PUBLISHED BY ALYSON BOOKS,
245 EAST 17TH STREET, NEW YORK, NEW YORK, 10011.
DISTRIBUTION IN THE UNITED KINGDOM BY TURNAROUND PUBLISHER SERVICES LTD.,
UNIT 3, OLYMPIA TRADING ESTATE, COBURG ROAD, WOOD GREEN,
LONDON N22 6TZ ENGLAND.

FIRST EDITION: APRIL 2007

07 08 09 10 11 **a** 10 9 8 7 6 5 4 3 2 1

ISBN 1-59350-015-7
ISBN-13 978-1-59350-015-3

COVER DESIGN BY VICTOR MINGOVITS.

Contents

Introduction

What is it about college and sex? Is it that first taste of free-dom, out of your parents home and ready at last for those years of self-discovery? Guess so, because you guys out there are either having a really great time at college—or you've got a healthy imagination. So, with that said, welcome back to school and another edition of *Dorm Porn*.

So, what's hot this year? Well, judging from the stories here, professors are always in, hiding their libido behind textbooks and reading glasses, and asking you to stay behind for "extra credit." Then there are those muscle-bound jocks who just hap-pen to shower together...and say they don't sneak peeks at their fellow teammates. What about that studly roommate who claims to boff girls and ends up doing you after a night of doing shots? The frat boy who wants to pledge...well, not his love for you, but certainly his lust! They're all here, as are many more gorgeous, sex-craved men, ready, willing, and virile.

So, sit back and relax. There's more than just studying going on at the dorms of Fisher U!

—Sean Fisher

A Work of Art
Lew Bull

I rushed into the art room, late for lectures as usual, to hear the professor's voice droning on about the merits and demerits of figure drawing. It was our first practical class on figure drawing as part of our Art 101 course, and I had overslept.

"Good morning, Mr. Reilly! I know that the elite always arrive late, but it is good of you to join us today," said the professor, giving me a sardonic look while the other students smiled or laughed at my lateness.

"Ladies and gentlemen, as you are well aware, today we are going to see whether we have the makings of a potential Michelangelo in our midst. Today we will have the privilege of having a live model on which you may base your works of art..."

While he carried on explaining to us the value of having a real live model from which to work, my mind wandered into the realms of figure drawing and wondered if this model was going to be some unemployed, voluptuous housewife with mountains of flesh falling over everything, draped on a platform in some unlikely seductive pose. Heaven forbid we should have to have this inflicted upon our young minds!

There was a platform in the center of the room. The students were seated around this with their easels in front of them, drawing paper on the easel and hands at the ready to start trying to interpret our versions of the model, who had not yet appeared.

"...Ladies and gentlemen," continued our professor, "it gives me great pleasure to introduce you to our model today—David."

The door to the professor's private office at the back of the art room opened and a young man of about twenty-one years of age walked into the room, dressed in a bathrobe. Immediately there was a reaction from the entire class—some of the girls gasped at his beauteous good looks, others giggled as they knew that he would have to, sooner or later, shed his bathrobe and their minds were all a flutter wondering what mystery lay underneath the confines of that material. For myself, my jaw dropped and my mouth flew open. I was speechless.

"Ladies and gentlemen, David will be your model for the three-hour period today and to fit in, rather appropriately I think, to the theme of Michelangelo and the fact that our model's name is David, I shall have him pose exactly like Michelangelo's David. Would you mind positioning yourself on the platform, please?"

David moved up onto the platform and disrobed. There was an audible gasp from both myself and the girls in the class. I was seated at the front of the platform, so when he removed his robe, I was blessed with the most magnificent front view of this young man.

Not only did he have good looks, but he also had obviously been working out at a gym and had a body to match. A gentle, warm smile emerged from his face as he became naked to the class, and I thought I caught a slight blush in his cheeks. In fact, I wondered if this was the first time that he had posed nude in front of a group of young people. Our eyes met and I gazed into his ice-blue eyes. I eventually moved my stare from his manly looking face, down the strong neck to his well-formed chest, which was void of hair. Then onto the abs, which flowed perfectly to a soft bush of light brown pubic hair that lay above the area from which a pendulous circumcised cock hung well below his firm balls. On seeing this, I suddenly felt a tingling in my groin and the beginning of an arousal in my jeans. Thank goodness *I* was wearing clothes! Amidst the giggles, sighs and comments that were being made by the students about this well-equipped young man, the professor was trying to regain a sense of decorum in the art room. The students who were seated around the back of the platform and were viewing David's back-view, started to try moving around to the front to see why everyone was reacting in such a way, but they were soon stopped by the professor.

"Come, ladies and gentlemen, it's time to start work and stop fooling around."

The class eventually settled down, and we began trying to capture the image of our David in much the same way that Michelangelo might have done hundreds of years ago. I sat there wondering whether Michelangelo might have gone through the same emotional and physical arousals that I was going through, when he sculptured his David: Or was he immune to these sorts of feelings? I doubt not.

I watched David intently, knowing that I wanted to touch that body, to run my finger tips across his chest—feeling its warmth—down his firm stomach and in particular, I wanted to touch that huge cock. As I watched, although he never moved, I noticed that his eyes focused on me quite often, and on one occasion I thought I saw a twitch of movement in his cock. Suddenly my mind raced. "Please God, don't let this beautiful man get an erection in front of all these people because I know it would embarrass him." Somehow, I think God was listening because throughout the entire time he stood there, as naked as the day he was born, he never got a hard-on, but I sat throughout the three-hour session with one!

I found it very difficult to concentrate on my artwork because my mind kept flitting to sex. I wondered what he might be like in bed, what sort of a kisser he was, especially when I focused on his full lips, and whether I could make a play for him. My mind was in complete turmoil, not to mention my throbbing cock.

I sat there studying David's nakedness, realizing that he was without disguise and wondering why he was doing this—nude modeling, I mean. Maybe his nakedness was not an expression of his own feelings, but rather a sign of his submission to the professor's feelings or demands. In a sense, a loss of mystery had occurred. David was naked for all to see and we became aware of every flaw that he might possess, although in my eyes, I did not see any. I remember once reading that the artist Albrecht Dürer believed that the ideal nude ought to be constructed by taking the face of one body, the torso of another, the legs of a third—and so on. But in David's case, I don't think we would have to borrow from anyone because he seemed to possess all the right assets.

As my pencil drew the outlines of his body, it felt as if I was caressing the paper on which my drawing was being done. Each line and stroke felt as if I was personally stroking David's body, and the more I concentrated on his physical features, the more I felt my arousal. In fact, my erection was becoming a little uncomfortable in my tight jeans, so I had to stand every now and again to surreptitiously try to adjust myself.

***

After three hours of hard work, if you'll excuse the pun, David picked up his bathrobe and left the platform for the professor's office, obviously to get dressed.

"That will be all for today, ladies and gentlemen. I think that you've all done some good work. You may pack up and leave."

Everyone applauded David for his stamina, having to endure our stares for three hours, and the students started to pack away and drift off to other classes or wherever they were headed. I didn't want to leave, so I took my time packing away. The professor went into his office and closed the door behind him. I could hear them talking quietly in the office as the last of the students drifted out of the art room.

Once I had packed my things away, I walked quietly up to the Professor's office door to listen to what might be being said. I didn't hear any talking, but I did hear a sudden low groan come from behind the office door. I bent down to see if I could see anything through the key hole, and to my surprise, I saw David sprawled on his back across the professor's desk, without his bathrobe and with the professor's mouth wrapped around his cock. I immediately started rubbing my crotch as I watched them, and as I watched the professor's mouth work up the length of David's cock, I could see how huge it had grown now that he had a hard-on. I could see David run his hand over the professor's crotch and I could see that he was saying something to him, but I couldn't make out what was being said. Suddenly, the professor pulled his head away from David's cock and disappeared out of sight. I kept posted at the keyhole waiting to see what was going to happen next. After what seemed like an eternity, the professor reappeared in the frame of the keyhole, but this time I saw that he too was naked. He ran both his hands over David's torso, caressing it lightly, as I lightly caressed my own swollen cock inside my jeans.

The keyhole formed the frame to the picture that was being "painted" on the desk in the professor's office. I saw how the professor climbed onto the desk and positioned his own cock over David's mouth while David's cock was being swallowed. After a short while, I saw the professor adjust his position and remove his mouth from David's cock. He disappeared for a moment and then reappeared, and I saw him place a condom over the full length of David's swollen cock. The next picture that emerged was seeing the professor slowly lowering himself over David's enormous length and impaling himself right down to the base of David's cock. The sounds that emerged from the office had been raised in volume as I witnessed the professor riding the full length of David's bargepole. By this time, my own cock had been pulled from my jeans, and I had been working furiously on it, getting myself closer to the edge of no return, when I heard a gasp and saw David thrust his pelvis upwards as he shot his load into the professor. Simultaneously, the professor erupted onto David's chest and I erupted onto the floor. As I did so, I lost my balance and crashed against the office door. Realizing what I had done, I zipped up my jeans, grabbed my art equipment and fled from the art room.

Three days later, David arrived again at the art class, stripped, and stood in front of us so that we could continue with our art. Our eyes met yet again, but this time mine had a knowing glint to them. I smiled at him and gave him a wink. He blushed slightly and returned the smile. My groin began to ache again, just as it had done the first day I set eyes on him. I tried to concentrate on my work, but found the going difficult.

For three hours I worked on David's contours, adding definition and an extra couple of inches to his dick. As I worked on my art, I smiled to myself as his form took shape on my paper. Just then the professor came up to where I was and looked at my artistic effort.

"Do you really think this looks accurate, Mr. Reilly?"

"That depends on what you are looking at, sir."

"Don't you think this is a little exaggerated," he said, pointing to David's dick on the paper.

"I'm sure when it's hard, it could be about that length," I replied, giving an impish grin as I said it.

Realizing that he wasn't going to get much more out of me, the professor wandered off to one of the other students. I could see that David was curious to see what I had drawn, but was obviously unable to leave his position to come and see for himself.

The professor's voice boomed over the gentle chatter amongst some of the students, telling us that the class was over and that it was time to pack up and go on our various ways. As David left the platform to return to the professor's office, he smiled at me, returning a wink. I wasn't quite sure what this meant, but decided once again to take my time in packing up. The professor went into his office and closed the door behind him. The rest of the class departed, leaving me in the quietude of the room.

I packed everything of mine together and crept over to the keyhole that had become my voyeuristic frame. I peered through but this time I saw David sitting up against the table facing the keyhole, with his legs apart, playing with his dick. I tried to see if I could see his face and when I was successful, I saw him looking straight at the keyhole and suddenly he winked.

"Oh my God, he knows I'm watching him," I thought to myself. I froze, not quite knowing whether to flee, or stay and watch; however, the better part of me said stay, so I did.

The naked professor knelt in front of David and, although his back was to me and I couldn't see David's dick anymore, I could see from the professor's head movement, that he was giving David a well-earned blowjob.

I was beginning to become uncomfortable, crouched on my haunches and peering through the keyhole, so I adjusted my position, and in doing so, I sneezed. No sooner had I realized it, when the office door flew open and a naked professor stood in the doorway.

"What's going on here?" he demanded.

I looked up at him from the floor, feeling very embarrassed, but replied, "I might ask the same thing, Prof."

"Get in here immediately!"

I rose to my feet and entered the office rather sheepishly, but when David and I caught each other's eye, we merely smiled at each other, knowing in our own minds what was going to happen. The professor seemed a little lost for words and tried as best he could to replace his clothes.

"Why bother with those, Prof," I said, crossing to him and grabbing his rigid cock and squeezing it. "I'm sure that we can all please each other here, don't you?" I winked at David as I said it, hoping that he would play along with my plan.

"And what did you have in mind, Mr. Reilly?"

"Well obviously you find David attractive, or you wouldn't have been glued to his cock, and I find both of you attractive, so I was wondering whether you would be keen to have a threesome!"

David's eyes lit up on hearing this. "I certainly don't have an objection to that," he said, leaping from the professor's desk. "What do you say, Prof?"

The professor eyed me, deep in thought, then looked at the beautiful body of David's and realized that if he didn't go through with the idea, he was probably going to lose David—well at least while I was also in the room. Before he had a chance to reply, David took control of the situation.

"Hop onto the desk, Prof," said David, guiding him onto the desk and pushing him into a prone position. "Tell me, little artist, what's your name?"

"Chad," I replied.

"Well, Chad, now's your chance to eat your professor's dick, and if you want to pass your exams, you'd better make it a good meal," said David, motioning me to move in between the professor's splayed legs.

I stripped off my clothes as fast as I could and stood in the office just as naked as the other two men. Both David and the professor stared at my body, which—if I say so myself—was in pretty good shape.

"I like what I see," said David. "Maybe you should get him to model for you Prof!"

"Maybe you've got a point there, David."

I moved in and lowered my mouth over the head of the professor's cock, running my tongue around the tip and then slowly sinking my mouth over his length until I felt my chin rub against his balls. The professor growled softly as I manipulated my tongue and mouth over his cock, which was a good length, but not nearly as long as David's. David, in the meantime, had moved to the other end of the desk and was feeding his nine inches into the professor's gaping mouth, thrusting deeply into the waiting throat.

After a while, I raised my head from the professor's cock and, looking at David, said, "I want that cock of yours in me. I want you to fuck me with that bargepole, please."

David smiled and said, "Only with pleasure." Moving to

where I was standing, he knelt behind me and started to rim my pucker. Feeling David's tongue dart into my waiting ass was driving me crazy and I wanted him in me; I wanted all nine inches firmly embedded in my warm, caressing chute. As David worked on me, getting my ass ready for his attack, I busied myself on the professor's cock, sliding it in and out of my mouth.

David pulled a condom from his jeans on the floor and slipped it over his engorged cock. I then felt the tip of his cock press against my opening and I anticipated his thrust, but he was gentle, and slowly slid into me allowing me to get used to his length and girth. Once he entered my chute, it felt like heaven as he slid slowly at first and then sped up a little more. As David began to pound my ass, so the thrusting movement forced me deeper onto the professor's cock. I could feel that he was getting closer, but then so was I. David's actions were driving me to the brink of no return and I was battling to hold on.

"I'm gonna come!" I shouted, firing my load onto the office floor.

As I shot my first load, so the professor groaned and I felt his warm cum shoot into my mouth as I swallowed as fast as I could to be ready for the next load.

My ass muscles clamped around David's swollen cock securely embedded in me, and I felt him give a deep thrust that nearly made me keel over as I felt his warmth shooting into my gut. A warm glowing feeling came over me as he pounded his last drops into my body and let his soft caressing hands run over my body. As I raised my head from the professor's cock and stood up straight, so David held firmly onto my waist, keeping his still swollen cock firmly safe in my ass.

"I don't want to leave you," he whispered in my ear, thrusting his cock into me as he said it.

"You don't have to," I replied, putting my arms around my back, holding onto his waist, and pulling him further into me. "I still have a drawing to finish, and I'm sure it'll take me a long time to get it finished perfectly, won't it Prof?"

The professor smiled at both of us, knowing that there would be many more "portrait sittings" between the three of us in the days—maybe years—to come.

The weeks that followed proved entertaining to all three of us; the professor and I saw each other on a fairly regular basis to discuss art and other matters pertaining to artistic creativity. Twice a week we had a practical class at which David modeled. The only problem was that now every time David came to class to model, he had to be draped in something because whenever our eyes met, he would start getting a hard-on and that would embarrass him in front of the others in the class. Of course, whenever David was in the class for a practical lesson, the professor and I would always look after David's needs when the lesson was over; the two artists taking particular care to keep the model looking fit and beautiful, and ensuring that every working inch of his body functioned to perfection at all times.

I still wonder to this day whether Michelangelo and his David went through the same passages of manhood as my David and I did, but we'll never know.

The Writing Tutor

L. J. Longo

After a day of crossing out commas, scratching "likes," and italicizing titles, the other tutors in the writing lab had gone, leaving the small conference room quieter than it had been all day. Going back to my dorm and my idiot floor mates meant braving the battle between Bon Jovi and the Black Eyed Peas, so I stayed behind, curled quietly in the corner of the couch, reading for my favorite class, World Mythologies. Besides, I was still recovering from a sorority girl's paper on the external benefits of toothpaste; I needed some time alone.

When the door to the lab opened, I didn't look away from the mythology. "We closed at six."

"Hey man, are you a tutor?"

I looked up, trying to appear aggressively annoyed. My glasses sat low on my nose, and I peered at him over the rim accidentally. My resolve weakened when I saw the man. It was September but he was still in athletes' shorts and a T-shirt, one of those boys that can show off their bodies all year long. He had a skateboard in one hand and a paper in the other. His eyes, darker brown in contrast to his sandy dreadlocks, pleaded with me to salvage his assignment.

Apparently, I hadn't mastered the evil librarian look. The tanned face broke into a smile. "Yeah, it's kinda obvious that you're a word nerd."

Any legitimate argument—and I didn't have one—fell away when he dropped onto the couch next to me and forced his paper into my view. "Please, it's due tomorrow and this guy is really tough on grammar."

Every muscle in my skinny body tensed at his nearness, smelling the spicy tang of his sweat. My nervousness was a good enough excuse for me to send the jock away, but I noticed his title: Homosexuality in Greek Mythology. "This is for Kinsella?"

11

"Yeah, you've had him?" His eyes darted down to the book in my lap.

"I have this class. You must be in the section after mine," I settled my glasses firmly on my nose, about to abuse this co-incidence in order to get him to leave. I read the title again and then looked at the man sitting on the couch next to me, biting his firm full lips from desperation.

My resolve crumbled, "You know, a paper about gay myths really needs a snappier title. It's an insult to the orientation."

The jock visibly relaxed when I took the five slivers of pa-per, as if in those few pages he had shrugged the weight of the world from his shoulders. Newly casual, his arm slung around onto the couch behind us, and he leaned closer to look at the title. He was looking into my face though when he asked, "Any suggestions?"

I glanced back at him about to suggest we move to a table. My eyes tripped along the path of muscle leading from his el-bow to his face, and my tongue stumbled. "I might have a few once I get to the end of the paper."

The name on the paper was Joshua, and the writing wasn't excruciating. True, he would not have been able to tell his com-mas from his colon, and his paragraphs were as scattered and rumbled as his coiled dreadlocks, but he had intelligent argu-ments. He knew the myths. I thought the title should be "Pat-roclus: Achilles' Cousin, Only His Cousin, Absolutely, Without Doubt, No More Than His Cousin...Maybe," but in the end Josh shortened it to "Achilles' Cousin and Lover."

When we finished it was an hour past closing time. His smile served as adequate wage, "It's really cool of you to stay af-ter like this."

I wondered about the sly glances he'd given me and his choice in paper topic. I took a risk, "Yeah, well, I have a vested interest in the topic."

Josh seemed surprised, "So, you're gay?"

I panicked, "Well, pretty much. I mean, it's not like...I guess it's just an assignment for you, but uh..."

"No, actually," He interrupted my mild hysteria with intense calmness. "I have...a vested interest too."

"Oh good, I was hoping that you were..." I realized what I was saying. "Um..."

Josh chuckled, amused by my shyness. "You wanna come over to my room? Hang out for a bit?"

I pushed my glasses higher on my nose as I nodded, too eager. "Sure."

He stood and casually slung his backpack over his shoulder. I tried to mimic his casualness, gathering my books. "Um... There's only two things I insist on: condoms and lube."

The backpack stumbled off his shoulder as he turned. "What?"

I clamped my teeth together, wondering why I was socially inept. "Oh...you actually meant to hang out."

"Well, I was hoping...but," Josh noticed my chagrin and stepped closer, settling his hands on the narrow waist of my jeans. "I wasn't sure what you were thinking."

At that moment, I was thinking about how easily his hands slid into my back pockets. I tried to separate his blatant sexuality from his flexible words. His fingers squeezed inside my jeans and I stopped trying, pressing closer against his chest and broad shoulders.

I was vaguely aware of the row of floor to ceiling windows framing the writing center and the mild pornography beginning to play inside. I was about to draw his attention to our exhibition when he kissed me.

The wet openness of the kiss scandalized me and I wasn't certain I liked it, until his hands squeezed tighter and I groaned parting my teeth, adding my own tongue to the moment. I gulped the scent of his body and tasted something minty in his mouth.

It was my fault we ended up on the couch. I tripped on my own weaknesses and fell. I sat down, forcing him to follow. His lips only moved from mine to laugh. He pushed me deeper into the stale popcorn smell of the cushions, and his waist sank between my raised knee and the leg that was falling off the edge of the couch. My knee crawled up his back and his hand traveled up my shirt exposing my flesh to the cool air in the lab.

Our kissing pushed my glasses above my eyes and when I tossed my head back to settle them again, I realized that I couldn't see through them anyway; his hot breath had clouded the lenses. Not being able to see the window and our potential audience worried me and I pushed him away as gently as I could. "So...uh...how far away was your dorm again?"

He grinned broadly.

***

Josh lived in one of the new apartments, which was considerably different than a dorm. For one thing, he had a roommate.

"Don't worry, man. Rich has a class at seven and he always eats dinner on campus. He won't come back."

I had never been in one of the new apartments before, and I wasn't certain how roommates worked these things out, so I just nodded and followed him into the bedroom. The room was small, stuffed with old clothes and two bunk beds. The bottom bunks had been removed from each bed so that a desk and dresser could be placed under the bed. Josh and his roommate had both thumb-tacked cheap bed sheets to the ceiling around their beds. The hanging sheets faintly reminded me of an Egyptian shrine. It seemed out of place next to gym socks.

While I was staring at the unmade bed, Josh put his hands on my shoulder and began to kiss my neck. I tensed from surprise, jolting as if it was the first time his mouth had touched my skin. He found my response amusing and his hands sank around my body, crossing over my chest. His lips continued plucking the muscles in my neck, until I had none left, and my head sagged back to his shoulder.

He reached his hands under my shirt, pulling his hands from my waist to my chest. His deconstructing fingers moved through the grooves in my muscles like he was forging something new from my bones, discovering something beautiful beneath my flesh.

My shirt hissed over my head and Josh returned, turning me around to face him. I laced my arms around his shoulders and lifted my mouth to his. He bit the side of my mouth playfully and his fingers itched down my bare spine and sank into my boxers. His fingers traced a line to the front of my body and his thumbs clamped on the button of my jeans. He rotated his pelvis against mine until I swayed and lost my balance, holding to this pillar of a man for support. His voice transformed into something smooth and sensual, "You know, for a word nerd, you're really sexy."

I smirked, amused and distracted. I couldn't remember how to speak, just went on filling my fingers with his shoulders and bunching his T-shirt in between my hands. I drifted outside of myself, centered only on the part of my bicep where his lips were pressing, until my jeans fell to the floor.

Nervous, I stood before him in only my shorts. When I dressed that morning, I didn't think anyone would be seeing my choice in underwear for that day, and I wore boxers that I had received as a joke. Little bastardized versions of Japanese deities flew around the pink and white cotton stretched over my ass. The tent in my shorts actually made the Fox stretch towards Josh's heavier body. He smirked. "Is that anime?"

"Actually, a...sort of, it's the Celestial Bureaucracy."

"What?"

"The Greeks had the Parthenon; the Norse had an Aesir; the Chinese had a Celestial Bureaucracy," I noticed the inappropriateness of my mini-lecture and chuckled. "Imagine getting into heaven when you have to sign forms in triplicate..."

He looped his thumbs beneath the elastic of my shorts. "Or I could just remove the Celestial Bureaucracy."

I choked on my nervousness as my last bit of relevant clothing slipped to my ankles. I was still bound by my jeans, not that I was going anywhere. I felt like Ganymedes standing before Zeus, a mortal paralyzed by fear, lust, and awe of a god. I wondered what this other man could possibly see in me.

Josh gripped my thighs until it felt like the only thing keeping his fingers from sinking in between my muscle and bone was the flimsy layer of my skin. My legs felt unsupported when he released me. "Climb up there."

I scaled the ladder next to the bed and sat at the edge resting my hands in my lap, watching him peel the shirt off his body. Half of my mouth twisted into a smile as the tight muscle of his chest glinted into my view. He noticed and immodestly ran his fingers across his abdomen. I felt my groin jump in response and glanced to the floor, suddenly embarrassed to look at the man undressing. His running shorts landed on top of my rejected jeans.

Josh sounded upset. "Guess I'm too ugly to look at, huh?"

"No! You're really hot. I just..." My eyes jolted up, stumbling on his hanging erection and struggling to get to his face. I saw his smug grin and remembered that he didn't know what insecurity felt like. I wondered if there was enough blood in my body to fuel my erection and flame my cheeks, "Oh, I thought you were serious."

He laughed and laid his head in my lap. He was still laughing at me, but I wasn't concerned anymore. I couldn't think of much besides that nose nuzzled against my stomach and the tongue tracing a maze over my erection. I moaned at the contact and squeezed his shoulders harder. I shivered when he pressed the lightest of kisses against my burning flesh.

Josh pulled away, leaving me gasping for more. I sat gawking at him, misunderstanding his gesture when he lifted his hands to my face and pinched my glasses away, setting them on the headboard. Blinded, I clutched the sheets of his bed.

He swung his body onto the top bunk gracefully. When he sat next to me, his legs dangled miles longer than mine. His mouth found my neck as he pushed me down to the pillow, my legs spreading in worshipful obedience around his thicker waist. His lips moved to my mouth, kissing like he was breathing new life into my body. His hands clasped my thighs tight as armor against his legs. When he rolled his body into the wall, mine followed.

On top of his thighs, I was acutely aware of my body: knees straddling him, legs spread wide, mouth melting with his, head bowed, a body genuflecting to the creator of my lust. His hands pet down my back, soothing my thighs. The slow caress was an erotic contrast to the speed of his mouth licking, sucking, and nipping my mouth. The obscenity of his lips on mine made me forget the immodesty of our naked erections rubbing together until my knees relaxed into the bed beneath us.

My mouth slipped from his lips to his collarbone when he stretched his arms behind him. His chest expanded as he arched back to reach for something hidden on his headboard. I tilted my eyes up and squinted until I saw the white bottle of lotion and the blue plastic of a condom. He smirked. "I remembered."

I felt all the tension in me spring to my lower body, but I let his touch ease that fear away when he dipped his fingers deep inside me. The chill of the lubricant gave me the same shock that his first minty kiss had inspired. I moaned into the sensation, cooing with a mixture of delight and insecurity. I continued to mouth his skin, sighing into the sweetly, sweaty spot where the empty skin of his neck budded into the compact muscle of his shoulders.

His knuckles slipped into me with less effort than I thought it would take. The tips scraped places inside of me that God hadn't meant to put there, creating a fire of forbidden lust that raced through every vein in my body. I clutched his ribs, laying all my weight on his pounding chest and panting into his biceps. He didn't stop until I begged him to replace his well-greased fingers with something harder.

I sat up on my knees when his hands guided me there and I pinched my eyelids until I could see the blur of his hands roll the condom onto his erection. I didn't have much experience, but I could tell that he was larger than anything in my dresser drawer. The head of his erection reminded me of an upside down heart, and I began rocking over his heavy legs, anticipating the feel of that spear inside.

He drew me back down to kiss me, preferring my lips against his as he began to push into my body. I moaned into his throat, accustomed to the fast and hard penetration of his fingers and unsatisfied by the slow, pushing of his thick member. I resisted the urge to throw myself back onto his erection, balling my fists up into his hair and transferring that pent up passion into the kiss. I whimpered when he moved his hands to my thighs but did not pull me onto him faster.

Josh laughed, teasing me, and even in the blurry haze, I could see his grin. He looked as mischievous as Loki in that instant, his mouth wide and his hair wild. I pushed against his hands, forcing the dull throbbing of his body deeper into mine. I kissed his temples.

A wave of pain and pleasure zipped up my spine and gasped out of my mouth when he allowed me to have my way and thrust sharply inside. He lifted his hands to my lower back and pressed me farther down until his entire erection impaled me. His control was amazing and I felt him swaying against my inner walls, ticking against me, purposefully driving me mad. I babbled incoherently and twisted my face down to his shoulder, pushing my nose into his soft skin until the pain in my face echoed the pain of his grip. I probably would have broken my glasses if he had not removed them.

His fingers lightened and his palms rubbed against my thighs and lower back, urging me to rock back and forth with him. I moved slowly at first, just arching at my pelvis and reveling in the stretch and roll of our bodies. I rose to my knees, pressing my face harder against his arm, hearing him groan as I dropped down and deepened his intrusion. I rocked faster, threatening to force him out of my body each time, but tightening my muscles and holding him inside. His pelvis lifted with me, bucking against mine. Our tailbones merged and in a blind panic inspired by the intense pleasure of that union, they thrashed away from each other.

His hands suddenly clenched harder at my back and inside his erection spasmed, trying to erupt but restrained by Josh's own will. He swore at himself, "Fuck."

I laughed in his ear and he forced me to slow down, reining me by his grip on my abdomen. His mouth veiled over mine, sucking away my laughter. He rolled away from the wall, tucking my body neatly beneath him.

This time my body fell into the position, melting like ice in the hands of the sun. I wrapped as much of myself around him, my legs twisting around his waist, my arms gripping at the raw power of his shoulders, my tongue sliding around his ear.

He grunted heavily, heaving into me, melding my pelvis to his. When he thrust into me, my back moved with him. Our arms locked our chests together, but our skin slipped with the sweat pouring out between us. Our bodies slid together, forged by the heat of his hands and united by the passionate lust of two young men.

His hard erection coiled deeper than before, until in my irrational thoughts, I imagined his tip scraping against my spine. My fingers gripped his flesh trying to hold him, when he bent his back separating our torsos and arched away. He pounded deeper, so close that I could feel him tremble.

Josh made sure I came first, playing his fingers over my bursting arousal as if it were his own. I held the flexing muscles of his ass so tightly my fingers went numb. He winced from the force of my grip when I came; a moment of brilliant pain that erupted suddenly, as if spontaneity was the only way to top the intensity of the build up.

His hands slipped away from my aching erection and locked around my hips. I continued rubbing my own organ as he rose to his knees and pulled me harder and harder into him. My entire body slackened into perfect relaxation as he came. He slipped away, the slow burn of the gesture leaving me with an aching emptiness. I was about to resist his abandonment when he gave a sigh as giant as his body and dropped onto me, blanketing my steaming body with the embers of his own slow-burning flesh.

The moment smoldered into ashes, and Josh rolled back to the wall, leaving my body where it was. He huffed out a steamy breath and I reached up on the headboard to find my glasses. Josh was smiling at me when he returned to my vision.

"Boy, am I glad I went to have that paper tutored."

"You should get an A for the effort."

He didn't say anything, just leaned over me and took some tacks out of the ceiling to allow the sheets curtaining around his bed to billow down and hide us from any roommate that might decide to skip class.

Dream Jock
Shannon L. Yarbrough

Through sleepy eyes I see the clock on my nightstand is striking midnight, and there is a cock in my face. I blink and rub my eyes to attempt to clear this illusion that lingers in front of me from deep within my dreamy fantasies, but it won't go away. Underneath the blanket, my own naked cock is already throbbing from a dream I was having of my dorm mate, Ross.

It was a reoccurring dream I've had quite a bit of Ross and I sharing a steamy shower in the community bathroom down the hall. Perfect timing, or not-so-perfect depending on who you are, had allowed me to share the shower quadrant many times with other guys. Those times were never quite as hot as it was in my dreams though. It was unspoken college boy etiquette that you kept your cock toward the wall, you didn't stare too long, and you avoided getting an erection as best you could. Although I had seen Ross semi-nude plenty of times in our room, I had not yet had the pleasure of seeing him standing beneath those shower nozzles outside my mind.

This was our second semester sharing a room together. We lived in Hayden Hall, nicknamed "Gay Den" hall—mostly because of all the hot guys with perfectly sculpted hair and chiseled bodies who lived here. None of them were openly gay that I knew of, but plenty would turn gay after a few beers. I had sucked a few hot cocks of guys who roomed on the second and third floors since I'd lived here. All it took was some constant eye contact and a few nods when you passed each other in the hall coming and going from class. Eventually, someone spoke up or they'd follow you back to your room hoping to get what their sorority girlfriends wouldn't give them.

I had already been here two semesters before Ross moved in. A mutual friend suggested me as a roommate when Ross was moving onto campus and needed a place. It was much easier to suck all the cock I wanted when I had a room to myself. There was always a place to go in case the guy had a roommate of his own, and we couldn't go back to his room. Some of my regular buddies gave up on me once they learned I no longer had a space to myself. A look of disappointment is all that I got out of them now when passing in the hall. No one ever told me I was a good cocksucker, but I knew I was since several guys always came back for more. And the look on their faces told me they missed having my hot mouth between their legs. I definitely missed going down on them too. That is, until Ross moved in.

Ross was a very studious jock-type, a business major who always went to class on time. When he wasn't in class, he was at the gym, the tennis court, or the soccer field. Our mutual friend even introduced us over a game of tennis, which I suck at. Ross took great pleasure in winning, but he wasn't a pompous jock who would continue to rub it in your face off the court. But it wasn't his gamesmanship that made me agree to let him move in. It was his body!

Ross looked a bit like a preppy jock. His brown hair was military buzzed with short-cropped bangs right across the top of his forehead. He was nicely tanned and had a cute moustache that was more like peach fuzz from his lack of ability to grow facial hair. He had probably spent all four years of high school trying to grow what he had now. The lack of facial hair gave him a cute baby face look with his icy blue eyes that made me freeze every time he caught me looking at him. He knew he looked good though, and definitely didn't seem to mind me looking at him.

His arms and legs were covered with a nice blanket of fuzzy brown hair, and his body was the perfect broad hourglass figure with a tiny waist and huge shoulders. Halfway through our tennis match, Ross peels his sweaty polo off. I had already been envisioning him without a shirt. The wet cotton fabric clinging to him left little to my imagination. We pause to take a break and like a scene out of an athletic shoe commercial, or out of a very teasing porno, Ross gulps half a bottle of water, then pours the rest over his head and down his chest. The droplets of water spill across his smooth skin like beads of rain on a sidewalk, falling down over his pecs and abs with only the grooves of muscle to guide them.

His upper arms are defined but still small. You can tell Ross spends more time on his torso and legs. He has colossal pecs with perfectly round dark nipples that are the size of half dollar coins. His six-pack abs are also flawlessly shaped. His chest is smooth, not a single blemish, except for a dark patch of hair right between his pecs and a bit of treasure trail beneath his navel, no thicker than his moustache. I had no second thoughts about sharing a dorm room with him after seeing him shirtless.

So, Ross moves in and I immediately began to wonder if I would ever get him into bed. We had opposite schedules, so I never got to catch him totally naked in the shower or before getting dressed in the morning. He was definitely not like the other typical guys I had hung out with from the dorm before. Ross was courteous, polite, and extremely neat. He never played his music too loud or stayed up late when I was trying to sleep. He often bought groceries for us and offered to help me with homework. He even offered to do my laundry once!

Although I had never approached the subject, I didn't think Ross had a girlfriend. He never brought any friends back to the room, at least not while I was there. I'd lie awake at night just watching him sleep and dreaming about being in his bed with him, but I was too chicken to say anything. By the time the next semester started, I had made up my mind that Ross had no interest in sex whatsoever. All he cared about was doing well in class, going to the gym, and practicing sports. Lucky for me, I was wrong.

Hayden Hall was a year round dorm, which was convenient for those of us who couldn't always make it out of town during long holiday weekends because our families lived miles away. Rather than having to move out at the end of a semester, or find friends to stay with off campus, we could stay right where we were. Ross and I both made plans to hang out together during Thanksgiving weekend because we would both be staying at the dorm. I was excited because I knew just about everyone else in the dorm would be leaving, so Ross and I would be completely alone. I secretly hoped this would give Ross room to open up and let go of any inhibitions. And I was right.

We spent Thanksgiving night at a bar not far off campus. We shared a plate of finger foods, played pool, and had a few too many beers. I even bought us a few rounds of tequila shots hoping it might pay off for me later that night. In the past when Ross and I would hang out with friends, he was always very cautious about his drinking habits. I guess he chose to loosen up tonight since it was a holiday, and we were within walking distance of the dorm. The bar was dead, of course, so we decide to call it a night and stumble back to our room just after ten p.m. to hang out or find something else to do.

Back at the room, I undress and decide to take a shower. Ross collapses on the bed to watch television; I bet he's probably going to fall asleep. Wrapped in my towel, I walk down the hallway to the showers, leaving Ross behind. I hang my towel on the wall while the shower quadrant quickly fills up with steam from the hot water. I step in and stand beneath one of the nozzles with my eyes closed, letting the hot water shoot over me and down my back. I hear the shower curtain rings slide against the rod behind me, the sound of someone else getting in the shower too. I don't even turn to see who it is, and the steam is so thick that I couldn't see them anyway.

"Hey, dude," Ross says, "mind if I join ya?"

"Oh, hey, I figured you fell asleep," I say.

My eyes open wide. I am shocked and elated that Ross is in the shower with me. I pray that he'll step close enough or use the nozzle beside me just so I can catch a glimpse of his cock.

"Nah, I'm too pumped up to sleep. You?"

"Nah, I'm not sleepy at all."

"Man, I feel so good after being at the bar, and I'm so fucking horny. Tequila does that to me, ya know?"

"Oh? Sorry, man. If I had only known," I laugh, but I'm glad now I chose the tequila shots.

"It's okay, man. I need to get laid though."

"Don't we all?"

I agree with him, anxious to see where he's going to go with this sex talk. He goes silent for a few minutes, and just moans a bit from the hot water falling over his body or from enjoying his buzz. It's as if he's forgotten I'm even there. I turn to peek over my shoulder, but he's facing the wall. I hazily get a glimpse of his plump round ass through the fog. I'm so tempted to reach over and give him a gentle slap on the butt, but I decide to wait.

"So, do you know of anyone else still on campus tonight?" Ross finally asks.

I find this question interesting because Ross knows that we live in the only year round dorm on campus. There isn't one for girls that I know of, so there would be no one else around the campus for us to hang out with anyway. And he didn't actually mention "girls" at all.

"Nope, dude, just us. Could be an exchange student or two from upstairs, but I think they might be out partying late. So, I guess it's just you and me tonight."

I worry that the situation might be getting a little awkward, and I don't want to push it. Plus, just being in the shower with Ross like in my dreams has started to give me an erection. I would love to stay in the shower with him, but I decide to leave him with that thought of us having the whole building to ourselves. I step out; towel off, and hurry back to the room. I turn off the lights and get into my bed naked, obsessing over the thought of seeing his cock after he comes back to the room. Ross must have stayed in the shower for quite a while, because I dozed off to sleep while lying there in the dark waiting for him. That's when I woke up to him standing over me.

He has a look of uneasiness on his face from what I can see through the dark thanks to a street lamp shining in the window. It was as if he was afraid he would get caught, but also as if he definitely wanted me to catch him standing there. The light from the window illuminates the outline of his body, presenting a long slender cock just inches from my grasp. From what I could see, it looks like he kept his pubes nicely trimmed, and he had nice low hanging balls. I reach for them quickly before he has a chance to hesitate.

His balls are huge, and the thought of Ross emptying his load across my chest gets me even more excited. I tug on his ball sack, pulling him closer to my face so that I can suck his beautiful cock. It reminds me of what I like to call a "pencil dick." It's long, thin, and very hard with a big mushroom head on the end like an eraser. Ross's cock is so long it even has a bit of a curve to it. I fondle his balls a bit more as I admire his rod, licking my lips for the taste of it.

"Do you want to suck it?" Ross whispers.

"Hell yeah."

Wasting no more time, I lift the head of his cock to my mouth and wrap my lips around it. It's so massive and definitely a mouth full. I slowly begin to engulf the rest of it, testing the waters to see just how much I can swallow. Once I reach the curve of his dick, I feel the head tap the back of my throat. With no gag reflex though, my cock sucking talents come into play because I keep going until my nose touches his stomach. I start taking some deep long strokes, bobbing my head back and forth as I suck his gorgeous cock.

Ross moans and puts his hands on the back of my head to force me down again and again, feeding it to me. I yank it out of my mouth to catch my breath, but Ross wastes no time at all. He collapses on top of me, pushing my blankets down to my ankles to reveal my own throbbing cock from under the sheets. With one gulp, he takes my entire cock into his mouth and begins to suck as hard as he can. Still taking a small break from sucking him, I roll his balls around in my mouth and tease them with my tongue. It drives Ross wild because he begins to suck me even harder. He eases his hands under me and grips my buttocks with his large hands, pushing me toward his mouth to fuck his face. I eventually take his own cock back into my mouth and begin sucking it some more.

My jaws are so sore from sucking his huge dick, but Ross hasn't once given me a hint that he might be tired of sucking me. It had been months since I had sucked any cock at all, so I definitely wasn't ready to call it a night just yet. I decide to give his rod a rest and see just how far Ross might be willing to go. I lean up closer between his legs, propping myself up with a pillow. This gives me ample room to play with his balls and make my way up his crack to his sweet little asshole.

I continue to tease his balls with my tongue and massage his ass with my fingers. I can tell this sends Ross into a fit of ecstasy because he begins to buckle his waist on top of me, pushing his ass closer and closer to my face, as if he was riding a horse. I slide my fingers up the slit of his ass working my fingers from both hands into his smooth crack until I find his tight pucker. I slowly knead it with my thumbs and can feel him flexing his ass muscles as a reaction to the pleasure.

Soon, I begin to test him by slowly pushing a finger inside his hole, fucking him gently with my finger. He lets up on my cock and leans up to straddle me, but he definitely doesn't seem to want me to stop. Ross moans so loudly that I'm definitely glad no one else is left on the floor to hear him. I decide to go full force and push my finger all the way into him, rapidly finger fucking him. Ross begins to moan even louder and bounce up and down to get me to fuck him harder. Instead, I pull my finger out and spread his asscheeks with my hands, exposing his hole to my face. I ram my tongue deep into him, eating his ass as he rides me.

"Oh, dude, I want to get off. I want to get off," he keeps saying.

"Go for it man," I mumble from behind him.

Ross is so overcome with pleasure that he begins to jack himself off while I rim him. He sprays his warm load all down my chest and even onto my cock. He uses his cum as lube to jack me off while my face is still buried into his backside just savoring this hot jock sitting on top of me. I stop just when I'm about to cum. The climax is almost unbearable. I flinch hard, spraying my load into the air and all over Ross.

"Oh yeah, man, give me that load," he says as he rubs my cum all over his chest with one hand while still stroking me with the other.

There would be many more pleasurable nights to "cum" between Ross and me. We ended up in bed with each other at least two or three nights a week from then on. He always wanted me to rim him and told me I was the only person that had ever done that to him. I was actually the first guy he had ever gone this far with. Although he had always wanted to experiment in the past, he had never met anyone he felt comfortable approaching. I thought that was funny because I had wasted two semesters living with him too afraid to approach him about anything. I guess a college guy's dreams really do come true!

Straight Jock's Orgy
Bearmuffin

A buffed dude in cotton briefs makes me so hot. You can imagine my predicament when Chad, my straight dorm roomie, always stripped down to his skivvies when he returned from his workout.

He was always on the cell phone talking to his football buds. I'd watch him from my room, padding back and forth, clad in a pair of clinging white cotton briefs. My eyes would be glued to his magnificent ass. I loved the way his briefs clung tightly to his firm, meaty bubble-butt.

Sometimes, I caught Chad scratching his nuts. He'd even squeeze his meat to create a whopping, eye-popping boner. I smacked my lips when I saw how lewdly it was outlined underneath the almost transparent cotton.

Thankfully, Chad was totally unaware that I was staring at him. But I'd have to go shut the door and beat off. I'd fantasize about having his delicious ass planted firmly on my face, my tongue waggling up his asshole. I'd wrap my lips around his kielbasa and suck it dry until he had spewed a huge man load down my throat.

Chad had a sizzling symmetrical physique, a real jaw dropper. He was Ivy League handsome with brown hair flecked with gold. His eyes were a light pale blue, and they enhanced his dazzling smile. I wanted to kiss his mouth for hours. I'd stick my tongue down his throat, grab his buns-of-steel and hold him tight. Then I'd rub my cock over his amazing, ripped midsection. I wanted to spooge all over those hard-as-steel six-pack abs.

One night, Chad was on the phone again. He always talked for hours, so I decided to watch a porn flick. It was fuckin' hot with three studs going at it full throttle, fucking, sucking and rimming like you wouldn't believe. Five minutes into the flick, I'd already greased my pole. I began fisting it, my eyes glued to the screen.

Suddenly, I felt a load rise inside my balls. I pinched my nipples and moaned, just ready to pop a big one, when Chad came into my room still talking on the phone. He wore a red baseball cap backwards and briefs. The minute he saw me, the phone fell with a resounding thud on the floor. He just stood there, his mouth wide open, his eyes bulging with amazement.

"Fuck, dude!" he gasped. His eyes were riveted to my cock. "That's the biggest piece of meat I've ever seen!"

Chad began watching the porn flick. I said nothing, wondering what the hell he was going to do next. As far as I knew, Chad was totally straight. I never dreamed he was bi.

"Scoot over," he said lying down next to me. "This is so totally awesome!" He continued to watch the movie with keen eyes as the bottom was being topped at both ends by two hot, muscular stud muffins.

When I glanced down at Chad's crotch, I noticed that his cock was jerking inside his briefs. Holy fuck! Was he getting a woody or what? Soon, Chad's hands found their way to his ever-thickening bulge. It wasn't long before he pulled his teeming cock through the pee-flap and began finger blasting.

Chad turned to me, sporting an evil smile. I couldn't keep my eyes off Chad's cock. Teasingly, he slowly stroked his meat. Thick blue veins encircled the shaft, throbbing lustily as his fingers glided slowly up and down, from his fat balls to the blunt tip.

Of course, Chad knew I was staring at him, but he just chuckled. "Go for it, dude," he said, shaking his cock at me. "It's what you want, isn't it?"

I couldn't fucking believe it. But my disbelief soon changed into complete and utter amazement when Chad gently grabbed my head and guided me towards his cock, which now bobbed tantalizingly before my eyes. I brushed my mouth against the head and a salty drop of precum oozed out, smearing my lips with hot jizz.

I hungered for more, so I greedily swallowed his cock, opening wide allowing it to glide smoothly down my throat. "Oh yeah," Chad moaned as his cock swelled inside my mouth, pushing past the roof of my mouth until the head was firmly lodged against the back of my throat. My nose was buried in his pubes, and I inhaled the ripe, musky odor of his manhood.

Chad's silky smooth cock thrilled me. The faster I sucked, the harder I got. Chad fastened his fingers around my pulsing meat. He squeezed it hard. "What a fuckin' stiffy!" he said.

Chad was obviously impressed because the next thing I knew he was licking it. I just lay there stunned as Chad's hot tongue snaked out to run along the sides of my teeming cock-shaft. He polished it from top to bottom. He even planted his sweet lips on the crown, wiping the tip of his tongue in my piss slit, lapping up the juicy precum.

Fuck! This obviously wasn't the first time Chad had sucked cock. No fucking way! The dude was a champion sword-swallower. My eyes were fastened on his hot ass as he blew me. I'd always wanted to play with his ass. Here was my chance. I reached down and began caressing his golden-tanned bubble-butt. My hands glided over the tight mounds so wonderfully sculpted by countless gym workouts.

By now, Chad had my cock all the way down his throat. His chin firmly wedged against my balls, his hot tongue stroked the root. My stiffy swelled between his hallowed cheeks. I ran a hand along the cleft of his ass, which felt all moist and sticky. When I boldly stuck a finger into Chad's crack, he responded by suctioning his sweet lips around the root of my cock.

I probed deeper and deeper until I reached his anal ring. Chad wiggled his butt back and forth. I felt his puckers dilate against my fingertip. It was just too good to resist. So I jabbed a finger right through the hole. It immediately disappeared into his moist anal crack.

Chad's head was flying over my cock now, hot sweat streaking his forehead. His cheeks were hollowed in as he sucked furiously on my cock. I stuck another finger up his ass and then another, until I had three hot fingers strumming inside his hot hole. It was fucking incredible! I was finger-fucking my straight roommate and he was blowing me, too!

I popped my fingers from Chad's ass and licked them clean. Fuck, his ass smelled so good. I just had to rim him. So I spread his mighty cheeks apart and dove inside. My tongue landed right on his anal ring. I began stretching the puckers wider and wider until it snapped open, letting my tongue go right inside.

"YO!" Chad cried, when I jabbed my tongue deeper into his hole. He pushed back with his ass until I was totally smothered by hot stinking butt. He pulled his mouth from my cock and began rimming me too. Fuck, it felt so good to have this straight dude's tongue up my hole. Chad could fuckin' eat butt! He circled his tongue around my puckers for a while until I was screaming with pleasure. He penetrated deeper, twisting his tongue inside my shit chute. Was he going to stick his head up my ass?

Then I pulled off Chad's butt and sucked on his balls. He responded with the same action, slurping noisily over my low-danglers, taking one nut and rolling it around his mouth and then both nuts, humming happily with macho pleasure. When he resumed sucking on my cock, I took Chad's mighty meat into my mouth again and sucked harder and faster. Soon, our heads were flying over each other's hot meat in a wild sixty-nine.

Chad's loud grunts were music to my ears. His nuts ballooned against my chin. They were filled with hot jizz ready to explode! Suddenly, he jammed a finger inside my butt until it banged my prostate. When I reciprocated, he cried out, "Awwwwww, dude. Gonna fuckin' pop my wad!"

Hot jizz surged within my balls. My cock was aflame, granite-hard. I was ready to spooge! "Unngh, unngh, unngh," I gasped. Chad sucked in his cheeks, squeezed the shaft, making my cock explode. My body thrashed uncontrollably as I filled Chad's hot mouth with wad after wad of sizzling man-jizz. Chad grunted as he spewed a torrent of straight stud-jizz into my gagging mouth. His cum wouldn't stop gushing, flooding my mouth, dribbling down my chin.

Chad's cell phone rang so he picked it up. "Dude," he said. "Get your ass over here, pronto! Got a surprise for you!" He hung up and winked at me.

Five minutes later, his buddy arrived. It was Mike, a hot, humpy jock with green eyes, steel-corded arms, plus the dick of death. Mike tossed his baseball cap off and stripped. Thick, rosy nipples capped his flawless pecs. His blond buzz-cut made him look so sinisterly macho. His big balls swung low. My cock bolted at the ten inches of man-meat swinging between Mike's thighs.

"I was horny as hell!" Mike said. He began stroking his cock. "I'm glad I called." You'd think Mike was as straight as they come. But gluing his lips to mine, he blasted his licker down my throat. My hands were running all over Mike's plated biceps as I sucked his hot tongue into my mouth.

While our tongues battled, Chad was kneeling behind his buddy and eating his ass. The faster Chad drilled his probing tongue up Mike's hole the hornier Mike got. Mike grabbed my cock. "Fuck, you weren't shitting me, dude. This fucker's got a primo piece of meat."

Mike was fisting it, churning his fingers all over my pulsing pecker until it was rock-hard. When he rubbed his abs all over my cock, I felt my meat throb angrily against his steel-like six-packs. I was moaning like a whore, in complete and utter ec-stasy. I could have shot another load.

Then Chad pulled his face out of Mike's butt and he climbed on top of me. He reached behind him, spreading his cheeks wide as he lowered his butt right over my face. My mouth snapped open and my tongue pierced his puckers.

"Dude! Eat my hole!" he cried. "YEAH, YEAH, YEAH!!!" He zigzagged his butt across my tongue, throttling his sweet butt over my lips.

Mike scooted behind me and pried my cheeks apart. I felt a cold rush hit my anal-ring. When he licked inside my hole, I moaned like a pig. Fuck, Mike was an ace butt-muncher! He ran his tongue all over my cheeks, inside and out, circling wide at first and then zeroing in on my hole. He buried his snout in my crack, tonguing it hard until it was totally up my shit chute.

Mike's stifled groans blasted against my cheeks. I grunted and shoved my ass against Mike's bouncing face. With a tongue hotter than hell, the dude rimmed the fuckin' daylights out of me. I chewed and chomped on Chad's butt as his brawny thighs closed around my ears. We were the gold medal champions of an olympic rimming marathon.

Then Mike and Chad exchanged places. I pried Mike's sweaty buttocks apart and watched his butt-bud twinkle with lust. He shuddered when I flicked my tongue-tip over his hole, later worming slowly into his ass canal until he was howling with macho pleasure. I was in fucking hog heaven eating straight ass. Chad's face was flush against my butthole, his wriggling tongue working overtime. He snorted and groaned, pushing with all his might against my bobbing ass. Finally, I couldn't bear it any longer. I had to have Chad's cock up my hole. "Fuck me, Chad!" I screamed. "FUCK ME!!!"

"Fuckin' A, dude!" Chad cried as he yanked my legs apart, tossing my calves over his brawny shoulders. His eyes were glittering with lust. I grinned at him. My heart was pounding. I was prepared for the fuck of a lifetime!

Chad smeared some lube on his meat. He grinned wolfishly as he grabbed his cock by the root and rubbed the head all over my twitching hole. I held on to his biceps for support. In a flash, he stabbed his cock inside me, going in for the kill. Mike mashed his hot ass on my face, so my screams of pain were lost inside his hole. When Chad noticed my hard, throbbing cock, he wrapped a hand around it. His hot hand flew over my meat while Mike's wily fingers tugged at my nipples. Fuck! My entire body was exploding with lust. I just lay there in complete and utter ecstasy being worked over by two hot, mega-buffed studs.

I reached up and began fisting Mike's hot cock while he and Chad leaned forward. Their tongues slithered out and joined as one. They deep-throated for hours. Our moans and groans of macho delight filled the room. We must have fucked for hours until we finally had to shoot our loads.

Mike was the first to spew, sending a torrent of salty stud-jizz rushing down my throat. I choked and gagged on Mike's hot sperm as Chad howled a mighty, "Fuckin' A!" and shot one steaming load after another up my ass until his cum dripped and soaked my balls. My cock burst in Mike's hot fist, wild orgasms rocking my body like an earthquake. My hot cum singed his fingers.

I couldn't believe it when Chad's cell phone rang again. He grinned and picked it up. "Yeah, come on over," he said. "Ya gotta meet my roommate!" He hung up and scratched his balls.

"How many friends ya got?" I asked him.

"'Bout twenty," he replied. A shit-eating grin played on his sweet butt-munching lips. Fuck! It was going to be a ball-slapping, dick-pumping, ass-smacking all-nighter in the dorms!

Tight
Michael Roberts

It was a pert ass.

The last thing I needed was a pert ass, especially one encased in tightie whities so tightie and so whitie that they might have been put on directly from the package. The guy these briefs wrapped so closely was on the ladder to the top of the bunk beds. His left foot was a rung higher than the right, and he was smoothing a sheet over the mattress.

The curve of the left buttock was simply breathtaking, leading to the angle of a well-muscled thigh. Through the middle of the shorts, stretched tautly across an enticing array of musculature, I could see faintly the indentation between his cheeks.

I was entranced. He didn't know I was there, and I didn't want to break into his concentration and have him turn around and have the face of a Holstein.

I did not need this ass. Last year, I had gotten involved with a pert ass, so involved that I failed three courses and barely squeaked by three others. The college dean had put me on probation. One of the conditions of that probation was that even though I was an upperclassman, a junior, I would live on campus under the watchful eye of the administration. Life in a college dorm is not conducive to academic excellence—or even academic mediocrity. A mass of over-energetic underclassmen yelling, squealing, and parading around in various stages of undress was not going to help my study habits.

And now it seemed that my sophomore roommate was going to be another pert ass, and I could only hope that he looked like a cow or that he had some feature that was so dreadful it would deflect any sexual interest I might have in him, and I thus might be able to concentrate on my course work and getting out of the collegiate cellar.

"Ahem," I said.

He glanced over his shoulder—his damnably broad shoulder.

Curses. He was lovely. He looked the way you would expect a student at a college in Iowa to look—so fresh and clean cut that I felt like the portrait of Dorian Gray, even though I was only a year or so older and had not led a dissolute life—well, not that dissolute.

"Hi, there," he said in a pleasant baritone that tingled through the hairs on the back of my head and gave me a smile so broad that I thought I might fall in. I could see my control of this situation sprinting away.

Then he climbed off the ladder and turned around and stuck out his hand. "I'm Sam," he said.

His grip was firm without being crushing, and I tried to return it with equal strength as I responded, "I'm Ethan." I did my best not to be obvious as I inspected him. I thought that I had mastered the fine art of checking out someone with reasonable subtlety, but it was difficult not to be pantingly transparent in my examination of my new roommate, for he was quite tastily put together.

He was not wearing an undershirt, and I had an unencumbered view of a chest that indicated hours of manual labor, not hours at a gym. His legs were strong, and the front of his tighties was just as alluring as the back.

"I hope you don't mind that I've taken the top bunk," he said.

"Not at all. I like the bottom." *Damn,* I said to myself, as I watched my exiting restraint go from a sprint to a gallop.

But he appeared not to notice my slip of the tongue and climbed back on the ladder to finish making his bed.

Thus began a semester that seemed destined to be even less successful than the ones that preceded it. I went from the academic cellar to some sort of sub-basement.

Sam's wardrobe in our room was jockey shorts, and he had a limitless supply, always tight, always blindingly white. It was impossible to concentrate as he sat opposite me with his delectable body on display, one leg over a chair arm, accentuating the tantalizing swell of his crotch.

I fled to the library, and when it closed I would stumble home, exhausted, realizing that I had retained not one iota of whatever I had been studying. He was frequently in bed, leaving semicircles of his perfect pert ass in the mattress, seductive in the white second skin, and I would lie in the bunk beneath, waiting for his snore, nearly bursting, so rigid that I was in pain, and often so overheated that I had to spring myself out of my boxers and beat off as quietly as possible, biting into my pillow so that my orgasmic cries wouldn't wake Sam and half of the dormitory.

I didn't know the specifics of his dating. Sometimes he'd return from a night out to say merely that he'd been with this or that woman. He didn't tell me any specifics, but he didn't need to; I'd fill in the lurid details in my imagination with a combination of disgust and desire until I was ready to shoot like Old Faithful.

And I was constantly presented the charms of his pert ass, as he lay in bed, as he bent to pick up something from the floor, as he stretched to get something out of a cabinet, as he did his daily set of pushups. Well, soon, I thought with a certain amount of satisfaction, I would be expelled, return home with my tail between my legs, and no longer have to worry about *his* tail.

The *pièce* that nearly destroyed my resistance, was arriving at our dorm room in the middle of the afternoon as he emerged from the bathroom after a shower, the only towel in sight the one with which he was drying his hair, and his cock, his exquisite cock, swung between his burly legs. It was neither too big nor too small, and it widened slightly as it extended down like an envelope of flesh hiding the head. I very nearly came right then and there, but I was able to control myself as he moved the towel from in front of his face and saw me. I answered his "Hi, Ethan," with a, "Hi, Sam," that was only slightly strangulated.

Then, with no apparent self consciousness, he walked over to the bureau and took out a pair of whities and leaned over to put them on, and I was treated to a spectacular view of his pert naked ass. It was perfectly proportioned and the same shade of light tan as the rest of his body. I swore that I could see a sign in the crease that read, "Here Lies Euphoria," and I wanted to fall down and worship this flawless butt.

I didn't. I think that I said, "Um—ah—oh," and grabbed the nearest book from the shelves and waved it at him, adding, "This—need—yes," and then I left as quickly as possible, ran to the communal bathroom on our floor, locked myself into a stall, and beat off frantically, not caring who heard my shouts— although I did wait fifteen minutes before I went back into the hallway.

For the next few weeks, I continued my inevitable decline into academic ruination. Every time the phone rang, I jumped several feet, sure that the dean was calling to advise me of my ejection from school.

And all of the time, of course, I was trying to avoid exploding in lust and attacking my roommate like a demented satyr.

When the eventful day arrived, I was sure that stress had caused me to lose myself in some sort of lunacy, and I could trust nothing that seemed to be happening.

That afternoon started with us both at home again and Sam once more in the shower. I listened to the running water and imagined it streaming down his fantastic body, and I tried to purge my mind of these pictures and instead concentrate on the novel I needed to finish for an English Lit test the next day. I was having scant success.

The water stopped, and I hoped that he would dry off and dress in the bathroom so that I would have a little less temptation to fight. But he stepped out wrapped in a towel that hung low on his hips.

"Good book?" he asked.

I marked my place with a finger. "Not at all."

"Would this be more interesting?" he said and opened the towel. There he was, in his shining glory, and I was sure that I had suddenly lost contact with reality. He stood in a mixture of sexuality and awkwardness, as if he wasn't quite sure about what he was doing.

I searched for a remark that would have at least a scrap of intelligence, but all I could do was gulp. I did that twice.

"You know," he said, "Sometimes you can be a bit dense."

Certainly part of me was dense. I gulped a third time and queried, "What?"

"I've been trying to let you know that I was attracted to you ever since the school year started. But I'm kind of new at this sort of thing, so maybe I wasn't doing things the right way. And now I think that I got things all wrong and I'm doing things all wrong, and I shouldn't—"

His cock was projecting at a forty-five-degree angle. Mine was at a rigid ninety degrees and threatening to push through my pants. He closed the towel around him.

"No no no," I said, "you're certainly doing things right, and I sincerely hope that you won't stop."

"Does that mean that you want me? Or have I been mis-reading you?"

"Have I been that obvious?"

"You weren't as subtle as you thought you were."

"Oh," I said. Was I disappointed that my skills at subterfuge were not as great as I thought they were, or—under the almost nude circumstances in front me—was I glad that he had fig-ured me out?

"And sometimes," he continued, "I saw you in the mirror, watching me. Sometimes, to be honest, I tempted you. You know, you can get chilly wearing only underwear."

"Hmm," I said, to interject some variety into my responses.

"And sometimes when you thought I was asleep, I wasn't."

"Oh?" I asked, returning to my major conversational gambit. "Oh!"

"Yes, oh," he responded and grinned at me in what I thought was an extremely lascivious manner. "Maybe you bit into your pillow to keep from yelling—yes, I checked and saw the teeth marks—but there's a certain slap of flesh that's unmistakable."

"Oh?" I inquired, abashed.

"Don't be embarrassed," he said quickly. "I've slapped my own flesh over you more than once."

"That's encouraging," I commented, glad to have something to say besides monosyllables.

"So I'm not wrong?" he asked, dropping the towel—nearly dropping the towel—which got stuck on his erection and was now jutting all of the way out from his groin. He flicked it aside—the towel, not the erection—and I was thunderstruck, staring at him with my jaw open like a fish gasping for air. As I watched, the foreskin glided up and revealed the head of his scrumptious organ, emerging as he was emerging into an unfamiliar life.

"As I said," he said, "I'm new at this. But wouldn't things work better if both of us participated?"

"No doubt, no doubt," I babbled, rousing myself from my slack-jawed appreciation of the manly magnificence before me.

I stood up and got out of my clothes as quickly as possible. When I was wearing only my boxers, my prick popped out the fly, drooling in anticipation. Sam looked at it and said, "At least I know you're interested."

I pulled the shorts down, and my cock went with them, then rebounded to thwack against my stomach. "Oh, yes," I said. "It's enthusiastic. *I'm* enthusiastic."

I followed the direction my prick was pointing until Sam and I were standing together, and our hard cocks were crossed, mashing our moist members against each other. We embraced, and he kissed me with a ferocity that I didn't expect from my shy, tentative roommate. I returned his passion, and the kiss was delicious.

After an extended moment, his lips trailed down my neck and onto my chest, and his tongue circled first one of my nipples, then the other. As he slipped to his knees, his tongue slipped down my stomach and into my belly button for a visit, then slipped out and continued its travel down to my stiff dick, and he took me in his mouth.

His technique was tentative and unsure, but that made everything more stimulating, more exhilarating. I looked down at him as he traveled along my prick, and maybe I was getting carried away with what I thought was the romantic fervor of the whole thing, but he seemed to want to please me. I was touched—in more ways than one.

As my gaze moved lower, I saw his cock sticking out, and I sort of gargled—because his oral ministrations, as unsophisticated as they may have been, were having a decided effect on my sexual equilibrium—"Let's try something different."

He looked a bit puzzled as I lay on the floor, but then he figured out what I had in mind, and he lay opposite me in the good old sixty-nine position, and we latched on to each other's dick with the force of vacuum cleaners.

The flavors of his cock were incredible. And he followed me, in a sort of sensual echo. As I licked his dick, he licked mine, as I traced the top and bottom of his shaft, he traced mine, as I rolled his balls around in my mouth, he rolled mine. I felt like a randy professor teaching an uninhibited student, and I gave him an A for effort, charm, and talent in learning so quickly. He enhanced his performance with several drops of his tart essence on my tongue.

Then he stared at me with eyes so liquid that I could have swum in them and said in a husky voice, "I think I'm ready."

Idiot that I was, I said, "Ready for what?"

He looked at me with both doubt and desire. "Ready to be with you completely."

"Oh, wow," I said.

"Don't you—?" he asked. "Yes," I answered, "Yes, I certainly do."

We moved as if we had been together for years, until he was on his back with his legs on my shoulders and I was looking down at his pert ass, his pert naked ass, his pert naked spread ass, and I had to pause for a moment and take a breath, because just the sight of this glorious gift was almost enough to drive me into eruption.

I bent and plunged my tongue into his warm, welcoming opening, tasting a little bit of soap and a lot of Sam, the combination was intoxicating, and I licked all around his sweet access, lubricating him for my entry. I put the tip of my cock against him, and I gently pressed.

One of my favorite moments in fucking a man is pushing through the initial resistance of his anal ring, the barrier to our pleasure, then the acceptance of me inside him. With Sam, the feeling was the same yet different. I didn't want to hurt him, so I moved gently, past the reluctance to fully accept what he wanted, entering him slowly, pausing before I went farther, and pausing again, watching his face for signs of discomfort. And they were there, but soon, they melted into pleasure.

He had closed his eyes; he now opened them and gazed at me, smiling. That smile nearly undid me. This act between us was not just his enjoyment and my enjoyment but *our* enjoyment, and I wasn't just fucking him; I was making love to him—I was making love to this beautiful man. We might not be moving quite together, but it didn't matter—we were in a special kind of concert, and that was what was important.

He held me closely, contracting tightly around my cock as I slid in and out of him, and sometimes his eyes widened as he looked at me, smiling, grimacing in a painful pleasure as I hit some new spot, gripping on my arms as I moved more deeply into him. He seemed almost to inhale me, and my ardor ascended, the intensity growing in my cock, balls, stomach, and chest. In some profound part of me, beyond the rolling, swelling of my sexual fever, he moaned as I fucked him, as I made love to him, as I plunged down and down into him and drove up, up into him. I almost couldn't breathe, lust and passion inflamed me and beneath me his body stiffened, and he cried out, cum cascading out of his cock onto his stomach, glistening, and consummation clutched me. I shouted and shot into him for what seemed a long time, too short a time, and for one glowing moment I was suspended in the magic of his body and being.

We lay on the floor, our arms wrapped around each other. As reality swept back in, I looked at the novel by the chair and conceded that the test on it tomorrow was probably a lost cause and that my making it through another year of college would be miraculous indeed. For the moment, however, I would let myself bask in the glow of sexual satisfaction, and my academic annihilation would just have to wait for another day.

Wanna Wrestle for It?
Stephen Osborne

I like my roommate, Nick. Honestly, I do. When dorm rooms are as small as the ones in Huff Hall, you've got to like your roommate or you'll simply go crazy by the end of the semester.

The trouble is that Nick likes me. I mean really likes me. In that way. Not that he's said anything, but I can tell. He'll start to say something to me, looking all serious and stuff, but then change his mind and ask something totally innocuous. It's like he's waiting for me to give him some kind of sign or signal, and I hate to break it to him, but it's never coming.

Nick's pretty hot, in that boy-next-door fashion. Unfortunately for Nick, hot just isn't enough for me. His wavy brown hair and dark, soulful eyes are nice to look at, but I just can't picture myself with him.

Truth is, I've got a wrestling fetish. Got it bad, to tell the truth. I can't even contemplate sex without a physical tussle preceding it. Maybe it stems from all those schoolyard wrestling matches with my friends as a kid, but whatever the cause, I'm stuck with it. And poor Nick, sweet Nick, wouldn't hurt a fly.

No, my crush is on Kirk Ramsey. Kirk Ramsey, college wrestling stud and all around ladies man, who would break my bones if he knew how many times I beat off imagining him getting me into a full nelson. Kirk Ramsey, who shares a dorm room with his buddy Matt just down the hall from us, but might as well have been staying on the moon for all the contact I had with him. Kirk Ramsey, whose shaggy brown hair and dreamy blue eyes are what I see in my dreams every night.

I yearned to wrestle with Kirk. Not that I stood a chance. I've got a tall, lean frame that just won't pack on muscle, no matter how hard I try. Still, in my wet dreams, I'm as buff and as much of a stud as Kirk. The wrestling is hard and the sex is harder.

Reality, however, shows a good-looking nerd type sitting at his desk late on a Saturday night, doing his homework. Most everyone else in the dorm is out at some party or other, but me, I'm cracking the books, sitting across the room from Nick, who's also working on homework. Every now and then, Nick steals a yearning glance at me. I ignore it.

Getting to a good stopping point, I slam my book shut. "I need a breather," I say aloud. "I'm going for a walk."

"Want me to come with you, Darren?" Nick asks, just a little too eagerly.

I shake my head. "Naw, that's all right. I won't be gone all that long." I'm just wearing jeans and socks, so I pull on a T-shirt and throw on my beat up basketball shoes before heading out.

Out in the hall, I'm really not sure where I want to go. I really just needed to get away from Nick for just a few minutes. Maybe give him a chance to jerk off thinking about me. That's mean, I know, but every now and then his puppy dog eyes annoy me. I walk slowly down the hall, not really having a destination in mind.

I slow down even more when I pass Kirk's room. The door is open and a light is on, but I can't hear any movement within. Stopping, I look up and down the hall. No one's around to see me. I peek into the room, careful not to hit the door or make any sound to give myself away.

As far as I can tell, the room is empty. Knowing Kirk and Matt, they were probably so busy rushing out to some drunken binge that they forgot to shut their freaking door. Feeling a little bolder, I push the door open even more.

The room is indeed empty. A sudden thought strikes me. I try to ignore it, knowing what would happen if I got caught. But how many chances like this would I get?

Just a quick rummage through Kirk's drawers to find one of his jockstraps and I'd have jack off material for months. I'd have to be crazy to try it, but I know I'm going to. Taking a deep breath, I walk in.

Kirk's room has that musky smell of dirty laundry. T-shirts are all over the place, and his bed is littered with assorted shorts, athletic socks, and a few pairs of jeans. Matt's bed, by comparison, is pristine.

I quickly look around Kirk's bed, but I can't see a jock anywhere. Several pairs of boxer briefs, yes, but no jocks. Funny, I hadn't pegged Kirk as a boxer brief kind of guy. I look around the floor. Still no jock.

I don't know which closet is his, so I just pick one. The wrestling shoes I find on the floor tell me I've picked the right one. Nestled on the floor behind the shoes is a laundry basket. Bingo. Right on top is a beautiful white jock.

I'm just about to grab it when I hear a noise behind me. Matt's laugh is loud and distinctive. I hear Matt say to whoever he's with, "I guess I did leave the door open."

"You're such a fucking doofus," I hear Kirk say.

I have only seconds before I'm discovered. I'm sure I must be as white as a sheet. I can feel my heart starting to thump loudly in my chest. Not stopping to think, I throw myself into the closet and close the door behind me. It won't shut all the way. I look down and realize I've kicked one of Kirk's wrestling shoes and now it's preventing the door from latching. I kneel down and hold my breath, listening carefully.

The roomies don't seem to have seen or heard me. I can see partly into the room, but just Matt's part of the room. Neither Matt or Kirk are where I can see them, but when Matt talks he sounds very close. "Like you haven't left the fucking room unlocked a million times." He comes into my view as he sits on his bed. He's got a beer in hand, and from the bleary look to his eyes, I'm guessing it's not his first.

"Well, it's shut and locked now, your majesty," I hear Kirk say.

Matt smiles. "Up yours, peasant," he says playfully.

"Peasant?" I hear Kirk chuckle. "Sounds like someone's getting pretty cock sure of himself."

"Like you could do anything about it." Matt finishes his beer and sets the empty bottle on the floor next to his bed.

Finally Kirk comes into my view as he stands over Matt in a faux threatening manner. "I don't have to teach you who's top dog around here, do I?" He's wearing jeans with a tear in the knee and a plain, white, very tight T-shirt. My dick starts to swell just looking at him. I carefully move back a little in the closet, careful not to make any noise. I sit my ass down. If I'm going to be hiding out here for a while, I might as well be comfortable.

Matt smirks up at Kirk. "Like you could."

Kirk springs, throwing Matt back onto his bed. Matt laughs and tries to maneuver out from under Kirk's body, but he can't. Kirk snaps a headlock on his roommate. Matt paws at Kirk's muscular forearms, but he can't break the hold. He starts to turn red as his airflow is cut off.

"I'm sorry, what did you say?" Kirk asks teasingly. "Did you call me your master? I thought you did."

In a strained voice, Matt gasps out, "Fuck you."

Kirk chuckles. "No, I think it's you that's going to get fucked, my friend."

Matt struggles, finally getting out form under Kirk. His legs fly over the side of the bed, flailing in the air. He must have loosened the hold on his neck, for I hear him laugh and say, in a strained but much more normal tone, "Not this time, stud. I'm fucking you tonight."

"You know the rules," Kirk says, shifting around to get his legs around Matt's torso. He squeezes hard. "Whoever says 'uncle' first gets the dick up the ass. And lets see...oh, wait! That's always been you!" He squeezes again. Matt grunts, trying to shift Kirk's massive legs.

"Not this time," he says, but there's no conviction in his voice.

"Just tell me you want my dick, and the pain stops, Matt old buddy."

Slowly, I unzip my fly. I don't care if I do get caught at this point. If I don't beat my meat watching this, I'll never forgive myself.

"Fuck you," Matt replies. He reaches up desperately, trying to grab Kirk's head. For punishment, Kirk gives a massive squeeze and for good measure, slams a playful punch into Matt's side. There's a trace of laughter to Matt's resulting cry. He's enjoying the hell out of this, and I can't blame him.

"Okay," he says. "Uncle."

Kirk slams a fist into Matt's stomach. "Wasn't loud enough," he says with a grin.

Groaning, Matt nearly shouts, "Uncle! Uncle! Fuck you, bitch, I said 'uncle!'"

"Bitch?" Kirk's grinning from ear to ear. "Did you call me 'bitch?'" He releases Matt, giving his side a kick. The boy rolls off the bed, landing with a thud onto the floor. He's facing me, and for a moment I'm afraid he's seen me, but his eyes don't show any surprise.

Kirk comes off the bed quickly and straddles Matt, sitting on his back. He pulls Matt's arms up and locks them over his knees. It's a move I've seen on a million Pro Wrestling shows, usually called a Camel Clutch. Giggling, Kirk puts his hands around Matt's head and pulls back on his chin. "I'll break your fucking back. Now who's the bitch?"

"I am! I am!"

"And who wants to get fucked?"

"I do," Matt says, the fight all out of him. "Please fuck me."

Smiling, Kirk releases his friend. Matt collapses flat onto the floor. Kirk raises up a little to loosen his jeans. "I've been needing this all week," he says. He's wearing black boxer briefs, which he yanks down, revealing a nice sized, very hard cock.

"Me, too," Matt says with a sigh. He reaches his hands down and struggles with his own jeans. He's hampered by Kirk kneeling over him, but he manages to pull his pants and underwear down to show a tight looking, very white and hairless ass.

My own cock is in my hands by now, and I'm pumping away. How they manage not to hear me is beyond me. I can only guess they've got other things on their minds. My breath is coming in short gasps, not unlike the sounds coming from Matt as Kirk sits back down on him. Kirk spits into his hand, then smears the saliva over his cock.

"Go slow this time, okay?" Matt asks.

"Fuck that shit," Kirk snarls. You can tell they've done this a hundred times, and Matt's loving every second. "You like it hard, and that's how I'm going to give it to you."

With a quick movement Kirk shifts so he's positioned over Matt's body. He uses his left hand to aim his hard dick towards Matt's waiting hole. Matt lifts his ass a little off the floor in anticipation.

When Kirk enters, I see Matt's body tense. He lifts his head in a silent scream. The pain in his face is quickly replaced with ecstasy. He smiles as Kirk slides the rest of his cock into his ass. Despite Kirk's hard talk, he waits until Matt's ass muscles have relaxed before beginning to move his hips.

I slow down on my strokes, wanting to savor the moment. My dick is throbbing in my hands, wanting to spill its load. I bite my lip.

Kirk starts to slam into Matt with increasing force. Matt grunts with each thrust. I can see his hands gripping the carpeting, the pleasure evident on his face. Who could blame him? Kirk's starting to really fuck him hard now, and a bead of sweat falls off his chin onto Matt's back. "I'm going to shoot," Kirk says through gritted teeth.

"Give it to me," Matt says in a groan. "Give me that fucking cum."

I pump my dick faster, matching the thrusts Kirk is giving Matt. With a final few hard thrusts, Kirk's face seems to go into convulsions. His mouth drops into an O and he moans. As a finisher, he slams into Matt one last time then stays there. It's suddenly hard to tell where Kirk ends and Matt begins. They look like one, coupled together in a sweaty heap on the dorm room floor.

I bite my lip hard, trying not to cry out as my own jizz shoots out, hitting Kirk's precious wrestling shoes.

As Kirk's gasps recede, Matt lifts his head up and Kirk leans down to kiss his cheek. Slowly, Kirk pulls his dick out of Matt. He slides off his roommate's body and lays next to him. Matt flips over, nestling against Kirk. Smiling, Kirk asks, "How was it?"

"Fucking fantastic," Matt replies, somewhat out of breath.

Kirk looks down at Matt's swollen cock. He reaches down and starts stroking it. Matt's eyes roll upwards. Kirk's hand is moving quickly. I can see Matt's balls bouncing up and down, then a white glob shoots out of his dick, hitting his chest. Matt moans as he shoots more cum over Kirk's hand.

Smiling, Kirk peels his T-shirt off and uses it to clean off Matt's juice. "You shoot more than anyone I've ever known," he says.

"You don't do so badly yourself."

They hug each other and then kiss gently. "Ready for bed?" Kirk asks.

"Sure."

They get to their feet, somehow staying in each others arms. They finish undressing, then climb into Kirk's bed. They move out of my line of sight, anyway, and I can hear bedsprings squeak. No wonder Matt's bed is so perfect. I bet he never even uses it. Just before they settle, one of them hits the light switch. The room plunges into darkness. I hear them rustling a little, and sounds of kissing. My legs are beginning to cramp up, and I find myself wishing they'd knock it off. Finally they grow quiet.

I wait for quite a while. I wish I could see them, or at least their shadows to know if they're moving at all. I can't hear any

snoring or heavy breathing, so I'm not sure if their asleep yet
or not. All I know is that if I don't move soon, my legs are going to fall asleep. Slowly I allow myself to stretch out, one foot
hitting the closet door. It swings open a little. I wait to see if
this is noticed. Nothing. Feeling bolder, I press the door open
all the way. Still no sound from the bed.

I get to my feet, trying not to let the pins and needles in my
calves make me grunt aloud. I peer into the darkness. There's
a dark shape on the bed. It's hard to tell who's who in the dim
light, but they're still entwined. Matt's one lucky bastard.

I reach back into the closet and feel through Kirk's laundry
basket. Since I came in for a jock, I might as well leave with
one, even though I now have more than enough visuals to keep
me jacking off for ages. Finding the one that had been on top,
I creep slowly out into the room. Neither of them stirs.

The door to their room is trickier. I start to turn the knob
and the damn thing squeaks. In the silence it sounds like a
bomb going off. One of the shapes on the bed stirs, so I just go
for broke and swing the door open quickly. In a second I'm out
in the hall, my prize in my hand. I close the door quietly behind
me and start back down towards my own room. There's no one
in the hall, and I don't hear any further sounds from the room,
so it doesn't look like anyone's coming after me.

Holy shit, I actually got to watch Kirk fuck his roommate.
I got away with it.

I slip into my own room, realizing at the last minute I still
have the jock in my left hand. I scrunch it up and try to hide it
with my body, because of course Nick is still at his desk. He
looks up when I come in.

"You've been gone ages," he says, mockingly accusatory.

"Something came up," I tell him.

He closes his book and gazes at me carefully. "What's that
in your hand?"

"What do you mean?"

"That thing in your hand. The thing you're trying to hide from me. What is it?"

I'm sure I'm red as hell. "Nothing."

Nick gets up and comes over to me. His face is set in stone as he grabs my arm. A slight smile lights his face as he sees what it is.

"Is that your idol's jock? Have you been sniffing around Kirk's room?"

I hadn't even realized Nick knew about my fascination with Kirk. Embarrassed, I stammered, "It's just...well, I...I just..."

Nick grabs the jock out of my sweaty hand. "I'm afraid I'm going to have to confiscate this. It's just going to have to become my property."

I don't know what to say, but I look at him to see how serious he is.

There's a twinkle in his eyes. "Unless, of course, you want to wrestle me for it. If you win, you get the jock back. If I win," he says, grinning slyly, "I get to fuck your ass."

My mouth drops open and my dick starts to stiffen all over again. I smile at Nick as he grabs me and wrestles me to the floor.

It's going to be a great semester.

Campus Steam
John Simpson

As the color of the leaves began to change, the sounds of yelling and doors slamming echoed though the dorms as the freshmen class reported for orientation. St. Aelred's college was waking up from its summer nap and coming alive with a couple hundred horny freshmen away from home for the first time and looking to party as well as learn.

As roommates found each other from the assignment list and located their rooms, everyone began to settle in for the fall term of 2006. Room 314 housed myself, Dale Garnet and Roger Houseman, total strangers but lifelong friends by the end of the first semester.

I was nineteen, with short blond hair in the "buzz" style, blue eyes, 6'1", 179, and hung like a mule. There was little doubt that I would be popular with whoever I wanted to party with during the school year.

Dale and Roger made a handsome pair as Roger was just as well built, but with black hair and green eyes.

"Do you want to get some dinner and meet some of the guys at the dining hall?" Roger asked.

"Sure, let's go and beat the crowd. Hopefully the food doesn't suck here."

As we finished supper, I excused myself to go to the men's room. As I entered, I looked around and noticed a brightly lit, medium size bathroom with five stalls. I went in, sat down and looked to my right, and saw that a hole had been drilled between the stalls on not just the right side, but also on the other side. The holes were big enough to stick two fingers through or any other similarly sized object. I started to grow an erection at the thought of letting another guy suck my cock in the men's room, especially one that I couldn't fully see.

As I thought about that prospect, another guy came in and

entered the stall on my left. I watched through the hole as the guy dropped his pants and pulled down his underwear showing a nice cock before sitting down. I became nervous, as I had never engaged in "tearoom sex" before. Neither of us moved so much as a foot as we sat on the toilets waiting for something to happen.

I finally noticed the other guy move forward and saw he was now looking through the hole into my stall to see what he could. In response, I leaned back so that the stranger could see my large cock. As the guy continued to stare, I moved my hand under my cock and pulled it up and out so that it could be fully seen. As I began to stroke my meat, the stranger became excited as he shifted his body around to better view the action. I contemplated feeding the guy my cock through the hole, but I didn't feel ready to do that. Instead, I just jacked my cock harder and harder until I was breathing hard. I could also tell that the stranger in the next stall was also beating his meat. Finally, I shot my load which went up and out over my legs hitting the back of the stall door and finally into my hand. The other guy then moaned and shot his load all over the floor.

I shook off the last of the cum from my cock, wiped, and stood up. I turned slightly so that my cock swung over near the hole and the guy could get a good view of the size of my cock. As I did this, a tongue came through the hole and I obliged by rubbing the tip of my dick down over the eager tongue, leaving behind a small trace of semen. With that, I put it away, zipped up, and left the rest room, not wanting to talk to my fellow jacker.

All of the guys were just getting back from dinner as I entered my room. I figured I would finish unpacking, make my bed, and maybe turn in early tonight. I blew a good load in the men's room and I felt a little tired.

"Hey, where did you go to Dale? I took my tray back and when I came back to the table, you were gone!" Roger said after closing the door.

"Ahh, I had to hit the men's room, and then I just took a walk."

"There's a big party tonight around ten, if you want to go," Roger said.

"Nah, I'm just going to take a shower in a bit, and then go to bed. I guess that walk really tired me out, and it's been a long day."

"Okay, maybe next time, stud."

I finished setting up my half of the room while listening to all the shouts and laughing coming from the hallway. Most of the guys had their room doors open and everyone was wandering in and out of the rooms. I lay down on my bed and thought about my encounter in the rest room. Why didn't I just feed my dick to the guy and get a good blowjob while I was at it? I started to feel a rustling in my shorts and realized I wasn't as tired as I thought.

I glanced over at the clock and saw that it was almost eight-thirty now, and I figured it was a good time to get a shower. I got up and stripped off my clothes, wrap a towel around my body, put on flip-flops and grabbed the soap. I headed out of my room, took a right, and headed towards the bathroom. I hadn't really inspected much of the dorm since getting there earlier in the day, and this was my first visit to the bathroom.

I was surprised to see, as I entered, that the shower was one big room with multiple heads so that up to twenty guys could shower at one time. The sound of rushing water greeted my ears along with the rise of steam coming from the shower room opening.

I looked in the mirror to check for pimples and walked over to the shower room, hung up my towel, and entered the shower. It was a little hard to see because there were several guys already in there getting ready for the party. The steam was getting thick.

I picked a showerhead next to a real hot guy who was soaping up his body and turned on the shower. As I soaked my body,

I slowly turned around enjoying the feel of the hot water washing over my body. When I opened my eyes I saw most of the other guys looking my body over and letting their eyes rest upon the sight of my cock. I was used to this happening, and it didn't mean anything because most men stared at my package.

I continued to enjoy the heat from the water when I heard a voice come out of the steam asking if I wanted my back washed. I laughed and turned around to see which clown thought he was being funny. What I found was three of the guys had moved from their positions and were now standing right in front of me. Their eyes continued to glance over my body, and I realized they were serious.

"Sure, if someone wants to soap up my back, that's cool," I said.

Before I got the words fully out of my mouth, two hands began rubbing my back with soap while one hand began soaping up my ass. It felt so fucking good that I couldn't stop the action and decided to see where it was going to go.

I had turned around facing the wall again so that the boys could do their thing when all of a sudden the guy that was standing next to me, dropped to his knees along side of me and looked up into my eyes. I knew what he wanted and just nodded my head. He turned my body so that I was now facing him eye level with my cock, and he quickly took my now hardened cock into his mouth and attempted to deep throat me. His sucking mouth felt fantastic in the middle of a heated shower room with as many as nine guys watching the action. All of the other guys were jacking their now stiff pricks as they watched the one guy on his knees servicing my cock. There was now a circle surrounding the action and me as I watched as these beautiful young guys jack their cocks slowly while watching me get head. I felt hands constantly moving over my ass, feeling its curves and brushing against my hole.

The guy on his knees stopped as his jaw got tired, and another of the guys quickly took his place. This guy was a far more experienced cocksucker as he worked my cock well and was able to deep throat me to the balls. I started to rub and pinch my nipples as the sucking got better when two guys replaced my fingers with theirs. Another guy spread my ass-cheeks and began to rim me, which almost sent me over the edge. They motioned for the cocksucker to stop, and then bent me over so that they could all eat my ass out. As this was going on, guys started going down on guys and it became an all out shower orgy.

I stood up and signaled that I wanted more head, and a new guy took over on my cock. He used his tongue well as he licked my balls and the underside of my shaft. As the new guy sucked away, I reached over and fingered a guy's ass that was nearby and cute. He reacted to my probing finger by pushing his ass into my finger harder.

What kind of dorm did I just move into? Was this some kind of unreal initiation for everyone, or were there a lot of gay guys on my floor? I felt myself getting ready to come as the steam caressed my legs and ass, while a sea of sucking was going on all around me.

I grabbed the lucky guy's head that was doing the sucking at this point and started to skull fuck him. I was now ready to dump my second load of the day. As I rammed my cock into the guys face, I heard him gag and gurgle, but he never motioned for me to stop. I was going to shoot my load down his hungry throat whether he wanted it or not. As guys started to come all around me, I finally gave up a hot spewing load myself, and flooded the cocksucker's mouth and throat to which he eagerly swallowed every drop of my load. When I finally stopped coming, I let go of his head, and he slowly let my cock slip out of his mouth, while squeezing out every last drop of the creamy white love juice that he could. He gave fucking great head and I would have to get his name because this would not be the last time that he serviced my dick.

As I leaned against the wall with the water still flowing over me, I caught my breath as I watched the remaining guys get off. When everybody had nutted, the water got turned off and we all exited into the towel area. Everyone just smiled as we checked out each other's bodies once again. I appeared to be the hit of the party as everyone introduced themselves to me almost at once. The cocksucker who finished me off whispered his name and room number into my ear and told me that I could have his mouth or ass whenever I wanted it. I responded by patting him on his bare ass and smiling.

After a few more comments, everyone disappeared after toweling off. I walked back to my room feeling quite good and not quite believing what a great year this was going to be. I didn't even have to go to the restroom to let some guy blow me through a hole! I had a floor full of cocksuckers.

I entered my room closing the door behind me and was startled to see my roommate standing by his bed...drying off.

"Were you just in the shower?"

Roger smiled and said, "I guess you didn't see me come in as you were quite busy, and I didn't want to disturb you. I quickly showered and left."

"You saw everything?"

"Oh yeah, I saw it all. I also noticed that you got one hell of a package on you, roomie!"

At that comment I just let the towel drop and collapsed on my bed.

"Don't worry, I'm certainly not going to spread it around that my roommate is the number one guy that every gay boy wants to suck off."

"Look Roger, are you gay? Because if you're not, then our rooming together is going to be a problem."

"There's no problem Dale, I am as gay as you are—and, if you will let me, I'll prove it to you," he said smiling as he looked at my cock. "Besides, I really want to fuck that sweet ass of yours this year."

At that statement I sat up. "You want to what? What makes

you think I'm going to bottom for you stud?" I asked with a grin on my face.

"Because, I'm that hot!" he said with a laugh.

"Well, I'm tired after that little party and I am going to sleep. So, behave and see you in the morning."

With that, I went to sleep still not believing the availability of sex with hot young guys. It appeared I had ended up in the gay dorm, as even my roommate was gay!

Studies ended up taking a majority of my time and so I had little time for other "activities." Roger never brought up again our having sex as he was as busy as I was with classes and sports. It had been a little over four weeks since the orgy in the shower when I felt that urge in my pants that just wouldn't go away. It was two in the afternoon and I had just finished my last class when I thought I would pay a visit to the restroom by the dining hall.

When I entered there was only one stall occupied and I took one to the right of it. I sat down after making a big show of dropping my pants and since I was wearing no underwear, my cock was free to swing as I stood up. I made sure that the guy in the next stall got an eyeful before I sat down. I heard a cough to let me know that he was there.

I leaned forward to see if I could see anything and what I saw was a nice hard cock sticking straight up. The guy had obviously been jacking before I arrived. I made it evident that I was looking through the hole so that if he wanted, he could now put on a show. I also noticed that he was wearing the school rugby uniform.

He didn't disappoint me. Before I knew it, he was slowly stroking his cock and I could even see a thick black patch of pubic hair surrounding the base of his impressive cock. I slowly jacked my own cock while watching him and even moaned a little by accident.

As I watched, the guy put his fingers through the hole in a signal for me to put my cock through the hole so he could play with me or suck me. Feeling horny, I decided to try this new avenue of sexual expression and stood up, turned, and found my cock was too big to fit through the damn hole. I swore and sat down.

I heard a sigh of disappointment on the other side, as it was obvious he wanted to blow me. Since his cock looked hot, and he had a decent body from what I could tell, I put my finger through the hole and motioned for him to put his cock through the hole.

A very nice dick barely came through the hole after a few seconds and hung out on my side about seven inches. I grabbed onto the cock and jacked is slowly and as I rubbed it with my thumb. I then moved over and took the dick in my mouth and began to suck it slowly, using my tongue to convey maximum pleasure. I was able to take the entire shaft down my throat all the way to the wooden wall that separated us.

His cock tasted nice, and I really got into sucking it. I looked up and saw that there were now two hands holding onto the top of the stall wall as he began to move back and forth, fucking my face. As his fucking pace picked up, I began to jack my cock faster as well. The entire scene became intensely erotic and I felt the churning in my balls that meant I would come soon.

"I'm gonna come, so stop sucking if you don't want to take the load," I heard the guy whisper. This made me suck harder as he rammed his dick into my mouth. As I felt the splash of hot cum hit the back of my throat and the roof of my mouth, I began to come myself, forcing me to utter unintelligible sounds that emanated deep from within my throat as I experienced a symphony of feelings. When the guy stopped coming, I withdrew my mouth and spit out his load into the basin below me. A sweet aftertaste of his cum lingered on my lips and tongue.

I had once again shot all over the place, and it took me a few minutes to clean up the mess. As I cleaned, I noticed that the guy didn't pull up his pants and make a hasty exit, as was custom when one was sucked off in the men's room. So, I got up, pulled my pants up, and exited the stall, stopping to wash my hands and rinse out my mouth at the sink.

As I did, the door to the next stall opened and as the guy emerged, my mouth fell open. I was speechless. There standing next to me, was none other than Roger, my roommate.

"Did you know that was me in there?" I asked with some irritation.

"No, not until your big fat cock couldn't fit through the hole, and when I looked closer, I recognized your sneakers. By then, I was very hot and horny and needed a blowjob!"

"Son of a bitch, you tricked me into sucking your dick!" I stated with some false shock.

"Yeah, wasn't it hot?"

This was going to be one hell of a year, and I had three more to look forward too.

Twist of Fate
Marcus James

"Alright class, I want your character comparisons in literature by the end of the day Friday, is that understood?" The cluster of students looked up at their professor, with his slight paunch of a gut and balding head, and nodded. He was an oblivious man, prone to wearing the same starched button up shirt and sweater vest. He was as boring as his voice was dull.

Zachary Blackmoore sighed and lazily threw his notes in his black leather messenger bag, ready to take advantage of the two-hour break before his next class. Though he knew that he was just going to torture himself by going down to the field to see the football gods practice on the lawn; namely one boy in particular. He stood and slipped between desks, completely unnoticed by the others. In a class of fifty-seven it was nearly impossible to stand out.

His skin was fair; almost milk white and his blond hair grazed his lids, parted in the middle and curtaining violet eyes, staring out from behind light blue eyes. He had been born with the disease known as albinism; though its only real traces could be found in those eyes, which he had learned to keep hidden for the majority of his life. His body was lean, perfected from years swimming on his own and for his high school, though upon his entering into college the year before, he had long ago packed away his Speedo.

The campus of Etherton University was sparse with students, all eager to be out of the rain, which covered the stately gothic grounds with its ancient spires and domineering statues. Decayed leaves of brown littered the walkways and grassy knolls, and students stood in the café and halls, under breezeways and inside the library, happy to be inside where they were safe and warm.

Zachary hadn't wanted to come to Etherton in the first

place, but his family was one of the most prestigious in the world, and he knew that he would have been hindering the Blackmoore tradition of excellence if he did not attend an Ivy League college. People here, in northern Massachusetts, were oblivious to the rumors of the Blackmoores, save for a few transplants. Rumors of witchcraft and ghosts had plagued the family for generations, and yet for the most part people felt nothing when they heard the Blackmoore name; though a library on campus was given his namesake.

He neared the stadium, with its coliseum shape and dominating walls; it always made him nervous, afraid that his target of interest would catch on and ask him to stop; or worse yet, kick his ass. He paid no mind to the rain, in fact he liked it; it was much better than the burning sun that stung his retinas, forcing him to hide in the shade.

As he entered into the bleachers, he heard the men calling out their plays and the sounds of their feet kicking up the soggy lawn. He liked this, seeing them move in their little shorts and tight tee's, when they decided to wear shirts, that is. There was something about the way their powerful legs moved that twisted his stomach into knots and Zachary would often break out into a sweat.

The one boy in particular was his roommate Nick Nolan, who seemed to move like a god amongst the rest of the sheep laid out for slaughter. His soft, tanned face, slightly round, big dark green eyes and long black lashes, a mole just above his lip on the right side and pouty lips that seemed like cushions drove Zachary wild, making him feel shameful. Nick's black hair was shaved short on top of his head, and his body was bulk, complete muscle, though he had the face of a baby.

They had known each other since middle school, growing up just outside of Salem, Massachusetts forming a solid friendship, one that would take them to the ends of the earth. That was the worst time for Zachary; being so close to the infamous witch-trial town had left him ostracized. In Salem, people had heard the rumors about the Blackmoores of County Mayo, Ireland, and on top of that he was an albino. As a result, he was anything but popular. Maybe that's why he had a hard time believing that someone like Nick Nolan, with all of his charm and celebrity, would want to hang around with him.

He threw his peacoat down on the steel seat and sat down, never taking his eyes off of his best friend and dorm mate. For years Zachary had tried to deny the attraction, through all of the girlfriends, through all of the homecoming games and formal dances, he had stood in the corner, watching Nick and loving him in tortured silence. No wonder he was doing his literary comparison to Mercutio of *Romeo and Juliet* fame. Mercutio had been so obviously in love with Romeo that he was willing to die for him, he was so needing of any and all affection that he got from the lovelorn teen, that he stood by and pretended to be supportive, though in reality he probably wanted to knock Juliet right off the balcony and smile while sending her to her death.

He definitely was Mercutio and Nick was his blinded Romeo.

The rain slowed up, and the smell of smoke from nearby fires fermented in the air, reminding Zachary of warmer places, like his mother's home on the water, with its classic East Hampton design and gracious gardens, just feet away from the sandy shores. Nick's tight white tee was covered in sweat, and his nylon black shorts were sticking to his defined tanned legs, the sweat dripping from his hair, dark around his butt. Zachary wanted so desperately to be able to turn away, to get up and go, but he couldn't. He had to watch Nick for as long as possible, in these moments when he didn't know, and when he didn't have to smile to his bitch of a girlfriend.

*I just wish he would look at me...totally see me and only me...*he thought to himself, picking at the skin at the side of his nail. His heart seemed to stop in mid-beat and his pulse quickened as Nick turned his head and stopped what he was doing; standing in place and locking eyes with Zachary. Nick grinned, his smile perfect, his dimples enticing, making him even more irresistible. He averted his gaze, inhaling and exhaling slowly, before lifting his head again, surprised to see that Nick was still staring.

Then, as if teasing Zachary, Nick reached up under the hem of his shirt and lifted it up to his head, wiping the sweat from his brow and at the same time showing off taunt abs. Zachary could feel his cheeks become flushed, and the blood move between his legs, stiffening his cock and painfully tenting his jeans.

Nick continued his little routine, and Zachary could not help but imagine what it would be like to run his tongue along the ridges of his abs, to taste the salt of Nick's flesh, to bite playfully on his nipples.

"Shit!" Zachary got up, forgetting his jacket and running to the side of the building, desperate to relieve the tension between his legs. He slammed himself against the cool stone wall; hidden in shadow and knowing that no one was in sight. Slowly he closed his eyes and with one hand he unbuttoned his light denim shirt, exposing a lean chest and stomach, with nearly white nipples.

"God forgive me...God forgive me..." he began to say over and over again. He unbuttoned his jeans and pulled down the zipper, moving his other hand into his white briefs, gripping the warm stiff flesh of his cock, pulling on it gently. With his other hand he teased his nipples, sighing and feeling his hair become damp from the sweat that seeped from his pores.

I want Nick...Oh God, I want Nick to love me like I love Nick... the heat moved through his body, and the sensation of tiny pinpricks moved along the surface of his skull. He began to move faster, feeling his knees buckle and the delicious, balance ending sensation that rode the course of his thighs and moved through his shaft before shooting out of his piss hole.

"Fuck!" it was warm and smelled slightly putrid. Clinging to his fingers and dripping on the ground. The great white pearly substance known as cum, something that he desperately wanted to see come out of Nick. Well, that was only half true. Zachary had seen Nick come once before. It was in his room, on one of the nights that Nick was staying over. They had just prepared to turn off the television when Nick, while flipping through the channels came across softcore porn on HBO late night.

Zachary didn't want to watch it, in fact the image of a woman naked, of exposing herself like that and getting fucked like that made him extremely uncomfortable; namely because if he watched for too long he began to picture himself in the place of the woman in the film.

"Don't you like that?" Nick had asked him, his fourteen-year-old face aglow with teenage lust. Zachary had just shrugged his shoulders and refused to comment. It didn't take long for Nick to close his eyes and slip his hand into his white Jockey's, tugging on his already nine and a half inch dick, the mushroom head already dripping with precum.

"Zachey...give me some help buddy..." He had hated being called Zachey; it was Nick's way of getting him to do anything. It was then that Nick pulled it out, perfectly tanned, reaching for Zachary's white, hairless arm, bringing his fingers around his stiff one. "Yeah that's it Zachey...nice and slow..." within minutes Nick was coming, shooting his load all over his chest, his thighs, and most importantly all over Zachary's hand.

Before anything could have been said Zachary ran into his bathroom and had licked Nick's sacrament off of his fingers and palm, loving the taste of it. Since then, nothing else had happened between them, though Nick has always referred to the incident as "a buddy helping another buddy out."

***

Zachary couldn't go to his next class. After what had happened at the stadium, all he wanted to do was sleep the rest of the day away. Lying in his bed in nothing but a fresh pair of black briefs, Zachary watched day pass into night and the hall continually fill in and out of students; going back and forth from their dorms for one thing or the other.

"Why did he do that?" he questioned, trying to understand his best friend's motives for the display on the field. He shouldn't have had to even try to figure this out, but here he was anyways, trying to find his way through a fog.

There was a tightening in his gut and Zachary knew that Nick was approaching; just seconds from the door...it was just his intuition, which often served as a warning for him to pretend that he was asleep.

The knob twisted and the door skirted across the floor, bringing in the hall light for just a moment before going dark. Zachary heard Nick's bated breath as he tried to be silent and not disturb him.

"Oh Zachey..." Nick let out with a sigh. In disbelief Nick moved close to him, hovering over him before moving down and lightly placing his lips on Zachary's forehead. He purposefully stirred as if he were waking up, and when he opened his eyes he found Nick grinning at him, his green eyes hidden in shadow.

"Hi..." Zachary said with a yawn and a grin.

"Hey back..." Nick returned the grin. "You know you left this out on the bleachers." Nick lifted his peacoat into vision.

"Oh thanks..." Zachary reached out for it but Nick pulled it away.

"Not so fast...what were you doing out there?" Zachary averted his gaze and shook his head.

"Nothing really Nick, I just go there to think...to clear my head...also people tend to look at me strange—"

"I know..." Nick interjected, saying this with the momentary closing of his eyes.

"It helps to see my best friend you know...you've always kinda been my superhero..." Nick laughed and stood up.

"Well I can't be a superhero unless I'm in my underwear!" Though it was supposed to be funny, it became something else for Zachary, watching Nick slip off his shirt and kick off his shoes, followed with his pants. His thick cock was tucked away in blue briefs with red stars all over them, the trail of black hairs moving from his navel down into the concealment of the elastic band of his briefs.

"There!" Nick curled his fists and put them against his waist in a classic superhero pose. "Here I come to save the day!" Nick jumped onto Zachary's bed, laughing and pulling off his comforter.

"No Nick, stop it!" he was already hard and the last thing he needed was for Nick to find out. He feared the end of their friendship right then and there.

"I don't think so...I have to save you..." Nick's laughter died down as he threw the covers over his body, staring down at Zachary, staring into his piercing violet irises. "I always save you..." His face became serious as he made his way closer to Zachary, laying out next to him, their heads sharing a pillow, their eyes locked together. "It's my job..."

Their breath was hushed as Nick moved his arm over Zachary's bare shoulder, running his fingers gently across his flesh, tracing his face. Nick moved closer to him, Zachary was surprised to find him hard, to feel Nick's cock-head press against his own.

Zachary closed his eyes as Nick's other hand moved down his body. His fingers running along the soft of his flesh before finding his stiff eight-inch dick, gripping on it and beginning to jerk him off.

"Why are you doing this?" Zachary asked him. He could already feel the shake of Nick's head.

"I don't know...but I need to..." he slipped his fingers into Zachary's undies and pulled them down just below his cheeks, his touch moving along his ass, making him reel against it. "I just need to do this...I have to..." Nick proclaimed in a whisper.

He feared where this would take them, but Zachary knew that he could not pull himself away, could not deny what it was that was happening and knew that it would be the worst mistake of his life if he put an end to it.

"Don't hurt me..." Zachary said, opening his eyes, gentle tears slipping down his face.

"I never could..." they moved closer now, Nick taking hold of Zachary and kissing him firmly, their tongues touching and his body smelling of his cologne. "I love you too much to hurt you..." Nick moved Zachary on top of him, his cock, still covered by his briefs, poking Zachary's ass, his hands cupping his soft, white ass, his fingers playing lightly with his hole.

"Shit..." Nick grinned when he heard Zachary say this, their tongues still moving erratically in their mouths.

"C'mere..." he pulled Zachary forward, opening his mouth and sticking his best friend's cock inside, teasing the piss hole with his tongue, smelling the scent of cum from earlier in the day on his balls, it only drove Nick to keep going.

Zachary's eyes rolled into the back of his head, and a grin spread across his face as he face-fucked his best friend. He hadn't known anything like this could happen, he hadn't thought that this would be real, but here it was, happening at this very moment.

He loved Nick's tongue as it slid up and down his shaft, curling around his skin. He knew that he was on the verge of coming, and he didn't care and neither did Nick, it seemed. Like nothing that he had ever felt before, like a moment that seemed could drag on forever Zachary shot his load into Nick's mouth and he took it down with a smile on his face while he moaned in pleasure.

"Shit you taste good....now lay on your back..." Nick instructed him and Zachary was more than happy to comply. He stared up at the ceiling, gripping his still stiff cock in his hand, allowing Nick to spread his legs. He thought that he was about to get fucked but instead he found Nick's face down in the crack of his ass, his tongue moving in all sorts of directions, forcing more precum to drip from his tip.

"I want you in me..." Zachary let out in a whisper.

"What was that Zachey?" Nick asked him, moving up to his mouth, their eyes locking. Nick moved his finger down to Zachary's ass and began to tease it, to move his finger in and out.

"I want you to fuck me...all night long..." Nick chuckled deviously.

"You want my cock inside of that tight virgin ass of yours... huh Zachey?" he nodded. "Is this tight ass something you've been saving for me?" Again he nodded. "Good." Nick reached for a condom in his wallet and a bottle of lube but Zachary stopped him.

"No condom...I want you to come inside of me...I trust you..." Nick smiled and popped open the bottle of KY, dripping it on his dick and spreading it around. "Just be gentle..."

"I know...I don't want to hurt you." Nick eased himself down, propping up Zachary's legs. He took a deep breath and slid himself inside, stopping only for a moment when Zachary winced in pain at being entered for the first time. "You okay?"

"Yeah...and you?" Zachary asked his best friend.

"Good. You're tight...but I like it...it's different. Better." Nick moved in and out of him, his hips grinding in a circular motion before going back and forth again. It seemed as if this could go on forever, and Nick wondered how deep into Zachary he could go. It was as if he could reach his organs, perhaps touch his heart, maybe even locate his soul, all of this accomplished with the power of his cock. Zachary's violet eyes seemed luminescent and glistened with the hint of tears.

"Are you sure you're okay?" he asked again, but Zachary only nodded. They were glistening with sweat and the air was becoming hot, Nick knowing that he was going to come at any moment. With Zachary, it was as if he was seeing everything. The universe, past the universe. He was seeing angels and demons, God and the Devil, all of them hanging out and throwing a party.

"Fuck…I'm coming…" It was a great rushing wave, moving through him and spilling into Zachary, filling him up on the inside. They had gone to a place never imagined and there was no reason to believe that they could ever come back.

"I know…I can feel it." He said in a whisper, feeling himself being taken over by Nick, being consumed by him, just as Zachary was consuming him. Nick pulled himself out of Zachary's ass and Zachary reached for him, pulling Nick close by the direction of his cock, licking his lips and smiling before shoving him inside.

The moist heat of his mouth was mind-blowing for Nick, who wondered if they could go on like this forever and never have to come up for air again. He could think of nothing else, nothing else mattered except for Zachary and making him happy. If he was only given one mission in life, pleasing him was all that mattered.

Zachary liked staring up into Nick's eyes, seeing his head roll back in pleasure, his hips thrusting back and forth, pulling that dick in and out. He could taste the tanginess of his own ass mixed with the saltiness of his cum and he wanted more. He wanted to feel Nick shoot his load in his mouth, to drink him down for the rest of his life. He never wanted to leave this room and he never wanted to see Nick Nolan in clothes again.

"God damn you're so fucking good…" Nick said with a chuckle, enjoying the pleasure of Zachary's mouth. "It's like you've waited for this your entire life…" Zachary was only half hearing him, continuing his goal of getting Nick to come again. "Shit!" and it came, in great waves it came, rushing out, hitting the back of his throat, slipping out of his mouth and sliding down his face, dripping onto his neck.

"I need that ass of yours again…I need you again." Nick said, pulling his now sopping wet cock out of Zachary's mouth. "I need to be in you again..." Nick took hold of Zachary and threw him up against the wall, shoving his cock inside of him once again, knowing that he wanted it too.

"Yes..." Zachary said in muffled breath, the strands of his hair dripping with sweat, his stiff cock pressed tightly against the wall as Nick fucked him from behind.

"You like that Zachey?" Nick purred in his ear.

"Uh-huh..." They were slamming against the wall, hearing it echo out into the hall, pictures falling from their nails and crashing to the ground but they didn't care. All that mattered was this very moment; everything else could go to hell.

Nick reached around and stroked him again, taking him through door after door in his mind. Memories, times spent together, all of it culminating into something else, something new, and something that could not be denied between them.

Zachary shot his load all over the wall just as Nick was coming inside of him once again, filling him up and taking him over, becoming a part of his very being.

***

They laid there against each other for several minutes, not sure of what to say, not even sure if any words were adequate to express what they were feeling. Their dorm was dark and the air smelled of sex, lingering around them like a ghost, and the silence between them seemed deafening.

"Why did this happen?" Zachary questioned, resting his head against Nick's chest, hearing his heart beat beneath the flesh.

"I don't know...I've never felt this way for you before...not for any guy actually...but it came on so suddenly." Nick sighed and kissed him on the forehead. "Like right after I saw you out on the field I couldn't stop thinking about you...I couldn't think about anything else but the idea of being with you. I didn't even go to class I just wandered around and thought about you...like I was seeing you for the first time...like I was taken over."

Zachary tried not to think about earlier, when he had been jerking off, when he had made his wish for Nick to love him completely and honestly as he loved him.

"It's like I'm under your spell..."

Zachary realized then that unlike Mercutio he had landed his Romeo, he didn't have to sacrifice himself for the love that dare not speak its name; the greatest love story never told. Nick had his Juliet, and Zachary wondered if Nick would leave her for him. Or was this just another case of "a buddy helping another buddy out?" For now it didn't matter, he was going to enjoy this moment with Nick, he was going to get honor for Mercutio; the doomed boy who had loved and died in silence.

It was a fitting end, friends into lovers and thoughts unspoken as hearts hit to the floor and this darkness washed ashore; he couldn't control this twist of fate.

Frank Fudgepacker, Teenage Whore

Simon Sheppard

I'm working my way through college, OK?

It's not my fault my cheap parents won't send me enough money, even though my dad's a professor and should fucking well know that college students have their needs. Man, he already gave me so much attitude about not being able to get into my top choices that I'm sure as shit not going to ask him for any more cash. But hell, I got to leave New York Fucking City and come to school in Florida. So what the hell, huh?

Oh, yeah...most of my clients call me Lance. Or Erik, depending. And sometimes, when I get all gothed up for the kinkier old men in my, um, clientele, I use the name Stiv. It's some old rock and roller's name, I think. One guy—he's not very nice, but he's rich as fuck—nicknamed me Frank Fudgepacker. You could call me Frank, I guess, but I'd rather you didn't.

So, yeah, I've always been attracted to older men. Sometimes *much* older men. I know, you'll probably say I have issues with my father. Whatever. Listen, a guy likes to fuck what he likes to fuck. You, as a gay man, should sure as shit understand that.

When I was living at home, I didn't do anything about that—about wanting to have sex with old men. But when I got to college, I started sucking them off, sometimes. Men I picked up down by the beach, or at the mall. Guys who used to be married to women, or still were. Men who'd lost their boyfriends to you-know-what. Sometimes they'd be all nervous till I showed them my driver's license, that I really was eighteen. I know I look young for my age, but dude, it still seemed comic.

I'd usually end up back at their house, down on my knees, sucking. Some of them had real nice cocks, too. And even though they were pretty old—OK, sometimes *very* old—a bunch of them could get it up pretty well. Even without those little blue pills—as far as I knew.

They all seemed pretty pleased by their luck, too, even the ones who'd been nervous at first, thinking maybe I was a police decoy or something. As if.

Then I met Bruce. He was one of those AIDS widows, living on his inheritance in a pretty nice place, though it was a little pissy looking, if you know what I mean, all antiques and shit everywhere. Still, Bruce was nice. And I found him sexy, though I mostly like 'em hairier than him. Nice cock, though. Big, thick cock, all veiny. And once he got his pants off, he did have hairy legs and a nice bush. So...

I sure hadn't intended to have anything like an affair. I mean, I was busy enough just trying to keep up with math class. But I started seeing him kind of regularly. It was nice, really, and he started taking me out to dinner and stuff, even though I had to explain to him what "vegan" meant. I think he was happy to be seen with a guy as young and—well, fuck, I'll say it—as cute as me. No, I *know* he was happy. Proud, even.

OK, once it got a little awkward when this straight couple, must have been in their seventies, came over to us and said hi to Bruce. I could tell he was trying to figure out what to do about me. He finally introduced me as a distant grand-nephew. That was that. I doubt that the Steins or Cohens or whatever suspected a thing. I'm not even sure they knew what month it was, if you know what I mean.

Not that Bruce was a mercy fuck. Far from it. He was attractive. Wasn't even very old, just in his mid-fifties. And he was actually hella good in bed. He was the first guy ever to rim me. Until then, I had no fucking idea. How good it felt. No idea.

He'd get my legs up and scoot down there and start licking my hole. It was amazing. He was really, really good at it. Lots of men have done that to me since then, so I know. Bruce was really good.

He'd always said he loved how furry my crack was, even before he started licking at it. Actually, my crack is one of the few hairy places on my body. Bummer, but there it is. I know...guys my age are supposed to all want to shave their bodies and be hairless as goddamn guppies. But fuck it. Guys my age aren't supposed to wind up in the sack with men old enough to be our fathers. Or grandfathers. Are we?

So he'd lick me and kiss me down there until it drove me totally crazy. Then he'd raise his head up and I'd look down between my thighs—OK, back then, I could have stood losing a few pounds, which I eventually did—and there he'd be, his spit all over his beard and a big smile on his handsome face. Then maybe he'd pull himself back up on the bed and lie on top of me, his stiff dick rubbing against my belly, his furry chest up against me, and he'd kiss me—a lot—and I could taste my ass on his mouth. Which was way hotter than it might sound.

Like I said, he wasn't a mercy fuck. He was a nice guy. Only I could tell he was pretty, well, romantic. Like he was always trying to avoid getting too affectionate, so he'd say stuff like, "Dave, I love...your hairy crack." Like he'd started out to say something else, but thought better of it. Which was smart, because when you're busy with classes, who wants some old guy to fall in love with you? Not me. But Bruce was nice, like I said, and not a mercy fuck. Actually, he was the first man ever to fuck me.

It had started out with him licking my asshole, as usual, then playing with it with his fingertips, just rubbing the wet flesh till it I was fucking squirming.

"I want you to fuck me." I said.

"Really?" he said.

"Yeah, just take it slow."

"How about if I just lay back and you can lower yourself down on my dick? At your own pace."

"That'll work," I said. And it did.

OK, well at first, when I looked down at his rubber-wrapped dick, I figured there was no way I'd be able to take it.

That big thing was just not going to fit inside me. No way. But Bruce lubed me up real good and just let me slide down on it slow. And it maybe hurt a little to start with, but he played with my nipples—I like having my tits played with—and told me to relax, so I bent over and kissed him and just kinda slid on down, feeling that big old cock enter me, inch by inch, like I could almost measure it with my ass. I swear.

"I feel like I gotta take a shit."

"That's normal. Relax."

"I *am* relaxed."

"Relax more."

And that's when it began to feel fantastic. Anybody who says anal sex doesn't feel good has just never been fucked right.

So Bruce started to fuck me on a regular basis, sometimes twice a night, though school was actually getting kind of tough and sometimes I couldn't schedule in sex with him, or I had to stay up late studying the nights that I did end up getting fucked.

Bruce was always going on about how cute I was and how I was good sex, so I decided to take his word for it, and about then was the first time I sold my ass. I needed some extra money all of a sudden—some asshole had stolen my iPod, and I hadn't backed up most of the music. And my mom and dad were *not* going to be sympathetic about me being careless enough to let someone rip off my new iPod. At least not sympathetic enough to cut me a check.

It was easy to set up, really, the hustling. I put up an ad online, and after some e-mailing back and forth, this guy and I spoke by phone. He asked me whether I was a cop, and I said no, I wasn't a cop, and yes, I had really just turned nineteen, and then he invited me over. He wasn't as good-looking as Bruce, but his house was a lot nicer—almost a damn mansion, really—and it was an easy 200 bucks, since I probably would have let him suck my dick for free. Probably. Not that I ever would have told *him* that.

After that, I started picking up some much needed funds, and it sure was easier than selling flat-screen TVs on the weekend or asking, "You want fries with that?"

I was still seeing Bruce, though. And things had gotten a little kinkier. He'd even drunk my piss a couple of times, once I got over being pee-shy, which was hot...Oh, he liked my foreskin, too. He was always going on about that. It's kind of long, see, even when I'm fully hard.

So one day during spring break, when I was still in my dorm room—because I didn't want to go north, and anyway, Florida is where everyone else *comes* for spring break—my roommate was gone. Bruce came over, and we did some role-playing, like he's my professor and he's come to see me because my grades have gone to shit. But, he says, there's one way I can pass, and I ask him how, and he tells me that he really needs his dick sucked. Kinda hot, right?

I had his big old piece of meat shoved all the way down my throat when there was a knock on the dorm room door. We kind of froze, hoping it wasn't somebody from the college who had the pass key. Actually, at some point I started half-hoping it was my roommate Shawn, coming back early, because he was actually pretty sexy, especially with his clothes off so I could see his big old dick and perfect ass, even though he was ostentatiously straight. Actually, though I mostly do go for considerably older guys, I'd jacked off every so often thinking of Shawn. That is, if I wasn't saving it for business. Thinking especially about spreading Shawn's cheeks and licking his hole the way Bruce liked to lick mine—maybe I'll be a good dirty old man someday. But anyway, after another knock or two, we heard footsteps going away down the hall, at which point Bruce started laughing pretty hard, which was kind of weird, seeing as how he still had his hard-on in my mouth. But that didn't stop him from coming...or from giving me a passing grade.

But by that point, I'd built up a pretty steady clientele. I'd been seeing three or four regular johns every week or two, and there were also the one-timers who obtained my services when the missus was out of town or something. Most of them were pretty good guys, though one of them, a rabbi actually, could only come if he spanked me—I charged him extra for that— and another one kept offering me speed. I mean, he's old enough to be my grandfather and *he* kept offering *me* crystal. But mostly good guys. And there was also my damn schoolwork to keep up with, on top of business. So I started seeing Bruce less often. Taking rain checks on dates. Just blowing him off. Seeing him a lot less often.

But one night, pretty late, I was feeling kinda weirded out because a potential john had decided not to hire me, after I'd gone to all the trouble to go to his hotel room and shit. And he was pretty nasty about it, too, really, like what I was selling was somehow crap. So I phoned up Bruce, just to talk, y'know? And that's when I first told him I'd been hustling a bit. And he acted all nice and understanding—because, after all, he'd occasionally been fucking guys besides me, as well. Maybe he was glad I'd just been busy, and it wasn't that I didn't like him any more, I don't know. Anyway, he was just so damn sweet that he managed to persuade me to head over to his place.

"OK," I told him, "but no hanky-panky. I'm beat."

But after we'd been lying around for a while on Bruce's bed, me talking, him trying to make me feel better, he leaned over and kissed me on the mouth, and pretty soon I had me a hard-on that was damn near peeking over the top of my jeans, and I knew that Bruce was going to fuck me, even if it was for the last time, and he did. And it felt great, no doubt about that. With experience, I've become relaxed enough to get fucked any old which way: on my back, doggy, even standing up and leaning against a wall, which is what this skinny, Mexican violinist who hires me likes to do. Still, I climbed up on Bruce and rode his cock, just like the first time, for old time's sake if nothing else. But then, while I was laying there with my head on his furry belly, smelling the drying cum, feeling safe and warm, he finally went ahead and said it: "I love you, you know."

And fuck, I didn't know what to say, so I said, "I love you, too."

And then he said, "I know." And pretty soon after that I got dressed and left.

So the weeks went by, and sometimes I answered Bruce's e-mail and returned his phone messages, and sometimes I didn't. I mean, I was busy with studying for finals and I wanted to earn some extra cash so I can travel during the summer, when Florida becomes an oven with hurricanes. Plus, I really needed a new car; my old one was for shit. So we never got together after that night, the time I got turned down by a john.

Eventually, Bruce sent me an e-mail that said, "I'm guessing that you don't want to see me again, but you just don't know how to say it. So I'll say it instead: Goodbye."

Well, though Bruce can be kind of a drama queen sometimes, the truth is that I was sort of relieved. It's not that I'd *never* have sex with him again, exactly, or that I want to hurt the guy. But what did he expect, really? I only have so much time and sexual energy, and business is business, y'know?

And also, here's something weird, it turned out that my roommate Shawn isn't really so straight after all. And hell, what's wrong with relating to someone my own age, somebody who won't die before I'm middle aged? I mean, sorry if it sounds cold, but it's true. So Shawn and I have started having this thing. I haven't told him about my work though, and I guess I never will, even though it's a bit of a job to keep it a secret from him. But he would never, ever be as cool about it as Bruce was. So I won't say anything about it, ever, and I hope he never finds out.

Bruce has called me a few more times recently, but I mean, what's the point? What's the fucking point? It's over, right? Not to be hurtful, but...unless he gives me cash...over.

And that's about it. That's the story. I know you said you didn't want to actually do anything, just beat off and talk. Oh, you wanted to do most of the talking? Sorry, sorry. But it's still the two hundred we talked about, right?

So you can finish up jacking off while I go piss, right? Hey, you want to come along and watch? No? You sure?

OK, whatever you want, right?

Because, yeah, business is business.

Be right back.

Driving Lessons
T. Hitman

Tyler felt Jason's gray-blue eyes narrow unblinkingly upon him, pinning him in their sites from behind the black lenses of his favorite shades, the expensive pair with the chrome frames. Also looming in his peripheral vision was Jason's well-traveled white baseball cap, its bill thready around the edges, turned forward to expose the lower half of an athletic haircut. If he were to focus on Jason directly, Tyler knew he'd see a face that was almost painfully handsome to behold, from the cocky smirk at the corners of his best friend's mouth, the bottom lip slightly plumper than its topside twin, to his neatly trimmed scruff of chin fungus.

White t-shirt under black hooded jacket and blue jeans with frayed cuffs, riding atop nasty sneakers whose funky odor routinely stunk up their dorm room after Jason returned from working out, kicking them off his size twelve feet, completed the image. This close together in the cab of the truck, however, Jason's scent was hypnotic: clean skin, the smell of soap from that morning's shower, and a hint of deodorant.

"Pay attention, dude," Jason admonished, exhaling the words on a gust of minty breath.

Heavenly distraction, Tyler thought as he reached his shaky right hand toward the radio.

"No," Jason growled.

Tyler recoiled, as though he'd stuck his fingers into the flames of a roaring campfire.

"Don't fuck with the radio. It distracts you from what the engine's telling you to do. You need to listen to it if you plan to nail this proper."

"Proper*ly,*" Tyler corrected. The lone word was out of his mouth before he could censor it, the result of nerves, and yes, distraction. Jason's scent had possessed him, unleashing hordes of butterflies in his guts and the nagging tease of an itch in that trigger of sensitive flesh along the underside of his dick's head.

"Whatever," Jason grumbled. "*Morely* to the point, how about you try to get this right instead of correcting my English?"

"Sorry, but that game face of yours is fucking with my head. And just so you know, *morely* isn't a word."

"Suck it up and deal, dude. And who doesn't learn how to drive a stick?" Jason asked no one in particular, easing the baseball cap off his head. He dragged fingers through his neatly buzzed hair before re-settling the cap on in reverse, this small action lending him an even sexier look. "Especially, a dude like you who likes having something long and hard in his hand." This came with a sharp round of laughter.

"Fuck you," Tyler said.

He opened the door and exited Jason's sport pickup, a cocktail of anger and embarrassment burning through his blood. As he started across the mostly vacant visitor's parking lot toward the path that would take him to the student-housing block, he heard the truck's passenger door slam.

"Come on, I was only busting your balls. Hold up!"

Tyler put on the brakes and turned around to see Jason standing doubled over, that cocky smirk on his sexy face now expanded to a full-on, shit-eating grin.

"What?" Tyler fired back. "What's so fuckin' funny?"

"*You are,*" Jason answered, righting. "Dude, you're having more of a problem with what you told me last week than I am."

"What I'm having a problem with is the fact that you're a shitty Driver's Ed teacher. Fuck you, fuck your truck, and *fuck the damn shift pattern!*"

As soon as he heard just how ridiculous the last part sounded to his own ears, Tyler began to laugh, too.

Jason caught up, pulled him into a headlock, and dragged him back to the truck.

"Let go of me, punk!" Tyler protested, though truthfully, he loved the feel of Jason's body against his. Their present closeness unleashed that wonderfully heady scent of deodorant and warm skin.

"No," Jason said. "Besides, I'd bet your dick is hard just from having me all over you."

"Fuck off."

"You master driving a stick, we'll both be fucking off, jack wad."

Jason released his grip. Tyler stood and smoothed out his shirt. "You're an asshole."

"Seriously, if we're gonna make it down to Daytona for spring break, my wingman needs to be able to drive a standard. Just think about all those spring break bitches, dude—or in your case, those spring break *boners* you'll be wrapping your pretty mouth around." Jason grabbed Tyler's chin.

Tyler punched his fingers away. "You suck."

"Yeah, well I bet you suck better. And at least I can handle a stick. This one—" Jason patted the truck's door. "And *this one*."

He then grabbed his crotch and shook it for emphasis, an action that scattered Tyler's focus, sent his already racing heart into a gallop, and pretty much killed any hope of him learning to drive a manual transmission on that sunny Saturday afternoon, a week before mid-terms.

Tyler stalled half a dozen more times before calling it quits. About the only thing he cared about was holing himself up in the bathroom stall and jerking some release out of his dick, which refused to soften.

***

The dorm housed two single beds, one desk, and a power strip feeding laptops, a banker's lamp with a green shade, the TV set, and a DVD player. Jason's masculine smell infused each shallow breath Tyler took upon his return to their room.

A college football game played on the tube, typical Saturday afternoon viewing when Jason wasn't jerking his dick under the blankets to one of the many adult DVDs piled around the television.

"Sup," Jason growled, tipping his chin upward in that standard guy's greeting. "You didn't have to whack it in the men's head, dude."

"I'm not gonna beat off in front of an audience."

"Since when?"

Tyler shot Jason a look and huffed out a sigh. The answer to the rhetorical question was simple: since he'd confessed his deepest, most painful secret over a six-pack the previous week, that's when.

Tyler sat on the edge of his bed and allowed his eyes to wander over Jason's body. After giving up on that day's driving lesson, Jason had kicked off his ripe sneakers along with his white socks. His hooded sweatshirt and pants sat crumpled in a pile on the floor. He was sprawled on his back across the bed, his naked legs crossed at the ankles, their taut athlete's muscles dense with a thatch of dark hair. One of Jason's arms was curled behind his neck. His other hand absently scratched at the meaty bulge of the package encased in a pair of gray boxer-briefs. Tyler had secretly masturbated with his face pressed into those very shorts on numerous occasions, usually following one of Jason's workouts after he'd hit the showers and when they were at their funkiest.

The football game droned on with Tyler not caring who lost or won. He and Jason would probably ace making the baseball team in the spring, just as they had in their freshmen year — unless, of course, word got out that he was a cock-hound, a cum-hungry dick-lover, a guy rabid for the taste of another dude's tool.

Tyler clamped down on his thoughts and did his best to not appear so obvious as he studied the topography of Jason's muscles. It wasn't easy to ignore those magnificent legs and feet with their long, flat digits, the nails cleanly clipped, sparse threads of hair on each big toe.

"So I figured it all out, dude," Jason said, his gruff voice slicing through Tyler's lust-filled memories.

"Figured what out? The Theory of Relativity?"

"No, dick weed, how I'm gonna teach you to drive a stick so we can head down to Daytona and party our rocks off."

"Oh yeah?" Tyler asked, his curiosity mildly peaked. "How's that?"

Jason swung his legs off the bed and stood, stretching to reveal even more naked musculature as his tee shirt rose with the effort. "Real simple. What's fucking you up is that fuckin' five-speed shift pattern on the head of the stick."

Jason strutted the few steps to the desk. There, he grabbed a pen and a sheet of paper from among the clutter. Tyler was only partially aware of the big double "H" Jason drew across the page; his eyes locked on the fullness in the crotch of Jason's boxer-briefs, a weight that looked far heavier than the usual meatiness created by low-hanging balls and soft dick.

No, Jason's tool was, at the very least, half stiff!

"Okay, check this out," Jason said. He drew a gear number to correspond with the top and bottom points on the "H" diagram, with "N" in the center middle, then squeezed the tenting lump in his underwear, confirming Tyler's suspicion: Jason's cock *was* swelling harder with each passing second. Its thickness now pushed the elastic waistband off his abdomen, exposing a lush patch of dark pubic shag. "Get up."

"What?"

Jason pulled Tyler off his bed and to his feet. "No questions. Just trust me. And kick off those sneakers."

Tyler hesitated for all of a second before Jason shoved him onto the other bed, its blanket messy with the still-warm relief of Jason's body. An instant later, Jason yanked off both of Tyler's sneakers, exposing the fluffy white cotton socks baking inside them.

"What the fuck?" Tyler huffed

Jason set the hastily drawn diagram on top of his pillow.

"You're gonna love this. Now sit up and look at the diagram. And spread your legs."

Tyler was forced to obey when Jason moved into the space between his legs, opening them wider while also backing him up against the dorm room's cement brick wall. Jason's masculine scent filled Tyler's next shallow gasp for breath.

"It came to me while you were jerking off," Jason chuckled. "The perfect way to teach a cock-worshipper like you to drive stick."

Tyler felt his face go red. He pushed against Jason's back to no avail. The brief, fruitless struggle stirred all of those incredible smells into motion: Jason's deodorant, the trace of shampoo at his hairline, the funky cum and sweat-infused bedclothes that reeked of balls, dick, and feet. "Fuck you. Let me up."

"No. Give me your right hand."

When Tyler refused, Jason took it by force, pulling it around his waist. Half high on Jason's musk, Tyler was powerless to resist what came next—not that he would have if given the choice.

"It struck me that a stick-shift is just like a dude's hard cock. And since you jones on cock..."

The sound of Jason's free left hand, fumbling with the elastic waistband of his underwear, somehow reached Tyler's ears through the drumming cadence of his heartbeats. "You've got to be joking!"

But Tyler quickly learned Jason wasn't, as the fingers of his shaking right hand closed around eight solid inches of erect dick.

"Now pay attention," Jason said. He encircled Tyler's hand with his own and maneuvered it forward. "That's first gear," he said, sliding their shared grip and his straining cock forward, into the imaginary upper limb on the left side of the "H" diagram. Jason pulled back. "This is second gear. Neutral in the middle. Going up, to third. Down to fourth. Up to fifth. Reverse is all the way to the right and down."

Tyler barely heard the instruction. Taking a heavy swallow and discovering his mouth had been drained of all moisture, he found himself instead focused upon the pulsating feel of Jason's rod in his hand, the full, throbbing life of it. How many times had he beaten his own dick to climax while fantasizing about Jason's? Smelling it. Kissing it. Sucking the seed out of its straining piss slit. The scrape of the coarse hair lining the sides of Jason's cock unleashed pins and needles along the underside of Tyler's wrist. The sweaty heat radiating out of the twin giants hanging beneath sent the temperature in the room skyrocketing.

"Holy shit," Tyler groaned, barely able to breathe.

"Pay fuckin' attention. I know it ain't easy, especially with that rod you're poking into my spine."

Tyler was so intent on squeezing Jason's cock, he barely realized his was standing at attention and drilling Jason's coccyx. *Coccyx*. How ironic was that? Some unaffected part of his dazed consciousness chuckled internally at that thought.

"Okay, plant your feet on top of mine."

"Huh?"

"Your left foot—place it over mine. Pretend my left foot's the clutch. My right one is the accelerator and the brake."

Tyler absently did as he was told to while stroking up and down on Jason's dick.

"Dude, you keep pumping the clutch like that, you're gonna stall out," Jason growled between sips for breath.

Tyler reached his other hand around and boldly fondled Jason's balls. He ogled the loose, damp skin, and in concert, Jason's hand over Tyler's ceased the shifting movement for something more enjoyable. Up and down, they stroked the thickness in their shared grip from root to head.

"Sweet," Jason groaned, leaning his head back. The right side of his face pressed against the left side of Tyler's.

"You're sure?"

"Fuck, yeah. Make me bust, dude."

Tyler unhooked himself and slid to the floor. Kneeling between his roommate's spread feet, he quickly sucked the helmet of Jason's dick-head and a few inches of hard shaft into his mouth. The tang of Jason's pre-cum ignited instantly across Tyler's taste buds. He gently tugged on Jason's balls, and after a few stiff gobbles on his cock, he showered them with sucks, one nut at a time.

Tyler again grabbed hold of Jason's length. "I think I got it. First gear," he said, giving his roommate's magnificent cock a shift to the upper left limb of the imaginary "H" diagram. "Second. Neutral. Third. Fourth. Fifth. Reverse..."

He was about to run through the gears again when Jason huffed, "*Fuck—!*"

The dick in Tyler's grip morphed from flesh to steel. The first blast of cum squirted all the way up Jason's chest and hit his neck, leaving a clotted line of whitewash across his t-shirt. Before the second salvo erupted fully, Tyler clamped his mouth over Jason's piss slit. He kept pace the rest of the way and didn't stop sucking until he'd swallowed the last salty, sour spurt.

Tyler knew by the wet itch between his legs and the widening stain on the crotch of his pants that he'd shot his load without even touching himself. "Damn," he moaned between laps at the dribble oozing out of Jason's pee-hole.

Jason settled back on the bed and exhaled a breathy grunt. "Good job."

"Just good?"

"For your first lesson, yeah. But it's clear to me you've got a ways to go before you master a stick. So I hope you're prepared to practice. *A lot.*"

"I am," Tyler answered. And for the first time since telling Jason the truth, he smiled.

Friday Night Video
R. K. Bussel

Every Friday night, the freshmen guys in my dorm with nothing else to do get together and watch a movie. Usually it's something silly, like *Porky's* or *Animal House,* and we get a senior to buy us beer and load up on chips and candy and generally make a mess of the rec room until it's time to go to bed. But last Friday, things went a little differently. Andy, who is generally the quietest one of the bunch, a pre-med student, brought in an unmarked tape. "Let's watch this," he said, with an unusual sparkle in his eyes. Andy's one of those guys who you never quite know what he's going to do next, and his surprises can be pleasant or not; he gives nothing away, so he didn't give a hint as to what was on the tape other than his flashing blue eyes. The eight of us looked at each other, shrugged, and agreed.

We didn't have anything better to do. Well, the minute that tape started rolling, our eyes were glued to the screen, alcohol and snacks long forgotten as we found ourselves watching real, hardcore porn. It wasn't some fancy, slick big budget picture with a title and credits, but simply launched right into images of people in various positions, naked and going at it with total abandon. I was riveted, staring at the screen as if my life depended on who was going to get plundered next, my cock instantly hard, pressing against my pants as I watched people screwing onscreen for real for the first time. Sure, I'd seen snippets here and there, glimpsed stashed tapes in my older brother's closet, but every time I'd started to watch one at home, I'd gotten so spooked, looking over my shoulder to make sure no one was watching, that I put it away. And I'd certainly never watched porn with a whole group of guys before. We all peered intently at the screen, as a buxom blonde went to town on a huge cock. She would take the entire thing down her throat, then ease back up and lick just the head, then spit on it, and start all over again. Her hand, with its long, painted-red fingernails to match her shiny red lips, was wrapped around the meaty cock. I was doubly fascinated, because unlike what a lot of the guys boasted about, I'd never had anyone suck my cock, though I'd certainly fantasized about it.

I didn't dare look at the other guys, too afraid they might cotton on to my growing erection. I continued to watch, too far gone to pretend to be blasé about it all, as the woman on the screen gave her man head like her life depended on it, smiling and cooing up at him on occasion. We barely saw the rest of the guy, just his dick, but that was enough. I couldn't have predicted my reaction, but I could tell that I was supposed to want to be the guy onscreen, the one whose cock was getting treated to a most elaborate, succulent blowjob, but in fact, I was picturing myself as the girl, sans lipstick and nail polish, just my mouth, sucking and licking, doing anything I could to bring my lover as much pleasure as possible. I could almost taste the anonymous cock in my mouth, feel my lips being stretched and pulled as I opened my mouth wide, wanting to do it perfectly. I swallowed hard, afraid the whole room could tell exactly what I was thinking.

I took the briefest of glances around and saw Andy staring at me. Maybe it wasn't the whole room I had to worry about. I noticed that his hand was in his own lap, his fingers seeming to idly play with his cock, stroking along its length. I looked away, back at the screen where the woman had stopped sucking his cock and had bent over, baring her smooth, shaved, pink asshole for him. He spread her rounded asscheeks even further apart with his hands and plunged his tongue inside, while she writhed beneath him. I knew that any minute now he was going to slide his cock into her tight hole, and I wasn't sure if I'd be able to make it. Because suddenly the video wasn't the only thing on my mind; Andy was there too. Andy and his probably-experienced cock. I'd never consciously thought about him like that before, never consciously thought about any guy, but at that moment all I wanted out of life was to be on my knees in front of Andy, taking his length down my throat.

My vision started to blur, the images before me shifting from the actual movie to my own fantasies, so I only idly noticed when Andy got up, moving quietly from his place near the TV toward the back where I was sitting. I took another peek around the room and saw some of my other friends, including Alex and Corey, with their hands in each other's lap, their hands moving silently underneath their pants to bring each other to orgasm. Apparently we were all thinking somewhat along the same lines, though probably none would have admitted it. Andy approached, moving steadily closer to me until I could feel the air around me change, now charged with arousal and electricity. I was still looking straight ahead but not seeing a thing. I knew that a glance to my right would find Andy, with his cock pressing hard against his jeans. Then I felt his hand on the back of my head, and I jolted, coughing lightly to cover it. His fingers sank into my hair, sending tingles of pleasure all the way down my back.

When his fingers made contact with my skin, I thought I'd lose it right there. Then his hand was grabbing the back of my shirt, tugging lightly to get me to stand up. As if in a trance, I followed his lead, and we both slipped out of the room. At that moment, I didn't care a bit what everyone else would think, and clearly the other boys in the room were occupied with their own fun, so I probably didn't have to worry. Andy kept his hand on my shirt, and I found that I liked it; any contact with him felt amazing, my body practically trembling as I realized that my fantasies about sucking a guy's cock were about to come true.

Andy's room was only a few steps away, a blessed single. We entered and he locked the door behind us. It was dark, but there was enough light streaming in from the moon that I could make out his outline. Suddenly, his nerdy exterior took on a whole new meaning. What had he been hiding behind his glasses and textbooks, behind those eyes that seemed glossed-over, glassy, removed? Maybe he was dreaming, plotting, planning just what he would do with dirty-minded boys like me. At least, I hoped so. He pulled me close for a kiss, and just that act right there—his hands holding me tight, his lips mashed against mine, his cock pressing insistently into the denim of my jeans—almost sent me over the edge, but I willed myself to hold out. "What were you thinking about during that movie? Did you know that I picked it out with you in mind? I've been watching you all this time and wondering when you'd realize that it was boys and not girls who did it for you. So tell me," he said, his voice dipping as his meager nails dug hard into the back of my neck, "What were you thinking about while you were watching? And don't lie—I'll know."

I'd come this far, and had no intention of lying. "I was thinking about sucking your cock." There was silence, so I continued. "Of how good it would feel to be on my knees in front of you, my mouth opened as you slammed your dick into me and I took it all the way down." I could have said more, but I paused, waiting for a cue, hoping against hope that this wasn't all just one long, elaborate tease.

He didn't say a word, simply stared me straight in the eyes for a few minutes, until the room felt like it had definitely shrunk. He shoved three fingers into my mouth, as practice, I guess, and I went to work on them, slobbering and sucking, licking and laving, treating them to everything I could think of to do with my mouth. With his other hand, he slowly undid his zipper, and even though my eyes were closed, I could hear him fumbling. When he finally pulled those fingers out and gave me a light but definite slap on the cheek, his cock was out. Wow. It was even more impressive than those of the guys in the video and had nothing at all to do with being a nerd. It was big and hard, thick but not misshapen, long, strong, and perfect. I couldn't believe it, because while I now wanted nothing more than to be his cock-sucking boy toy, even I could acknowledge that Andy wasn't exactly Mr. Hunk. But his cock more than made up for any scrawniness elsewhere, and with a quick glance at him for permission, I sank to my knees.

He held his dick at the base and fed it to me, and I eagerly gulped, trying to take it all in. He pushed his fist up so only the tip was in my mouth, so I concentrated on that sensitive part, letting my tongue lightly trail over the crown, getting used to its nuances against my taste buds. My own cock was going crazy in my pants, but I tried my best to ignore it. I closed my eyes again and put my hands along the sides of his legs to steady myself and then went to town. I gave everything I had to that blowjob, wanting to memorize the feel of his cock against my tongue in case I never got to feel it again. From his moans, I figured out which strokes and licks he liked best, and he gradually fed me more and more of his cock. I let my throat go, let my whole body relax, and before I knew it my lips were nuzzled against his pubic hair and that cockhead I'd just been sucking was somewhere halfway down my throat. He stroked my cheek encouragingly, and I swallowed, tightening around his dick, working on pure instinct.

I tightened my lips around him and slowly slid back up his shaft, amazed at how warm and alive he was. His cock felt amazing, and I gave myself over to him, let his cock invade me, teach me, show me everything I'd been missing. I must have sucked his cock for half an hour, and it's to his credit that he let me, because I'm sure he could've come at any point. My mouth was filled with saliva and lust, and I just couldn't get enough of him; I felt like I could have two cocks in my mouth at once. I reached down briefly to undo my jeans and let my cock fall loosely in front of me, then put my hands back to work holding the base of his dick and fondling his balls. I was thrilled that I could sense when he was about to erupt, and redoubled my efforts, rocking back and forth and taking him as deep into my mouth as I possibly could. When the time came, he held my head still and pumped his juice into my mouth, and I swallowed every salty, delicious drop, before beating off myself, only needing a few fast strokes to shoot a load of my own.

We spent the rest of the night trying all sorts of other experiments, some we'd seen in the video, some we hadn't. We ended up disbanding our weekly movie night, because everyone had paired off and had better things to do than sit around and wait till we could be alone. Andy still looks like a nerd on the outside, which I'm kind of grateful for. If everyone knew how impressive his cock was, I wouldn't stand a chance. Right now, though, he's all mine.

Jimmy in Me
Jeff Funk

I'm about five strokes away from pumping my meat to a creamy explosion when I hear a key in my dorm room door. "C'mon, c'mon," a guy's deep voice says in frustration. I pause and listen. My cock pulses in my hand, hot and throbbing. The guy in the hallway drops something heavy, sounds like a bag full of gym shoes. His keys jingle as he tries again. Who the fuck's out there? *Wrong room, buddy.*

My roommate dropped out the third week of school. Couldn't take the pressure, which suited me just fine. He was a sad-sack son-of-a-bitch. I hated the way he tried to keep track of me. "Where are you going?" he'd say in his prissy tone. "Out," I'd say as I left to go to a movie on a Saturday night, leaving his ass in the dorm room to scribble in his journal, no doubt whining about his dreary life. God, he drove me nuts. Even my mom didn't have her nose up my shit as bad as this mo-fo. So when he flunked a couple tests and spent hours boo-hooin' to his mama back at home, it didn't shock me none when his ass was gone. And I had the place to myself.

I made myself at home. Spread my shit all over the room. Walked around naked anytime I pleased. And I stroked my cock—lots. The dormitory wasn't air-conditioned, so my windows were always open, except when it rained. My room was on the third floor. Many nights, I stood there with the lights all off, letting the night breeze blow through my thick patch of red pubic hair, my balls bunched up close to my dick. I'd watch the guys cross Fairfield Avenue and come walking up the steps to the dorm building, laughing and slapping each other on the back. Good-natured ribbing, especially among the football jocks—all that camaraderie. I heard a joke at a party this semester: What's the difference between a straight guy and bi guy? About four beers. Maybe I need to pay a senior to pick me up a six-pack sometime. Truth be told? Even though I've wanted to, I've never messed around with a guy before. Unless you count the close call at the adult bookstore, which scared the *hell* out of me. But also intrigued me.

Now, I hear the door lock turn. Whoa, shit. I got porn mags spread out all over my bed. I can either grab for my boxers, or...

I take my comforter and toss it over the glossy images of guys' dicks.

The door creaks open. I see a big guy bend down and grab a duffle bag. He steps into my room, but stops when he sees me sticking my right foot into my boxers. With a surprised look on his face, he says, "Oh, I'm sorry."

I finish pulling up my blue plaid boxers. My rod peeks out of the fly and I have to stuff it back inside. "What are you doing coming into my room?"

"I just...I guess I'm your new roommate." He looks at a pink piece of paper. "This is room 307, right?"

I take the paper from him and study it. "Yeah, looks like you're in the right room." I try not to sound too pissed off. Here I was just getting used to being on my own.

He extends his hand. "I'm Jimmy."

"Nice to meet you, Jimmy. I'm Greg," I say with a nervous chuckle. He gives my hand a squeeze. When I try to let go, he keeps holding on, looking at me with interest. He's a good-looking guy, built like a football player. He wears a wife-beater T-shirt to show off his meaty pecs and big friggin' biceps. Curly, dark hair. Five o'clock shadow. I look down at his hand engulfing mine. Fine dark hairs curl over the side of his hand and trail up his manly forearm. My dick's still hard. This hot jock ain't helping matters. I feel weird standing in front of him. He's fully dressed and wearing shoes. Me, I'm damn near naked, barefoot, and with my penis barely tucked away. The fly on these boxers gapes like a son-of-a-bitch. Jimmy's blue eyes sparkle with mischief. He blinks and lets go of my hand at the same time.

I can feel myself blushing. "Here, let me give you a hand with your stuff." I go out into the dimly-lit hallway, grab a large suitcase, and haul it into the center of the room.

"Which bed's mine?" he asks.

"Sorry. Let me get my shit corralled." I start grabbing clothes, flinging them toward the laundry basket in my closet. Jimmy pitches in. Then I crack the window. It's a damp fall afternoon. He talks happily about the campus, what he's majoring in—blah, blah. I ask what he's doing changing rooms; usually, people are settled in by October. He hesitates, then says that he and his other roommate didn't get along. *Is this guy trouble?* I wonder. I try to get out of him what his beef was with this other guy. But he's tight-lipped. Says he'll tell me about it sometime, but he's not in the mood to "get into the whole thing."

Then Jimmy turns and grins at me. "So did I catch you jacking off?"

"What? Hell no."

"Aw, don't be embarrassed. I like doing it right before bed. It's my sleeping pill." I'm mortified. But oddly turned on, hearing him talk about stroking himself at night. Will he do it when I'm in the room? I sneak a quick glance at his crotch and see the outline of his cock stuffed into his sand-colored cargo shorts.

I look at the clock and see it's getting close to three p.m. "Fuck, I need to get goin'. I gotta get to class." I pull on jeans and a T-shirt and step into flip-flops. Jimmy announces he's gotta take a piss. When he turns to leave the room, I notice his round, firm ass. "Damn," I say under my breath. Taking advantage of the moment alone, I move swiftly over to the bed, gather my porn mags, and hide them in a drawer under some clothes. Then I put my backpack over a shoulder and head to the bathroom 'cos I gotta piss myself.

Jimmy's at a urinal. He turns and looks at me. "Sucks that you got a class now. We could hang out together and do something fun. Why don't you skip it?"

I step to the urinal beside him. "Can't. I've skipped two classes already. Dr. Cahill drops you a letter grade for every three classes missed. She takes attendance, if you can believe it."

"Hmm." He looks down. "So are you going to the Halloween party Saturday night?"

Just then, the toothbrush guy comes into the bathroom. This guy's an asshole. He'll stand there with headphones blasting while he brushes his damn teeth for twenty minutes or more, letting his frothy slobber drip all over. I roll my eyes at the sight of him. *Fuckin' dickhead. Why don't you clean the damn sink when you're done?* I once saw him talking to a girl and his teeth were freakishly white. He's got some kind of psycho condition if you ask me. OCD at the very least.

The dorm's bathroom culture was weird. Guys would stand stark naked, talking about computers and weird shit. I'd think things like: *Really? Moog, eh? Nice cock. A Mac iBook? Great. Let me see your ass again. Yeah, like that.* This one guy would almost dare you to look at his long penis which swung like an elephant trunk. He'd parade around buck naked. Then if you looked, he'd frown and act offended. I didn't know whether to look at it or feed it a peanut.

One time, I went to the crapper around two in the morning. Someone was taking a shower. Guys shower at all hours, so I didn't think much of it. Until I heard moans. Dude had a girl in there, fuckin' her in the hot water. Barefoot, I stood on the toilet to see who it was. I had a clear view of the guy's dark, wet hair. And through the opaque shower curtain, I could make out the shape of him thrusting into her. I stood there and jacked off while they fucked. Every time I heard the guy's rhythmic grunts, I'd feel a wave of lust wash over my body. Made my nipples hard. How I wished I coulda been the one in there with him instead of his girlfriend. What would his dick feel like, moving in and out of my ass? My breathing mimicked theirs while my hand stroked my hard-on in a feverish frenzy. When I cracked my nut, the cum splattered onto the tile floor. I crept down off the toilet, opened the door to the stall quietly, then I flushed and scampered out of there, knowing full well I sent a blast of scalding water in on them. I heard the girl let out a yelp, which made me laugh like a maniac as I ran down the hall back to my room.

Now, I hear Jimmy pissing, a strong stream which goes on and on. Just when I think he's done, he pisses some more.

I say, "I'll probably go to the Halloween party. You're talking about the Kappa Sig party, right?" It's a campus-wide party, held in the bottom of Richard's Treat. Anyone can go.

"Yeah, they're co-hosting it with the Tri-Dels."

"Try Dels. Try 'em. Everyone else has."

"Dude, I have heard that joke fifty million times."

"So did you ever make it with one of 'em, Jimmy?"

"Them skinny bitches ain't my type."

"Not even Haley?"

"She's the skankiest one of 'em all. Say, you ever been with a girl?" Jimmy says, raising an eyebrow.

"No," I say with a shrug, a bit embarrassed of my virgin status. I flush the urinal. Mr. Toothbrush is brushing like an idiot, oblivious to our conversation.

"Ever been with a guy?" Jimmy looks at me with a crooked smile. He's done pissing, but he's still standing with his dick out. *Is this a trick? He's just messing with me, right? Trying to suss out the new roommate. Or does he know I'm into guys?* I look into his eyes. The way he looks back makes me horny. I force a short hiss of air through my nostrils and shake my head like *get a load of this guy*, hoping to seem calm. The wind comes up, blowing a burst of rain against the window. I leave the bathroom, go down the back stairs and walk to my class with an umbrella.

I say "hey" to about twenty classmates as I walk, which was weird to get used to. "Hey" must be an Illinois thing. Like the way they call soft drinks "soda." In Indiana, we say "hi" and we drink "pop." Also, on a bigger campus, I probably wouldn't speak to anyone. This is a small campus, attended by about eighteen hundred students. And gossip flies like crazy. I wasn't so sure I wanted others knowing my business. I wouldn't cry brokenhearted if they found out I'm into guys; but on the other hand, I wasn't going to advertise it. In class, Dr. Cahill drones on and on. I spend most of the time staring out the window, thinking about my new roommate. Every time I close my eyes, I picture us grinding our cocks together, which causes tons of dick drip.

After class, I go to the parking lot at the dorm and get in my car. I need to clear my thoughts, so I drive through the rain-slicked streets to my little newsstand. I dig the lady who works there. She's real slick, doesn't let any of the other customers see what I'm purchasing. What she does is she'll take the magazines out of my hand, hold them down beneath the counter and punch in the price on the cash register. I give her my money. She bags them discreetly. And off I go. The fuckers at the mall made a big production one time when I bought three magazines, with the one I *really* wanted sandwiched between. They waved that magazine around like lunatics, wanted everyone to take a gander. So I go here, and I buy only what I want. It's an adventure figuring this stuff out. The adult bookstore's a couple blocks away. But I haven't been there in a while because a guy scared the crap out of me.

As my eyes scan the magazines at the newsstand, I peer into my memory of what happened that night at the bookstore.

Here's what went down. I went there, okay? This was a couple weeks ago, back when my old roommate would ask where I was off to. I was there browsing around midnight. I saw a sign that you could pre-view a video for five bucks. I didn't want to risk renting them because then I'd have to put a credit card on file with the joint. And wouldn't my old man shit a brick if he saw charges from this place? So I thought, hell. I'll just watch one here. So I paid and stepped into preview booth number five. I closed the door and sat on the bench. There were controls to fast-forward the video. I scrolled through the opening credits. And when the action started getting good, I pulled my cock out and started stroking. Then I had this creepy feeling: someone was watching me. I just felt it, man. Eyes on me. I looked around. Didn't see anyone. But then I saw a crack in the booth where a couple boards were parted slightly. And I saw a dude's eye, I shit you not. My heart raced. "Excuse me!" I said, real mean-like. The guy scurried away.

Determined to get my five bucks' worth, I went back to stroking but by then I was paranoid. Then I saw a piece of white paper come sailing under the door. I bent down and picked it up. Here's what it said: "I need a blowjob. Or I'll give you one. Open the door if interested." So I stood there, not moving for a good five minutes. Guys were sucking Latin cocks on the video screen while I planned my escape. I put my hand on the door handle. Flung the door open. And I bolted out of that place. Outside, I ran to my car, which was parked in front of a Chinese restaurant. I was worried that whoever wrote the note would try to follow me. Then later that night, I couldn't stop thinking: what if I'd opened the door? It became the feature presentation in the ole spank bank. What if...

Now at my little newsstand, the cool lady's watching the rain. I pick a magazine. The guy on the cover reminds me of Jimmy.

***

And so, Jimmy and I settle in as roommates. I get to know his habits. I watch with interest as he does crunches each day, sculpting his abs. He makes me watch game shows while we eat lunch together in our room. He laughs his ass off as people race through a grocery store, chuckin' food into their carts. After a couple days of hearing his deep, booming laugh, I find myself laughing along. For whatever reason, I never laughed out loud while watching television before. A couple times, we go to a used bookstore and on the way he tells me about his hometown. I love his stories. I didn't know having a roommate could be so much fun. I catch myself worrying about future college years—would we be roommates? What about beyond college?

He does jack off at night before he goes to sleep. He's not vocal about it, but I can hear him. I could so easily cross those few feet between us and give some assistance, but he hasn't put the sex moves on me since that first day. He was probably just joking around. Or maybe he's waiting for me to approach him, which I almost did the other night...

I couldn't sleep, see. Kept thinking about Jimmy as he lay close to me, his manly scent filling the room. I got up and went to the bathroom for a sip of water. Then I quietly slipped back inside. The curtains were open. The moon and a lonely street light filled the room with a grainy, blue glow and inky shadows. My eyes adjusted. I stood over Jimmy, watching him sleep. His muscular arm was up over his head, exposing the silken armpit hair. His other hand rested just above his navel. Could I touch him lightly, my fingertips caressing the length of his manhood, without waking him? I listened to his breathing and let out a hot breath of my own. Then I crawled into my bed and fell into a dream of him.

***

On Halloween night, I carry a late supper in a Styrofoam box back to the dorm, which is decorated for the holiday. Skeletons and jack-o'-lanterns. I smell warm fabric softener coming from the laundry room, mixed with the scent of microwave popcorn. I stop at the vending machine and get a soda. Then I climb the stairs to my room.

Jimmy's getting dressed for the Halloween party. "You're gonna be late, Greg. Eat up so we can go together." He's naked with his back to me. He drapes his body with a white toga and uses a gold rope to hold it in place. He steps into sandals. He's a vision of male beauty. "What are you wearing?"

My mouth's full when I answer. "Goin' as a pirate." I dig in my pocket then hold up a cork from a bottle of wine. "Got a lighter?"

"Yeah, why?"

"Cheap makeup."

He fishes in his drawer and finds a lighter then hands it to me. I light the cork, let it burn for a few seconds. Then blow. I smudge my face. "See?"

"Aw, that's so cool."

"Let me run down to my car and get the rest of my outfit." I stuff the last bit of food into my mouth then get up and leave the room.

As I begin down the first set of stairs, I hear some fellas making one hell of a ruckus. A little guy races past me with a group hotly in pursuit, spraying shaving cream at him. The last guy bumps me hard. I feel myself start to fall. I reach for something—anything—to stop myself, but I tumble down half a flight of stairs. I lie on my back, disoriented. When I open my eyes, I look up the stairwell from this odd angle. I can tell something's wrong with my left ankle. No one stops to check on me.

With effort, I stand. But I can't put weight on my left leg. I grab the railing with both hands and skip a step at a time back upstairs. When I get to my room, Jimmy sees me limping. "Greg, what happened!" I tell him. Deep lines of worry form on his face. He mutters the word "assholes" when I tell him about the guys. Then he says, "I'm taking you to the hospital." He slips into jeans and helps me out to my car. I give him my keys and he drives.

We end up going to the emergency room. It's pandemonium there. Halloween's a bad night to be at the hospital. We wait three hours before I finally see someone. They wheel me down to get an X-ray, then we have to wait for that, too. Turns out, I have a bad sprain. They wrap my ankle, hook me up with some crutches, and give me a prescription for painkillers.

When we get back to the dorm, Jimmy surprises me when he scoops me into his arms and carries me up the stairs to our room. I start to protest, then feel myself melting into his massive chest, my face against his neck.

He gently puts me on my bed. I look at the clock. "I'm sure the party's still going on. You can go without me. It's cool, really."

Jimmy just stares at me. His eyes are glassy like they're filled with a sort of "love dew." For what seems like a minute, we look at each other. Then he bends down and kisses me. Tentative at first and then more insistent. I love the endearing way he holds the side of my face. He brushes his cheek against mine and the friction of whiskers against whiskers sends goose bumps capering across my skin. He pulls away from me and yanks his toga out from his jeans and tosses it to the floor. With fumbling fingers, he unzips my pants and takes my dick out and plays with it. Then he takes it into his hot mouth. I arch my back and whimper from the pleasure. I grab a handful of his dark hair while he performs his ministrations. I feel like crying out, but I hold it in. Just then, his mouth covers mine. He kisses me hungrily. Urgent, like he needs my lips as badly as he needs air.

"Get these off," I say in a husky voice as I tug at his jeans. He sheds them and stands before me. His penis is something to behold. I kiss the tip then work it with my mouth, slurping at it. I run my tongue up the shaft and lick the head, tasting the precum which leaks from his piss hole. I'm rewarded with the sound of his moans and the dirty words that fall from his pouty lips. He grabs my head and shoves his hard-on down my throat. I choke but keep going at it with pure lust as he rocks his hips.

Then he stops. "Let me try something. Do you trust me?" I nod at him. He goes to his closet and shuffles till he finds what he's looking for. He rolls on a condom and gets on the bed with me, kneeling between my legs. He lifts them, taking extra care with my bandaged ankle. He places my feet against his chest. Softly, he kisses my toes. He squirts lube on his fingers and works my hole until I relax from his probing.

With a lazy smile on his face, he teases my pucker with his cock. "You ready?"

"Yes." The word flows hotly from my mouth. Slowly, he pushes into me. I gasp when I feel his girth. He keeps going until he slides in all the way. I swallow hard. I take deep breaths as I squirm under him. Soon, the pain turns to pleasure. When he sees the shift take place, he moves in and out of me, increasing the pace as he goes.

"You feel so good," he whispers.

My cock gets harder every time he thrusts fully into me. If he keeps this up, I feel like I could shoot a load up my chest and maybe hit my face. "Jimmy, oh Jimmy. God...*damn*...ooh."

He takes both of my legs and has me wrap them around his torso. He brings his body closer to me. I feel his cock go deeper inside. Through hot breath, he jams his tongue into my mouth.

As I close my eyes, I think of how much I've yearned for Jimmy. And all the men I've longed for but felt I couldn't have. Tonight my wish came true.

So long, virginity.

And now as we fuck, I relish the feel—

Oh, God.

—of having Jimmy in me.

My Final Semester
Shane Allison

I can't stop thinking about him as my dick glistens with cooking oil beneath a ceiling fan of hot lights. I can't stop thinking about him in the aisle of tit clamps and butt plugs. I can't stop thinking about his dick dipping into the special sauce of my dirty thoughts. He's the cutest professor in the department, you know. He hates being called doctor anything. Says doctors belong in hospitals, not the classrooms of Twentieth Century American Literature. He prefers his students to call him Professor Barry, but I always referred to him as Mr. B. I haven't seen him in damn near two years. I'm anxious to find out what's been going on in his corner of the world.

After several exhausting climbs up several flights of stairs, I saunter down a maze of hallways. I'm about to give up hope of finding his office, but as I veer around a corner I'm thinking will never end, I spot his name on the slightly jarred door.

***

I rap on its walnut frame. Barry is sitting, staring at pages of text on his computer screen.

"Come in," he says.

He doesn't turn around to notice that I've knocked. Every corner of his office is strewn with fat stacks of research papers, some bound neatly in a rainbow of report covers. Barry's chair squeaks as he turns to face me.

"Hey," he says, looking down at his watch. "You're here early."

"I am? I wasn't sure if I was too early or too late. I didn't want to risk driving around campus for an hour looking for a parking space."

"No, you're fine. I still have a few papers to grade and another hour before heading off to teach my next class," he says. Nothing has changed about Barry other than the fact that he's put on a few new pounds, which is a good thing considering I like my men thick. I've always adored his garbage bag-gut that bulges unapologetically over his belt pinched beneath an oxford shirt. What's left of his hair is combed down in sleek, pitch-black streaks. I've always been a cocksucker for brunettes.

"It looks like you might be here all night."

"Looks that way," Barry says as he shuffles papers and folders in search of the letters of recommendation.

"Ah, here they are. For a second there I thought I lost them. I'm forever losing or misplacing things in this mess. I have to get this place organized one of these days. Have a seat."

I'm able to find a spot on the sofa that isn't covered in white. Barry's thumb grazes against mine as he hands me an unsealed oatmeal-colored envelope with black, English department letterhead in the top left hand corner.

"Let me know if there's something I forgot, or anything you would like me to add," he says, as I stick the letter in an unzipped pocket of my gray Gap bag.

"So, how was your Thanksgiving?" I ask.

"It was nice. I went to Chicago to visit my mother for a week."

"What part of Chicago?

"Urbana-Champaign."

"I have an aunt who lives up there. She's been bugging me about coming up to visit. Says it would be a change of pace from Tallahassee."

"You should go. It's a great city, and you never run out of things to do," says Barry.

"I'm gonna try to get up there in the summer. Right now it's colder than a dead man's dick up there this time of year."

"True," he says. "But the city's beautiful during the winter with everything covered in snow."

"I can imagine, but I'd rather wait until it's hot. I'm too thin-blooded," I told him, "for them Midwestern winters."

"So how was yours?" he asks.

"Same old shit. My sister and her bad ass kids came up from Orlando. My mother slaved away in the kitchen complaining while seasoning ham, shearing chitterlings and baking sweet potato pies—about all the food she felt obligated to cook. My dad did what most men do on Thanksgiving: watched steroid-induced tight ends kick a piece of pig skin around a field for two hours."

"I would love to have been at your house." Barry sits on the edge of his desk facing me with his arms folded at his chest.

"We had to be the only family in America who didn't have a turkey this year."

"I doubt that," he grins.

"I mean, come on, turkey is the mascot of Thanksgiving. I told her that next year she better have a bird on the table bigger than my thigh."

Barry sits in a chair opposite me; his face redder than a porn star's spanked ass.

"Thank you for writing a letter of rec. I really appreciate it."

"No problem. You were a good student. Quiet most of the time, but a good student."

Barry's letter is the last thing I need to complete my applications to grad school.

"So, other than Temple, what other schools are you applying to?"

"East coast places mostly: NYU, Columbia, Syracuse has a great English Lit. program. I haven't decided yet, but maybe UNLV in Las Vegas."

"You know, I have a friend who teaches there part-time. I could put in a good word."

"Wait a minute...what's his name?" I ask.

"Jarret."

"I know Jarret. We had Multicultural Lit. together. He's a good friend of mine. I call him at least twice a month."

"So how's he doing?" Barry asks.

"He's good. He's an arts and entertainment editor for a newspaper up there."

"Jarret's a nice guy," Barry declares. "So, have you thought about going to graduate school here? We have a pretty prestigious program ourselves."

"I've considered it but I really want to get out of Tally." I rest my chin in the cup of my palm.

"I would stay if I had something going for me here."

"What about your parents?" he asks.

"I love them and all, but they can drive me nuts. Things haven't been the best at home lately."

"I understand," Barry says.

I notice Barry looking at the clock above one of the bookshelves.

"Well, I hate to rush you off, but I have to finish grading these papers."

"Can I check my e-mail?" I ask.

"Sure."

"I'm not inconveniencing you am I?"

"It's not a problem," Barry replies.

I walk over and sit in the brown executive desk chair where it's still warm from Barry's ass.

"It's just that the library is all the way across campus."

The thought of sitting my ass in the very spot he sat his in is enough to make my dick curl. My feet hover above the floor like a little boy as I lean back playfully typing hotmail.com into the search engine.

"Whoa!" I yell.

Barry jumps behind me to break my fall. "Sorry. They've been promising me a new chair for months now." He hoists me up, his hands tenderly touching my shoulders.

He sits on the edge of the desk next to me as I punch in my password. I glance nonchalantly from the corner of my eye at the bulged impression through his polyester crotch. I click the words *Check Mail* in bold blue lettering. *Unread Messages: (0).* "No messages," Barry says, standing over me with musky underarms.

"You trying to rush me off?"

"Not at all; I just have tons of work to do," he replies.

I grab Barry's stiff package.

He jerks it objectively away, but I know he wants it. I've dreamt of him the whole semester looking down into my coffee-brown eyes as I drench his dick with spit.

I want to tell him of French-kiss-dreams, of bubblegum-lips suckling my nipples like chocolates. I want to speak of dicks plunging in and out of bottomless butts. I want to tell of wide-ruled love letters that were later ripped to pieces and tossed into the wasteland of wide-ruled love letters. If Barry only knew of the countless e-mails that met a deleted demise. I want him to throw me across his desk of papers, lift my legs to the heavens, and fuck the living shit out of me. I want to be his honey-dip baby; his all-day dick-sucker, crouched beneath his desk, between his legs, servicing his boner until he spews white fire all over my four-eyed face while holding office hours with English Lit. undergrads.

***

"Oh come on," I say. "Stop playin' hard to get." I fondle his dick through dark-blue polyesters. I called them *church pants* as a kid. "I remember how you use to switch that ass in class; you were such the tease. I use to daydream of how warm it would feel with my cock stuffed between that ass of yours."

"I think you need to get the hell out of my office," says Barry, as he walks toward the door.

I head him off, and shut the door, locking it behind me.

I push Barry out of the way, throwing my weight against him, shoving him in the middle of the room.

"Sit down!" I holler, pushing him forcefully against the desk; the edge burrowing into the small of his back. I can tell he's scared. "Shut up and take off your clothes."

I thrash Barry across the face. I hit him hard enough to knock his glasses off. He stands stunned and disoriented.

"I'm not going to tell you again."

Blood trickles from the corner of his mouth as he starts to unfasten the first two buttons of his shirt. I charge at him like a red-eyed bull pulling away at his buttons. They pop from their thread onto the desk. Barry tries to tear himself from my grip but I jerk him forward like he's nothing, clutching his crotch.

***

"Don't fucking play with me," I say, yanking his shirt down around his fat arms.

"All right, all right! Jesus, calm down."

Barry barely finishes unbuckling his belt before I start fussing with his pants. I noose my hand around his throat, mouthing skin. My dick stiffens as I fondle myself with pliant fingers.

Barry's powerless. I want him to put up a struggle, to try to break free from between the grizzly-bear-grip of my legs. I pull my knit top over a pot-belly caked with hair, and grab Barry unyieldingly by the wrists, sliding his unwilling hand across my nipples.

"Squeeze 'em," I demand. He grabs hold of them grown with silken waves of fur.

"C'mon, squeeze 'em."

"Harder." I order. I'm sensitive to his abuse. I gawk at my aching dick that has popped from the flannel slit of my plaid boxers. I slide my hand through his zipper, along his bulge. I hook my fingers over an elastic band and fish his dick out of his briefs. Barry's dick is circumcised with a pale-pink head.

"Damn you're big!" I hold Barry's ball sac within his undies of sweaty ass-crack.

"When was the last time you had a blow job?" I ask, massaging his balls.

I push Barry back onto the desk of papers and stationery and squeeze his dick's head.

"I said...when was the last time this dick was in a mouth?" I repeat. He bends to my tactic of ball-breaking torture.

"Couple of weeks," he tells me writhing with pain.

"Did you like it?" I ask. I hold his balls in my hands like dice.

"Ye-ye-yes," he replies, squirming.

"Yes, what? I say aggressively.

"Sir. Yes, sir."

I dip down giving the head a few licks; fat lips 'round a firm dick.

"Stand up. Get out of the rest of those clothes."

"Yes, sir." Barry pulls his slacks from argyle-covered feet.

I fling the snow of papers off his sofa onto the floor, many of them sliding beneath the water cooler.

"Lie down," I demand, whacking him on his butt. I crouch on the floor running my fingers between the trench of his ass.

"You're tight," I tell him. I pull the phone cord out of the wall to bind his wrists.

I knew I didn't have a snowman's chance in hell of getting in Barry, but that was the fun of it.

"How would you like to be my pig-boy? Wanna be my dirty little piglet?" I ask, embedding my middle finger forcefully between his ass.

"Yes. Yes, sir," he squeals, gripping the sofa's arm.

"Don'tchu move, pig.

I search his desk, pulling out drawer after drawer until I come across a bottle of syrup.

Of all the things to keep in your desk.

"This might be a bit cold going on, so just relax."

I flip the red top on the bottle, pouring it on his butt. I can smell the syrup as it runs within the gully of Barry's ass. My fingers slip within the torrid ditch of him.

"I love syrup on my 'biscuits,'" I say, smacking his booty.

My dick throbs hot. He winces to my finger pressing against his sticky sphincter.

"Fuck me," he whispers.

"What's that, piggy?"

"Fuck me, sir," Barry pleads, as his leg slides to the foot of the sofa.

"I knew you'd come around."

I used to daydream of sucking his dick under a podium booth.

"You like that, piggy?" I ask.

"Yes, sir," he replies.

My breath tickles his ass.

"Spread 'em; I want to taste you."

I slobber and slurp within him. Good and warm, just how I like my biscuits.

"Like that, pig?" I snort through his butt.

Barry bucks forward with each flicker of my tongue licking syrup out of his hole. My thatch of facial hair brushes against his syrup-scented behind.

I reach around, smearing his dick with syrup. I lather Barry's insides.

"Roll over," I order, stroking his dick. "I want to taste you."

He turns over on his back. I move within his inner thighs and smear him onto the couch, his butt teetering on its edge. I hold the open bottle of syrup high above his groin and squeeze. A web of thick topping pours from its spout.

"Yes, sir," Barry says. I tip Barry's angry inches up to the rich, sticky stream that runs down his shaft into a jungle of musky fur.

I hold his boner at the base as I suckle its crown clean of syrup.

"Work the head," he pleads. He thrusts his pelvis into my face. His sticky bushel tickles my nose.

I cock his thighs on the temples of my shoulders as I run my lips down his shaft. Barry's legs shiver as I work his middle. A thread of slobber runs from his dick to my mouth when I slide up and off his boner.

"I'm about to come, sir," he heaves.

He can barely catch his breath.

"Not yet, don't come for me yet, pig."

Barry's legs slide off my shoulders into the inside creases of my arms. I pull his butt smack dab at my dick and work it through his ass. He claws my elbows as I slowly pork his hole.

I want to look into his eyes while I fuck him, but they're hidden behind fogged wire frames.

I quicken my pace like the beats of my heart as I rope my arms like garter belts, around his thighs.

"Beg for it," I say as I take him from behind.

"Fuck me, boy," Barry says.

He can barely hold on as I ram my glazed dick up in him; his dick grazing up against my stomach. The mixture of booty, sweat, and syrup gives off a sickly sweet funk throughout the office. My juices trickle out of him with each thrust of my dick spiraling through his soul.

"Damn, you're wet!"

Sweat rolls down my face into the crevice of my lips. I can feel the juices flowing through me.

"Gonna come, piggy!" I say, screwing Barry steady. I work my dick giving special attention to the sensitivity of the head.

My thrusts are in perfect synchronization of my self-inflicted hand-jobs.

"Me, too!" He shouts. A stream spurts forth. Barry's eyes are closed; his face is flushed as he lets out groans of satisfaction. I slide out of Barry and shoot across his hefty ass.

I collapse on top of him with a drenched dick between our bodies.

"Your ass felt good on my dick," I say heaving.

I slide off of Barry, turn him over and free his wrists from the phone cord.

"What time is it?" He recovers his torn shirt off the floor.

"It's a quarter 'til three." Barry wipes his dick clean with the tail end of his shirt.

"I gotta go," I say, stepping into the leg of my underwear.

I fasten my jeans and the buttons on my shirt.

"Where's my bag?"

Barry stands, content and relieved, tucking his dick back into the recesses of his pants.

I pull Barry to me and kiss him. I can taste his lips seasoned with syrup and ass-funk.

"Why don't I come by tomorrow, help you get this place organized," I say. "It's a *pig sty*. Besides, I want some more of that butt of yours before I leave Tallahassee."

"That's fine," he says.

"See you tomorrow, pig."

Outside Chance
Tony Pike

Matt pulled up the two pints from the hand-pump with a practiced hand, adjusting his action at the last moment so as to deliver just the right amount of foaming head. He rang up the items and named the prices. There was an exchange of money and change and then his customer, with a friendly "Thanks mate", picked up the glasses, turned around, and walked out with them into the sunshine by the riverside where his companion presumably awaited him at one of the tables.

They all preferred to sit outside in this weather. Pity, Matt thought. Good-looking guy, that one. He stroked his be-denimed crotch meditatively. For a moment he was alone in the college bar. Nice place. Among the dreaming Oxford spires; door opening onto the bank of the Cherwell. The only thing was (Matt's hand strayed lightly over his prominent package once again, absent-mindedly) his dick had seen no action whatever in the three weeks since he'd come up to uni. At least, no action that involved anyone else. Taking the bar job had been a step in the right direction, he'd thought even if up to now it hadn't brought him into contact with the kind of fellow students that he and his dick needed to meet. Still, he thought hopefully, you never knew who would be next to push open the old oak door, ducking under Tudor beams, momentarily disoriented by the relative darkness.

"Oh, hallo." Here was the next customer already, ducking and blinking. "Are you open?" They often said that.

"Sure we are," said Matt brightly.

"Only it looked so empty."

"It's the sun. Everyone goes outside." Matt had just time to size up the new arrival and decided he liked what he saw. Another first-year student, he guessed, bright-eyed and with an open smile. No time to surf the package though: the boy was at the bar, which cut him off an inch or two below the waist. As to whether he was blessed with the well-shaped, jeans-moulding butt that Matt rather suspected (hoped for?), that information would be tantalisingly withheld until the stranger turned away to take his drink out into the sunshine, affording him only the bittersweet pleasure of a parting glance. Matt hoped he could engage him in conversation for a minute or two longer. "What can I get you then?" he said. "We've six real ales," he gestured expansively, "three kinds of lager, or..."

The boy touched one of the polished pump-handles. "A pint of this one." He paused and added, "Please."

"Haven't seen you in here before, have I?" Matt asked as he drew the ale. "What college are you from?"

"Worcester," said the stranger. Then, unbelievably, "I think I'm going to say something stupid, and you'll think I'm a complete asshole." He paused, stuck.

Matt giggled. "I promise I won't think that. Just say it."

"Your name isn't Matt, is it?"

"Matt Fuller. Yes it is."

Then they both gaped at each other, as the ramifications of this discovery began to penetrate their minds.

"Jay," Matt said, and then was silent again. Memories came tiding back in rolling waves that rushed and overlapped, pulling away again with a delicious, sexy, dangerous tug of undertow. Jay was babbling something about old times at primary school, naming teachers and old classmates. Matt hardly heard him. They had been lovers, Matt thought. Lovers at the age of ten? Certainly they'd played naked in the woods and fields together, exploring each other's contours, tickling miniature balls and squeezing precocious, non-productive erections, competitively comparing size. All this. But lovers? Matt had felt so even at the time, though never said, of course. But how had it felt for Jay? Did he even remember now? Very possibly not. People do air-brush their pasts.

Now they were talking amiably. Jay had offered Matt a

drink. He'd accepted just a half— that being the rule—and now they stood face to face, but separated cruelly, Matt thought, by the metre of polished mahogany bar. Unconsciously he pushed himself against it, and then felt the stir of his cock in his jeans. He found an excuse, a moment later, to join Jay on the customers' side of the bar—miraculously there were no new arrivals just then—where they faced each other on high bar stools, legs spread wide apart as if to focus attention on what absolutely could not be displayed there and then. They talked still, of this and that, of times past, the present, and everything that had happened in between, but Matt's thoughts were not engaged in the conversation. He tried to read the signals of Jay's body language. Confound tight jeans! He couldn't see if Jay was getting hard, as he was, though he saw clearly that he had developed a promising package in the time (ten years!) since he had last had the pleasure of fondling his cock. Then, with the arrival of a new group of customers, Matt had to return to his station.

The bar got busy and stayed that way. Matt hardly had a chance to speak to Jay. Finally Jay leant over. "I can't stay drinking all lunchtime. What time d'you finish?"

Matt's heart and cock both leapt. "Half past three."

"See you outside. By the river." Then Jay abruptly turned and left, giving Matt the bittersweet parting glimpse that he had visualised hopefully a little earlier: an impeccably pert backside.

***

Half past three came slowly, but at last Matt was free. He strolled off to the washroom to piss and check his hair before his assignation with Jay. He was not surprised to find his cock was heavy and sticky when he pulled it out. He eased his jeans a few inches down his hips to give his balls some air. It felt sexy. He gave his thickening dick a couple of experimental tugs as he was pissing, easing the foreskin to and fro, the way a pilot checks his wing-flaps on the taxiway, ready for the main action to come. But what action, he asked himself. Probably Jay was straight (most students were) and only wanted to talk. Perhaps he was exciting himself for nothing.

Two boys walked in and stood unzipping, one on either side of him. Matt recognised one of them. He was a third-year student from Matt's own college and he'd served him two pints of beer earlier, before Jay's arrival, but he had taken them out onto the riverside. The other was his equally handsome companion who had come inside later to buy the second pint. Matt had idly wondered if they might be gay. No doubt of it now, as they too pulled their jeans down a couple of inches more than was strictly necessary, showing their dicks off to him and to each other, stroking themselves gently as they recycled their lunchtime beer. Their fat cocks were at half-stretch: one had a foreskin, which its owner played with so that his bluish dick-head appeared to wink at Matt; the other was circumcised, his dick-head like a shiny dark plum. Matt thought of his assignation with Jay, waiting outside. Three weeks of nothing, he thought, then more than you could deal with all at once. He took a gamble on Jay's intentions and zipped himself back up— no easy matter: he was hardening by the second. Ducking backwards between the outreaching arms of the two older boys he made his excuses ("Things to do") but allowed himself a back-stop ("Another time—you know where to find me") then found himself outside.

"Thought you weren't coming," said Jay. "I nearly gave you up."

"Did I ever let you down before?"

Jay smiled, indicating no. They wandered up-river in the sunshine.

"Remember our walks all those years ago?" Matt asked, exploratively.

Jay giggled. "I wasn't sure if you did."

"And all the things we did?" Matt was getting bolder.

"Like what?" Jay stopped and turned to face him. He was smiling teasingly.

"The pissing competitions, for a start?" (Subconsciously disappointed by the non-orgasmic nature of their fumbles, they had compensated by finishing their sessions with a contest to see who could pee the highest arc. Jay had usually won.)

"For a start," said Jay. "Just for a start. Remember anything else?" For an answer Matt grabbed the front of the waistband of Jay's jeans, then slid his fingers and back of his hand down into the tight depths, enjoying his first encounter with the crop of springy hair that the more adult Jay had grown down there, before he felt the sudden upswing of his grown-up cock. "No knickers," Matt observed, approvingly.

Jay pulled Matt towards him. They kissed long and hard, pressed up against each other's bodies, feeling the bounce and tension of their hot cocks through fabric—two muscular prisoners aching to get free.

"I wasn't sure if you were..." Jay began.

Matt cut him off. "I wasn't sure if *you* were."

"And now you are?" Jay teased.

They were standing in a little grassy clearing, among scrub beside the stream. No one ever came here—except (in more ways than one) Matt, who sometimes walked here after work and would vent his frustration by stripping off and wanking, naked under the sun, spraying his cum indiscriminately among the plants. Now there were two of them to do it. They undressed themselves, item by item, as if it was a game—remembering a ritual of long ago. ("Now you." "No, you go next.") So intent they were on watching what they saw that they almost fell over while simultaneously removing their jeans.

"Wow, you're big," said Jay.

"So are you," said Matt, watching in wonder as Jay's thick-based, tapering dick finally reared away from its prison, a glistening pool of clear juice spilling from the hidden source beneath its crowning, protective foreskin. "You're so wet," he said.

"You too," said Jay. "You're dribbling on the grass."

Matt looked down. An unbroken dewy thread, like gossamer, connected his ramrod hard-on to the grassy floor.

For a moment they stopped and wondered what to do. None of their pre-pubescent gropings had prepared them for the question: who fucks who?

As they both felt instinctively in pockets for the small packets whose contents would protect them, Jay said it. Just like that. "So, who fucks who now? Toss for it?" They both laughed at the double entendre.

"Tell you what," said Matt. "Biggest dick gets to fuck first."

Facing each other they held their cocks together, side by side, dabbing wetly at each other's groins, and agreed that, whereas Jay's was fatter, Matt's was longer (something that had been true in childhood too) but that there was no clear-cut winner in terms of overall size. "I can't hold off much longer," said Matt suddenly, urgently.

"Nor me," said Jay. They both collapsed together onto the grass, clasping each other's dicks and pressing their tummies together, just as they had done years ago. Their hands moved quickly, briefly: foreskins flicked back and forth, exposing quick glimpses of ripe-cherry dick-heads. It took just a few seconds and then they came together in two creamy spurting floods that spread hotly between their two bare chests, gluing them together like the lovers they were meant to be.

But, even as the last convulsions died away and their copious spurtings dwindled to a gentle ooze, two shadows fell across them. "Well, well, well," said a voice with some amusement, "You naughty boys."

Pressing themselves even more tightly together—solidarity in the face of intrusion—they twisted their heads to see...the two older boys who had stood either side of Matt in the washroom.

"Relax," said Matt to Jay. "They're friends."

As if at a signal the two new arrivals, now standing right over them, undid their belts and let their jeans slide down to their knees. Their massive cocks rose to full attention. Jay and Matt reached up with their hands and explored the two pairs of warm and furry, muscular thighs. Then, rising to a kneeling position, they began to caress a cock each with their fingers. Both were equally enormous. Matt hadn't realised, seeing them half-hard at the urinal, what their full potential might be.

"I'm Gary," announced the owner of the circumcised organ that Matt was struggling to get his hand around. "I'm David," announced his foreskinned friend. And Matt and Jay introduced themselves while fondling the strangers' chunky balls.

Inspired by the examples of nakedness crouching at their feet, Gary and David also started to strip off completely; shirts, shoes and jeans were flung to the ground—though not before each had extracted a tiny packet from a back pocket, Matt noticed. Then they joined them naked on the ground and the four found themselves rolling and squirming together like a litter of puppies.

Gary and David were two years older than the other two; it showed in their physiques: more muscular, more hairy. As for their drooling cocks...

Matt felt at a disadvantage as far as his own organ was concerned. Having just come, it was only half hard and looked a little smaller than usual. He took comfort in Jay's identical condition and appearance: everything matted with slippery cum and bedecked with a few stray bits of grass. As a pair they looked both vulnerable and very cute, which did not go unnoticed by the newcomers. "Couldn't help overhearing your earlier question," said Gary with a chuckle— though not an unpleasant one. "About who fucks who. Though shouldn't it be whom?" He paused. "Of course, things don't always go according to plan, and events have a way of taking over—rendering your question a bit academic. Might I suggest that, since you two have already come—and a very stimulating sight it was too..." He looked down at his own jerking, copiously juicing cock. "...Anyway, seeing as you've come and we haven't, perhaps the two of us could fuck the two of you...I mean one each," he added hastily, seeing a look of alarm cross the faces of the younger pair. Then he opened the little packet in the palm of his hand and deftly slipped the rubber over his wet cock-head, stroking it into place down the shaft. On the other side of Jay, David was doing the same thing.

Matt and Jay lay on their sides facing each other, their cocks hardening up again, while Gary and David lay behind them, a muscular chest pressed against each of their backs, exploring moist assholes with gentle fingers until the younger two were relaxed enough to take their two massive pile-driving dicks. Matt felt Gary enter him like an explosion. His gasp of surprise and shock met Jay's own, and so they found themselves kissing each other, their two cocks, rigid but slippery, thrust towards and against each other under the impact of Gary's and David's piston action from the rear. Gary and David's greater experience showed: they knew how to enjoy the younger boys slowly. Even so, it was only a matter of time before everybody came. It was just a question of in which order. In fact, David was the first. While thrusting deep into Jay he shot his load, at which Gary, spurred on by his partner's ecstatic peal of laughter, ejaculated too. For a moment or two they rested, then both of them rolled gently onto their backs, rolling the younger pair round with them, carefully keeping their spent but still standing dicks inside them. Lying back now, with Matt lying back on his chest and impaled on his plunger, Gary now grabbed Matt's excited cock and pointed it towards the sky. With a spittle-moistened hand David did the same with Jay.

"Let's see which of these beautiful boys we can make come first," said David laughing.

Gary giggled. "And which of their pretty pricks can shoot its load the furthest."

That was all it took. Jay's cock quivered, he gave a little moan and shot. A little spurt of white gobbets that landed on his chest. Immediately on seeing this Matt felt himself starting to climax too. And how he surprised himself—and the others— just as Gary's fist drew back his foreskin, by squirting his little milky fountain a full foot into the air. He rolled, smiling broadly, into Jay again, embracing in warm white wetness. Jay said: "Like a rocket launcher, you. Impressive. And your second one in about ten minutes!"

"Have you been practising for this event?" asked Gary, quite impressed himself.

Matt looked at Jay, grinning. He said, "I think we were in training for this years ago."

Practice Pony
Lawrence Schimel

I couldn't help thinking about the sign I'd torn down from the post office door:

PUT A BEAST BETWEEN YOUR LEGS!
JOIN THE YALE POLO TEAM.
INTRODUCTORY MEETING
TONIGHT AT 9 P.M.
IN THE DAVENPORT LOUNGE.

The yellow Xeroxed sheet with this information was riding in my back pocket, folded into a tiny square, as I crossed campus. I imagined myself astride a horse, the feel of withers pressing up against my asshole, rubbing back and forth.... I was getting so hard I was sure that everyone walking past must notice my erection, and I swung my books loosely in front of my crotch, feeling like I was in high school again. Nostalgia 101.

I'd grown up on horseback, riding competitively in dressage and hunter-chases until I hit high school and decided it wasn't masculine enough. Even then, I knew I was gay, but I was afraid people would find out. In high school, it's just not accepted. So I did everything I could to pretend that I wasn't. In college, things were different, but I still wasn't comfortable being completely out. There were these football players who lived on my floor, who I had to share a bathroom with, and I was afraid of what they might do to me if they knew I was gay and thought I'd been watching them in the showers all this time, desiring them.

But the idea of polo was sexy—and very, very masculine. Despite the wording of their sign: Put a beast between your legs. Did they know what that sounded like? Could they mean...? I was afraid to finish the thought, lest I jinx myself. I glanced at my watch, then thrust my hand into my pocket. Just eleven hours until I can find out, I told myself, hopefully, as I squeezed my hard cock in my jeans and walked into my Anthro class.

***

I'd gone to the meeting for the Yale Equestrian Club during the first few weeks of my freshman year, but when I walked into a room full of women I just pretended I had stumbled into the wrong meeting and fled. My heart pounded in my chest as I hurried back to old campus and my dorm; no way was I going to be the only boy on an all-female team! That would've been like running through the streets shouting, "I'm a faggot! I'm a faggot!" and I wasn't ready for that. I'm still not, although I'm much farther out of the closet than I was last year.

I didn't think the polo team would be anything like the equestrian team. It didn't seem like a women's thing, so I was surprised to see four or five girls in the Davenport Lounge when I walked in a little before nine p.m. But there were also a dozen guys sitting about, half of them in riding pants or chaps and boots. There was one man—and he was a young man, not a boy like most of the people in the room—who seemed to dominate the whole room. His skin spoke of some exotic clime: Brazil or Argentina, someplace Latin, someplace where heat and passion are a way of life. He had liquid black eyes and lips that curled in a small pout when he stopped talking. Obviously tall, even though he was sitting on a couch, his long legs were casually spread wide....

I quickly looked away. Great first impression, I berated myself, drooling all over the men.

But as I scanned the room and my eyes fell on him again, talking with a group of three very frosh-looking guys in jeans who stood facing him.

I struck up a conversation with someone I recognized from

one of my Poli Sci classes, and after a moment Mr. Drop-Dead Gorgeous stood up and called the room to order. He was even more attractive when standing, I thought, as my eyes traveled up and down his tall frame. The bulge in his crotch seemed even more enormous on his thin waist.

Turns out he wasn't just on the team, he was captain. Which meant I'd suddenly developed a new hobby.

***

The smell of wood shavings always brings back the memory of the first time I sucked another man's cock: it was a hot summer afternoon when one of the stable hands took me into one of the back stalls and dropped his pants. I'd been so enthralled by that huge, veined piece of flesh that swelled between his legs. It reeked of his sweat as I knelt down to examine it more closely. The whole barn reeked of strong scents: cedar from the shavings, the stale bite of the horse's urine, steaming mounds of manure baking in the heat. Precum was leaking from the tip, and I reached out to wipe it away; my fingers burned as they brushed against the swollen, throbbing gland, but rather than pulling back I grabbed hold of his cock with my fist. It was easily twice as thick as my own, I marveled, and half again as long. I'd hardly imagined cocks could be that size. "Suck on it," the stable hand commanded, pulling my head toward his crotch. There was no way I could take it, I thought, but as I opened my mouth to protest his cock pushed in and—

I shifted uncomfortably in my jeans, suddenly very aware of my surroundings in the Yale Armory. My cock was as stiff as a polo mallet and feeling far too confined in the jockey shorts I was wearing instead of boxers. I'd want the support, I knew, once I was on horseback; I hadn't made allowances for getting such a raging hard-on. And staring at the captain's tight ass in his riding chaps as we followed him to the arena wasn't helping it go away!

After listening to the requirements for being on the team and the commitment we'd have to make if we joined, there were eleven of us left. We were now about to try getting up on horseback. Many had never ridden before, so it was a chance for them to see what it was like, to get used to being astride a living creature. There were only four horses saddled up in the arena, so we took turns getting on and walking around. To keep us humble, as if simply staying astride weren't battle enough, we had to walk forward and try to hit a ball. I rode English, but you had to keep the reins bunched in one hand and neck rein like in Western styles, so that your right hand was free to hold the mallet. It looked so easy when the team did it, but when I tried to hit the ball I must've missed by four feet!

I kept guiding my horse around again, in tight circles, again and again, trying to hit that damned ball. But I never did. The mallet struck too high or too low or too far to one side. I was really impressing the captain like this, I told myself each time, trying hard to fight the blush of shame and embarrassment that colored my cheeks.

To my surprise, as I dismounted the captain said, "You've got a good seat and you ride well. But you can't hit the ball for shit. Meet me in the practice room at the gym tomorrow at six-thirty."

My heart was beating so hard and loud that I couldn't hear my own reply. I must've mumbled something. He hadn't offered anyone else a private lesson, so he must actually see something in me. My cock felt pinched in my jockeys again. I wanted to climb up into the hayloft and jerk off, but I didn't know how to get up there yet. I went into the bathroom instead. My hand was covered with grime and horsehair but I didn't care; I fisted my stiff cock until I came, whispering "Alberto" as I shot my load against the white ceramic of the sink.

***

Classes were done for the day, so the gym was crowded not only with sports teams practicing, but also with a large number of people who were there simply to work out, jog, or swim. I wished I had an excuse to cruise through the locker rooms and get an eyeful of the sweaty jocks going into the showers, but I was fully dressed in my riding gear, even though I wasn't about to be on horseback, just the wooden practice horse. I thought it would make a better impression on the captain, however, to show him I was seriously interested. Which I was—in him more than the sport!

I wandered down corridors, following the directions the guard downstairs had given me. Past the squash courts...there, on the end: a normal sized door with a small window at eye level. I peered in. It was empty, save for the large wooden horse in the center of the floor. I tried the handle and the door swung in. The air was stale; the room hadn't been used in a while. Mallets lined one wall, along with a few old balls that had lost their firmness.

I walked over to the horse, a simple wooden frame with stirrups on leather straps dangling from either side. I swung up onto it and just sat there for a moment, enjoying the feel of such a wide body between my legs. I put my hands on the wooden withers and rubbed back and forth, scratching my asshole through the fabric of my jeans and underwear. I imagined Alberto licking my ass, working my hole with his tongue to prepare the way for his cock....

I checked my watch, wondering where he was. I was still fifteen minutes early. In my excitement to see him, I'd made certain I wasn't late!

I ran my hand up the inside of my thigh, rubbing the side of my swollen cock, which had poked free from the confines of my briefs. I wondered how soon he'd show up: did I have time to go jerk off? It would let me concentrate on the lesson at hand. But even if there was time, where could I do it? I looked over my shoulder at the tiny window in the door. Even though not many people came all the way down to the end of the corridor, it would be just my luck that someone would.

I dismounted and walked over to the wall to select a mallet. I would practice my swing to take my mind off my aching cock. If I didn't lose this erection by the time Alberto showed up there'd be no way he couldn't notice it. I chose the longest mallet and climbed back on the wooden horse. I stood up in the stirrups like they'd shown us yesterday and took swing at an imaginary ball. The mallet cracked against the side of the horse, and I winced at the sound. I was glad no one else was here, and also that I wasn't on a real horse! I took another swing and this time managed to avoid hitting the horse, although I still couldn't direct the mallet where I wanted it.

Again and again I swung, trying to get accustomed to the heavy weight at the tip of that long stick, its arc as it traveled toward the imaginary ball.

"Your mallet is too long."

I was on the follow-through of a swing and I almost swung myself right over the side of the horse.

I turned around. My heart was beating from fear, and it wanted to stop completely as I stared at him. He was so hot! He was a tall shadow in the dusty light; dark hair, dark skin, and those liquid dark eyes....

So much for having forgotten my erection, I thought, as I twisted back to resume my proper seat and break eye contact. "I didn't realize you were there."

He walked toward me; I could feel his presence behind me, just beside the horse. He exuded an energy, something sensual that sent an electrical charge through my body. My swollen cock thumped against my leg each time he spoke, vibrating to the timbre of his voice.

"I told you six-thirty. That was ten minutes ago."

My eyes flicked to meet his; he'd been watching me for ten minutes! I couldn't read anything from his expression, so I looked away, down at my hands in my lap, the reins bunched between them and the mallet jutting off to one side like a giant erection. I let the tip of the mallet dip; it helped to hide my real erection.

Alberto took hold of the mallet and handed me another one. "This is a better size for you." The new stick was half a foot shorter. I leaned over the side of the horse and stretched so far toward the floor that I almost slid off.

Alberto laughed, a short quiet burst of sound. "Much better." I turned to look at him, and he met my stare. I couldn't read him at all, which was part of what I found so sexy about him. He was a cipher.

"You've got to stand up in your seat when you swing."

He offered no more explanation, so I went ahead and tried it, assuming that's what he wanted me to do. I stood up and leaned forward to take a swing, and it *was* much easier to keep the head of the mallet focused where I wanted it to go. I wasn't entirely convinced it was the length of the mallet, although the shorter mallet was lighter. However, I'd just spent a good twenty minutes swinging that first mallet, so I felt some of my skill was simply the result of my own practice.

I took another swing with the new mallet and then another. Alberto didn't say anything, just watched me from beneath those dark, brooding eyes. I kept practicing. Occasionally he would comment, in the form of an instruction. "Slow down the swing." "Lift your arm higher."

"Take off your jeans."

I looked at him, surprised. Had I heard him correctly? My heart was beating so fast I could hear nothing else. At last, this was the moment I'd been hoping for! Why was I hesitating?

I dismounted and looked up at him. He hadn't moved. He was watching me, casually, almost disinterestedly, waiting. But he was watching me.

I stripped down for him, peeling off my chaps slowly, giving him a bit of a show. I undid the buttons of my jeans and re-

membered suddenly that I'd shaved off all my pubic hair the
other week. What would he think? I worried, as I stripped off
my underwear with my pants. As I bent over to step out of
each leg my erection was pointing straight at him, so hard it
was throbbing like a discotheque. I couldn't believe what I was
doing; this was a public gym! What if someone walked past and
looked in? But right then, I couldn't care about anything but
Alberto and what he wanted from me.

Naked from the waist down, I climbed back atop the practice horse and stood up in the stirrups, my ass up in the air as
it had been when he asked me to take off my pants. My sphincter twitched, anticipating the feel of him sliding into me. I
thought of him using his crop as a dildo, thrusting the long
black leather whip into me.... A bead of precum dripped onto
the saddle.

Pain flashed across my buttcheeks!

I spun around, almost falling to the floor before I realized
where I was and caught my balance in the stirrups. I sat down
and gripped with my knees to keep my seat. My ass burned
against the wooden horse, a strip of heat-pain.

He'd whipped me!

"I didn't tell you to take your chaps off," he said.

I dismounted again. He was standing much nearer to me
this time. I could feel the closeness of his body, making my own
respond strongly. He saw all of me, naked before him, so obviously desiring him, but he made no move toward me. I had to
wonder what he planned to do with me, or to me. Whatever it
was, my body wanted it and was ready for him.

I bent down to pick up my chaps and couldn't help looking
at his basket, which always bulged so prominently that I
couldn't even tell if he was hard now or not. I climbed back
into my leathers, pulling them over my legs. My ass and cock
were left bare, and it felt as if a sudden draft snuck through the
tiny window, deliciously cold and making me even harder.

I climbed back onto the practice horse and resumed my position in the stirrups, leaning forward over the neck, my ass thrust into the air.

He tapped the inside of my leg with the crop and I tried not to flinch. Slowly, he tapped his way up my inner thigh, sending goose bumps across my skin.

He tapped my balls, on either side, making them swing.

He didn't say anything about the stubble.

Suddenly the crop was gone. I wanted to turn around and see what he was doing, but I stayed where I was. I strained to hear what he was doing, listening for a rustle of fabric, a footstep, anything, but there was no sound of any sort—I couldn't even hear if he was in the room with me.

There was a rush of movement behind me, and I sat down to turn about—I sat right onto his cock. I cried out, unprepared for this impaling. Heat flared through my gut. I hadn't even heard him move, not to unzip his pants, or unroll the condom he was wearing, nothing. His cock was long and thin, like his body; I could feel it inside me, well above my navel, it seemed.

"Grip with your knees."

I did so, pulling myself up off his cock a few inches. I held there a moment, and then he stood up in the stirrups to slide into me once more, pushing me forward with a grunt. I leaned into the wooden neck again, wrapped myself around it and held on for dear life.

He laced his fingers through my hair and jerked my head back, so his hot mouth could more easily find mine and force it open. My jaw ached as his long tongue snaked its way down my throat. He reached under my shirt and seized a nipple between his thumb and forefinger.

I arched my back with the sudden pain. Alberto thrust into me, grinding forward. My cock slapped painfully against the polished wood. I reached down and grabbed the reins; I looped the leather cords over my balls so every forward thrust made them tug my cock.

His breath was hot in my ear, pulsing rapidly in horse-like bursts from his nostrils. I couldn't hold back; I'd been so excited thinking about him for so long, I shot my load onto the horse's neck, letting it ooze down the wood. He didn't stop thrusting into me, riding my ass relentlessly, thrusting into me deeper and deeper. My insides felt like they were being torn apart. But he didn't stop, and soon my cock grew hard again with his filling me up.

At last, he too came, crying out in a short bark as his body spasmed, then silence. His long cock was still within me, upholding me and holding me up.

He dismounted, and I slid down against the wooden horse. My ass burned; it twitched against the smooth polished wood. I collapsed against the wooden neck, my cock slicked by my own cum as it slid between my stomach and the wood.

"You've got a good seat," he said. "But you've still got to practice your swing."

A Late Workout
Armand

Working as a monitor in the gym on campus, I got to check out all the hot guys and their hard muscles. My classes were in the daytime, and I usually worked in the evenings. I wasn't really *out* to the guys in the fitness center, so they thought I was straight. Though I never set out to deceive them, it was easier to get along with these macho jocks if they assumed I was another hetero.

One night, towards the middle of the semester, my favorite jock, Jacob, came in very late looking stressed. We only had ten minutes before close. I was disappointed that I would have to run him off, because it always gave me a rush to watch him.

I had first seen him almost a year before in the bookstore, and I couldn't believe his body. The man was a demigod. From the size of his arms and chest, it was clear that he worked out, but he didn't have that puffy bodybuilder look. It was his green eyes that really drew my attention. I followed him around the bookstore, eventually coming face-to-face with him in the mechanical engineering section. As a History major, I felt like I had wandered into foreign land. When Jacob looked up at me, I was stunned by his sweet, sun-kissed face, the wind-tossed hair and those amazing emerald eyes. He smiled and nodded as I passed. When I glanced back, I realized that his shorts hid nothing of his perfect, round ass.

When I started working in the gym, I heard him talking with another student about his upcoming semester and the Archaeology class that he was taking, so that night I registered for the same course. The plan worked, and we became study buddies for the term. During that time, I heard a great deal about his on-again, off-again relationship with his girlfriend Meredith, and I tried to encourage him to look for greener pastures.

Jacob and I didn't really hang out after that semester ended, but he usually chatted with me when he came in to work out. The night he showed up late, I was surprised he didn't even acknowledge me. Something was wrong.

Ten minutes after he arrived, I began closing things down. Most of the other patrons had left, but Jacob was really hitting the weights hard. He was benching 375 without a spotter, so I walked over and stood behind him to spot. After seven clean repetitions, he struggled through two more with my help.

"Thanks, buddy," he said as he jumped up from the bench.

"No problem. Actually I wanted to remind you that we're closing."

"Man, I didn't realize it was so late. I really need to finish my workout. Is there any way that you could let me finish my chest and triceps? I hate to ask, but I've got to burn off some energy."

"Is everything okay?"

"I'll tell you after my workout. So can I finish up?"

That smile and those eyes! How could I deny him anything?

"Don't tell anyone. I'll wait around."

While Jacob moved from one machine to another, I watched him surreptitiously. As he did his set on the decline bench, his shorts rode up, so I could check out his massive thighs. Jacob was one of those guys with a smooth upper body and hairy lower body. While he did triceps presses on the cable crossover machine, I checked out his round ass.

When he finished his workout, sweat dotted his bare arms.

"Thanks, buddy. I really appreciate this. I owe you."

"I'm glad to help. Hope everything is okay."

"It will be. I'll tell you what happened."

Following Jacob into the locker room, I tried to appear casual and uninterested. He opened his locker and pulled off his shirt while he began to tell me about his problems.

"Meredith totally freaked out today and broke up with me. She thinks I have something going on with one of my group partners for my class project in Communications. First of all, the girl in my group has a boyfriend and secondly she isn't really attractive. Meredith just gets crazy sometimes, and you can't reason with her."

"That's too bad. You're a great guy, Jacob. You shouldn't let her treat you like that."

He looked away as if contemplating what I'd said, and then responded, "She can be a bitch. To top it all off, I had a midterm today and I know I failed it. I was so stressed out that I really needed to lift. Thanks again for staying."

By this point, Jacob was standing there in only his underwear. The moment felt precipitous, because I knew that against all my powers I could not resist looking at his crotch. When his underwear came off, I would look at his dick, and he would catch me. Then he'd freak out and our friendship would be over. In my head, I kept saying, "Don't look at his penis. Don't glance at his crotch."

In the locker room there were two massage tables that nobody used for massages. Usually when the athletes needed a muscle wrapped, they sat on one of the tables while the trainers worked on them. Jacob was looking at the tables.

"Do you do massage?" he asked.

"Not professionally. I know some simple things."

"Would you mind giving me a rub down?"

"Not as long as you don't expect anything fancy."

It was a dream come true! During our many chats, I had never touched Jacob, but I thought about it every time. He lay face down on the table, and I began to squeeze his neck and shoulder muscles. Inside I was trembling and I felt a stirring in my pants.

"That feels great," he said. "If I didn't know better, I'd swear you'd done this before."

"Not much. Tell me if I rub too hard."

"Nah, man, it feels great."

I made long strokes down his back to the edge of his underwear and back up his sides. Each time I pushed my hands down his back, I tried to push his underwear a little lower on his ass. Part of me felt guilty for being so turned on by his body, and the rest of me was trying to figure out how to go farther.

"Do you mind doing my legs?" he asked.

"Sure."

Again, I rubbed a little higher each time, and eventually my hand would slide underneath the edge of his underwear and over the cheek of his ass. I watched for him to exhibit signs of discomfort, but Jacob seemed to be completely at ease with my touch. After I finished one leg, I moved onto the other. This time, my hand was able to explore a little more of his ass. Then I threw caution to the wind and began rubbing his asscheeks with both my hands. I wished his underwear were off, and I tried to imagine his beautiful bare ass.

"This feels so good."

Clearly he had no problem with me touching his round glutes. Then he turned over suddenly, and I felt like I had been caught doing something bad.

"Would you mind doing the front, and then I won't bug you anymore?"

Rather than speak and hear my voice crack, I just nodded and walked to the end of the table. Jacob's chest was so hard and round that I was fascinated by it. For a brief moment, I forgot that I was massaging my friend and not exploring a new toy. When I realized that I was actually flicking his nipples with my thumbs, rather than rubbing his chest, I panicked. What was he thinking? Immediately I returned to proper massage behavior.

I ran my hands down his sides and into the waist of his underwear and then I dragged them back up his body. His dick was clearly outlined in the white briefs, and I could tell that the head of it rested just below the waistband. Each time I ran my hands down his sides, I moved farther, and each time his underwear stretched a little more. I wanted so badly for the band to slip over the head of his dick. Though it was subtle at first,

I noticed that his dick became thicker, and his underwear began to strain a little more against his cock.

I continued down his body to his legs. Again I pushed the limits of my reach and was careful to go as close to his crotch as I could without actually touching his penis. Twice my fingers bumped against his balls, but he never flinched. My dick was so hard that I would have to hide behind the table when he got up. As I was finishing his second leg, I noticed his dick had grown even more. He clearly had a semi-woody now.

"That was great, dude," he said, breaking the silence.

Jacob sat up and dropped his legs off the side of the table. At that moment I thought that he was the most beautiful thing I had ever seen. He sat there leaning slightly forward, and I worried that he was feeling freaked out about the extent of my massage.

"Are you okay?" I asked.

"Yeah. It's just that I don't want to go home."

To comfort him, I placed a hand on his back and squeezed his shoulder.

"The worst part is that I've been horny as hell and Meredith hasn't been putting out."

"Women are like that."

"You ever have that problem with a guy?"

I could not move for what seemed like an eternity. Suddenly, I pulled my hand from his neck and I said nothing.

"What's wrong?" Jacob asked.

I still could not speak. Inside I was certain that this whole situation was going to end terribly. I began to chastise myself for going so far during the massage.

"You didn't think I knew you were into guys?" he asked.

"No."

"It's cool. I've known since the first time we studied for Archaeology together. I saw a gay magazine in your book bag, and it made sense. Seriously, dude, I have no problems with it."

"Jacob, I didn't know that you knew. I'm sorry that I didn't tell you. I wasn't trying to keep it secret."

"Oh, I know. I figured you'd tell me when you felt like the time was right. You know it doesn't bother me, right? Would I have let you massage me if it bothered me?"

"I'm sorry if I made you uncomfortable during the massage."

"What? Hell no! I loved the massage. Almost gave me a woody."

"Maybe I should go now."

"Can I ask you something? What do you like about me?"

"What do you mean?"

"I just want to know what people like about me. What do you think I have going for me?"

"That's easy. You are kind and smart. You're funny, generous, easygoing. Unlike a lot of guys who try to hide behind some macho facade, you have a good heart and it shows. You have great eyes, great hair, perfect teeth and a killer body. What really draws people to you is your personality."

"Wow. Thanks, man. I needed to hear that."

Jacob slid off the table, walked over and gave me a hug. I was so worried about hugging him back, but I did it anyway.

"It'll all be okay," I offered. "I promise."

My hands slid down his back to the edge of his waistband. If he leaned even a little closer to me, he would feel my dick straining against my pants. I couldn't tell if he was crying, but he was deathly quiet. We remained in a hug for a long while, and his arms never moved.

What happened next was beyond my expectations. Jacob shifted his hips slightly and I felt his dick against my leg. He was rock hard. I wondered if he had rubbed his dick against me for a reason, so I ran my hands into the back of his underwear to see what his reaction would be. He moved closer and I felt his butt muscles clinch. I squeezed his globes in my hands and kissed his neck. Then he clearly moved his hips to rub his dick against me.

I kissed his neck some more and he moved his head aside. He looked like a victim inviting a vampire to drink. First I licked his neck and tasted the salt on his skin, and then I kissed him lightly from his ear to his shoulder. All the while I felt his furry asscheeks in my hands. Finally, I slid my hands around to his front and felt his thick, tumescent cock.

His embrace was still so tight around my neck. I wanted to break free and look at his dick, but Jacob didn't let go. Clearly, he enjoyed me stroking his cock in my hand. I heard him moan.

"Are you okay?" I asked.

"Yeah. It feels great."

"Tell me if you want to stop."

"Can I kiss you?"

Without responding, I moved my cheek closer to his. Then our lips met and began to explore. I could feel his tongue against mine and the passion of his kisses surprised me. He held the back of my neck with one hand, and I thought that I might kiss him like that forever. His dick in my hand was rock hard and I felt precum on my skin.

"Will you suck me?" he asked between kisses.

"Sure."

I dropped to my knees and gazed at the most beautiful cock I had ever seen. His cock was thick and evenly proportioned, and it had the best curve. His black pubic hair was trimmed but still full; large balls hung underneath. I pulled his briefs down to the floor, and he stepped out of them.

I wrapped my lips around the head of his cock to suck out the precum. His whole body convulsed, and he groaned out loud. I slid my mouth all the way down his cock until I felt the tickle of his pubic hair on my nose.

"Fuck yeah," he moaned. "Oh god. That feels so good."

I worked my mouth up and down on his cock slowly and evenly so he could experience the full sensation. While I gave him the best blowjob he had ever had, I gently rubbed his balls and the sensitive skin between his legs. I could feel my finger getting close to his hole, and my dick was about to burst, so I freed it from my pants.

"Oh god, I'm going to come if you keep it up."

I think that Jacob was warning me, in case I did not want his cum in my mouth, but I didn't mind. In fact, I rather liked it.

Now that he was really into the blowjob, I began to suck faster on just the end of his dick while I jerked the base of it with my hand. He was breathing in short gasps as I worked his cock like a pro. I felt his balls pull up close to his body and his dick get as hard as possible. It was going to happen. Suddenly, his body spasmed as he declared, "I'm coming!"

I tasted his semen in my mouth, and he spurted several times before stopping. Once he stopped squirting, I sucked one last time on his cock. He jerked as his cock fell free from my mouth.

"That was hot," he said.

"Yeah it was. I can't believe this is happening."

"I've thought about doing this before with a guy, but I just never did."

"I'm glad you picked me for your exploration."

He snickered. "I guess maybe I'm gay too."

"Or bisexual. Are you okay with what just happened?"

"Yeah. I love women, but I need something more. There are things guys will do that women won't. I didn't know if I was really gay, or bi, until I felt your hands on me."

He kissed me again. All the while I cupped an asscheek in each hand. Our hard dicks were pinned between our bodies and rubbed against each other.

"There's something else I want to try," he said coyly.

"What?"

"I don't know if you'll do it. I want to have my ass licked."

I nodded my head emphatically and turned him toward the table. He leaned forward as I knelt behind him and spread his furry cheeks. The sight of his pink pucker made me swoon. I blew a breath to tickle his ass and then I licked it with my tongue.

When I heard him say "Yeah," I knew that I could dive in and have a good time. I love to eat ass, and this ass was prime grazing land. I worked my tongue up and down the entire crack and kissed his cheeks. Then I wiggled my tongue up against the hole as if I were trying to get inside him. From his moans, I knew he was enjoying it. Wishing beyond all hope, I wet one finger and worked it in a circle against his hole. I didn't know if he'd let me inside him, but I wanted to find out.

"Can I slide a finger inside?"

"Fuck yeah."

So I spit on his ass and pushed my middle finger inside his warm ass slowly. At first, he seemed to tense and I worried that he would stop me, but eventually he relaxed and pushed his ass back toward me. Once I had the finger inside him, I reached around to feel his dick. It was still rock hard.

"That is so fucking hot," I gasped. "I love your ass."

"Yeah. It feels good."

"I'd love to fuck you." There. I'd said it!

Jacob didn't respond. I was certain he was trying to figure out a polite way to say "no way." I licked his ass and wiggled the finger some more and said, "It's okay."

"I've got a condom in my locker."

"Are you sure?"

"Yeah."

I pulled my finger from his tight hole and stood up. Jacob kissed me and stroked my cock a few times. Then he walked to his locker and came back with a condom and a small tube of lube. Like a true gentleman, he put the condom on my dick and lubed it up.

"Do you mind if I lay on my back?" he asked.

"No. That would be great."

"Good, 'cause I want to see you while you're inside me."

Jacob lay back on the table and I climbed between his legs.

"I guess I'm really queer now," he said.

"This doesn't make you anything. We don't have to do this, if you're unsure."

"No. I don't give a shit if it makes me queer. I want you to fuck me."

I rubbed my hands over his thighs, across his hips and to his abdomen. Our eyes met and I wondered if he had any fears. I leaned forward with my hand on his cock and my hard dick resting against his ass and kissed him. He wrapped his legs around my back and kissed me passionately.

"Are you sure about this?" I asked.

"I wouldn't do it with anyone other than you, buddy. Take it slow at first. I'm ready for you."

The hot stud lifted his legs toward his chest and I smiled. I rubbed my dickhead up and down his crack and playfully poked the head at his pink hole. Then I pushed my hips forward and felt the pressure of my dick trying to enter his virgin ass. I moved very slowly and let him gradually open to me. Eventually, I felt the head pop inside. Before pushing in any farther, I jerked his cock to keep it hard. While I continued jacking him, I leaned forward and watched my cock slide inside him. Once I was all the way in, I leaned over and asked if he was okay.

"Yeah. It's good."

"Let me know if you want to stop."

"I'm ready. Fuck me."

So I obliged. I began to slide my dick slowly out and in while I watched his face. He winced a few times and then smiled. I nodded at him and he nodded back. Then I plunged in harder once and watched him gasp. I did it again. The third time he said, "Yeah, that's it."

I lifted his legs higher and started to pump his ass. The sight of his hairy ass opening for my invading dick made me hotter than hell. I wanted to fuck him hard. Without stopping, I leaned over him and rested his legs against my arms. Once I could look into his eyes, I began to pump harder and watch him bounce with each thrust. He never broke eye contact as I invaded his ass at full speed.

He said, "You feel so good in my ass. I want to come while you're fucking me."

"Yeah."

"Does it feel good to you?"

"Does it ever! I've never felt anything so good."

"Yeah. Tell me how much you like fucking me so I can come for you."

"Jacob, your ass is so hot." I looked down to watch my dick sliding into his body; his massive thighs were resting against my arms. Never in my wildest dreams did I think that I would have sex with Jacob, and never could I have imagined that I would be fucking him. He rubbed his balls and then began stroking his dick.

"I can't believe how good you feel. I love being inside you."

"Yeah. Are you going to come while fucking me?"

"I'll pull out just in time."

"And shoot on me?"

"Yeah. You feel so good. I don't think I can last much longer. You are so fucking hot. Your ass is amazing."

Then Jacob tensed. I looked down and saw cum flying from his dick. I couldn't believe he was shooting such a big load for the second time. I pumped harder, and he responded by groaning loudly while he emptied his cock onto his belly.

I couldn't take it any more. I pulled out of him and yanked off the condom. Then I stroked for a few seconds before I shot my huge load onto his belly and crotch. It was the hottest fuck session I'd ever had.

"Thanks for taking care of me tonight," he said.

"Thanks for letting me. It was amazing."

"I never thought it would be like this."

"Like what?" I asked.

"So hot. I'd never really thought much about it before."

"And now?"

"Now I know it can be just as hot with a guy as with a girl."

"This won't ruin our friendship, will it?"

"What?" he asked, incredulous. "No way. In fact, my room-mate is going to be out of town tomorrow, and I thought maybe we could do this again tomorrow at my place. You could spend the night."

"Really!"

"Yeah."

Jacob grinned wide and I leaned over him. We kissed again, and then I looked into his eyes. He brushed my hair with the back of his hand and then said, "So tomorrow night can I fuck you?"

"We'll see," I laughed. "We'll see. If you're a good boy."

We hopped off the table and headed for the shower.

The next night I showed up at Jacob's with flowers, a case of beer and a full pack of condoms. We didn't even make it through dinner before we were exploring Jacob's sexuality some more.

Looking back, Jacob and I are both glad that he decided on that late night workout.

Skateboarder Loves His Toys
Jay Starre

Glen watched Mateo out of the corners of his eyes as the slim sophomore performed on his skateboard in the empty plaza behind the Science building. It was hot as hell that afternoon with the California sun beating relentlessly down on the concrete. Besides Glen, there was only Mateo in the plaza. The sophomore raced back and forth, leaping on and off his skateboard, twisting, turning, and flipping the thing with a teeth-rattling clatter. With the heat and Mateo's noisy show, no wonder no one was around.

Glen sat in the shade of a wilting oak and pretended to be working on his papers. He was actually nursing a big hard-on and covering it with his notebook. Sweat trickled down his armpits, just like it trickled down the slender brown sides of the sophomore playing tricks on his skateboard in front of him. Glen's eyes wandered from his work, to Mateo, and back again.

Mateo sported baggy shorts and a sleeveless shirt that hung on his frame. Damp with sweat, his nipples showed through the white material. Mateo's ass jutted out from behind his narrow waist in twin mounds of firm flesh as he pumped across the plaza on his skateboard. Glen bit his lip and forced himself to look down at his work.

The sophomore raced closer. And closer. Glen didn't look up until he heard the skateboard screech to a halt and a surprisingly soft voice break the sudden afternoon silence.

"Are you a teacher or somethin'?"

Glen looked up at bold brown orbs and a flashing white grin. The fucker was as cute as hell. "No. I'm a grad student." For some reason he added, "I'm only twenty-six."

"I'm twenty. I know I look younger. You're hot. I like big jock types. Want to come to my place and fuck?"

Glen sputtered out a laughing reply. "Uh, sounds like a plan, maybe. I'm not getting much work done with all the noise you're making. I'm Glen." He rose and reached out to shake the skateboarder's hand.

Mateo slapped the offered palm playfully and laughed back. "I'm Mateo. And I love to get my ass worked over. Sound good to you?"

Glen blinked rapidly, a little jolted by the younger student's brazen and nasty forwardness, but liking him because of it. He made an instant decision.

"Lead the way." Glen grinned as he dropped his notebook and displayed the huge tent in his own shorts.

Mateo eyed the bulge and raised his dark eyebrows. "Let's not waste another fucking minute."

Glen followed the globes of Mateo's ass like a fish caught on a hook as the sophomore skateboarded ahead, just slow enough so Glen didn't actually have to run. The blond grad student was breathless by the time they travelled the ten blocks to Mateo's apartment building. Mateo expertly flipped his board up to standing and lifted it in one arm as he unlocked the door to his first floor suite.

Glen crowded close, touching the lean body from behind for the first time. It was sweaty, warm, and firm. His dick rubbed up against Mateo's rounded asscheek. "I can't wait to get a look at this," he growled in Mateo's ear as the door opened and they tumbled inside.

"My ass is all yours, buddy," Mateo promised. He shoved his butt back into Glen's crotch briefly before he moved away to shut the door.

Mateo immediately begin stripping. He tossed his clothes aside on the cluttered carpet carelessly. Glen glanced around and was shocked at the mess. It was a small bachelor, with only the one room, a kitchen, and bathroom. The bed was in the corner and unmade. The floor, couch, and coffee table were covered in discarded clothes, books, and papers.

Glen's attention was diverted from the pigpen surroundings.

His eyes zeroed in on the hot sight of Mateo naked and bounding across the room toward his bed. "Come on, Glen. Let's do the nasty! I'll start by sucking your big cock!"

Glen didn't need any more encouragement. He threw off his own clothes and added to the mess without a second thought. Once his underwear was off, his pink and leaking cock jutted out in front of him.

Mateo grinned. "It's a fucking bat! Huge!" He sprawled on his belly on the bed facing Glen. He licked his bowed lips and stared up with his big brown eyes, and then he wiggled the mounds of his ass seductively and spread his legs.

Glen moaned. Satin flesh. Dark where the sun hit and softer amber where it hadn't. The creamy brown butt was a work of art! The punk was hairless and slim, but his shoulders were broader than they had appeared, and his thighs were solid muscle.

He was hot, hot, hot!

Stumbling over Mateo's scattered belongings, Glen made it to the bed. His hands on the base of his cock, he pointed it at Mateo's waiting face. Mateo laughed and then opened wide with his fat tongue lolling out obscenely. The sophomore was certainly uninhibited.

Glen was about to find out how really nasty the skateboarder was.

In the meantime, the older grad student humped forward with his hips. He buried his cock in the open mouth as he bumped into the side of the bed. Mateo gurgled and slurped. He tongued the mushroom cap in his mouth and wrapped his lips around the thrusting shaft. Glen shivered from head to toe as the wet warmth enfolded his cock.

Mateo's head and shoulders hung over the edge of the bed. His hands were down on the floor and reaching under the bed even as he smacked his lips over Glen's dick. He pulled a box out from underneath and flipped off the top. Glen looked down at the contents on the floor between his spread feet.

A big bottle of lube. Dildos!

Several of them, in fact, and some grossly large. Glen's mouth dropped open. Once again he found himself shocked by the sex-hungry sophomore's uninhibited attitude. Mateo, though, wasn't waiting around for Glen to say or do anything. He snatched up the bottle of lube in one hand and one of the dildos in the other.

Glen watched in shuddering amazement as the amber-skinned punk swallowed his cock noisily while managing to squirt a vast amount of lube all over his perky asscheeks then toss the bottle aside along with the other discarded items in his messy room.

Mateo's hands were behind him. One clutched the lengthy rubber dildo while he used the other to open up his own ass-crack. Mateo aimed the blunt head at his asshole.

Glen leaned over and stared with his eyes wide open. He had a perfect view of the hairless crack and the pink hole. Mateo rolled his hips and spread his thighs wider apart to offer Glen a better look. He still sucked away on Glen's cock. The sophomore rubbed the dildo up and down his crack lewdly, while wiggling his butt for Glen in a nasty exhibition.

The little fucker was a real performer—and not just on his skateboard!

Glen's eyes focussed on that nasty display, while at the same time his cock throbbed with pleasure in Mateo's hot mouth. The intensity of both experiences multiplied each other. Mateo gurgled real dick deeper while he thrust the fake dick up and down his slippery crack and wiggled his plump, but solid can.

"Fuck! That's so nasty," Glen managed to gasp out.

Mateo gurgled something unintelligible as he aimed the realistic looking dildo head at the puckered lips of his asshole. Glen leaned over farther to get a closer look while placing his hands on Mateo's buzzed scalp. The sophomore kept his auburn hair closely trimmed, and from the looks of his apartment did it, so that he wouldn't have to bother combing it. The bristling feel of that short hair under his fingertips only added to the sensual elements bombarding Glen.

Glen was mesmerized as he watched Mateo begin to feed himself the greased dildo. Mateo's thighs sprawled wide apart, he rose on his knees and arched his back, then began to shove with the palm of his hand on the flat base of the dildo. Tight asslips parted, sphincter relaxed, and with a deep grunt, Mateo forced the head of the fake cock up his ass.

He didn't stop there. With more grunts, and lewd slurps around Glen's cock in his mouth, Mateo pressed the dildo deeper, and deeper. And deeper. Glen was impressed! Lube oozed around the length of the pink rubber as it rode ever farther up Mateo's puckered asshole. Mateo used his free hand to work more of the slippery stuff along the dildo shaft and his tender butt lips.

The skateboarder wiggled his ass and humped upwards, using the movement to drive more of the dildo up his hungry butt. His throat opened at the same time, and suddenly Glen was getting sucked right to the balls.

"Oh my god. Oh my god," Glen moaned. His hips drove forward into Mateo's face.

Throat muscles pulsed around his cock as he leaned over. His face was close to the lewd sight of that foot-long rubber disappearing up Mateo's quivering butthole. The skateboarder didn't let up until he'd fed himself the entire thing. Only the base remained visible between his perky asscheeks.

And Mateo was just getting started.

Slowly and deliberately, Mateo began to pull back, which allowed Glen's cock to slide out of his pulsing throat. At the same time he began to pull the dildo out of his ass. Inch after inch of flesh-colored rubber cock reappeared. The dildo glistened obscenely with lube. Mateo's stretched buttlips clung to the dildo as it slid out, as if unwilling to release it.

Mateo drew back so that just the head of Glen's cock hovered between his lips. He tickled the buried crown with swipes of his tongue while massaging the head with his full lips. He pulled the dildo all the way out of his hole with a nasty plop. Left behind was a swollen gash Glen stared down at with his knees shaking.

Mateo's free hand snaked out to grasp one of Glen's. He yanked it down into the slippery valley of his spread crack. He crammed Glen's fingers up against the maw of his own lubed hole and gurgled as two of Glen's fingers were forced deep into the hot orifice.

Glen gasped. The hole was still snug and the asslips clamped over his buried fingers. The insides quivered and the lips throbbed. Glen wanted to ram deep with his fingers, or his cock, or even the greased dildo discarded between Mateo's firm and squirming buttcheeks. He wanted to drill that slick hole with anything and everything!

The blond grad student instead chose to go along with Mateo's nasty guidance. The younger student pushed against Glen's fingers with his own hand. They were forced farther up his asshole. Glen obligingly dug deep. He twisted and explored, probing and finding prostate, and then tapping it with his fingers.

Mateo squirmed and grunted like a gored pig. His lips tantalized the head of Glen's cock while his asshole convulsed around Glen's buried digits. The obscene dildo remained in plain sight, ready for more action, between Mateo's creamy brown buttcheeks.

Mateo apparently was thinking of that dildo too. He moved his hand from where it pressed against Glen's fingers and groped for the discarded rubber. He snatched it up and before Glen realized what he intended, crammed the thing back between his parted asscheeks and back into his own asshole.

A squishy spurt of lube splattered from between the stretched asslips. The dildo slithered between Glen's buried fingers and pushed deep into Mateo's bowels. Glen felt the firm rubber sliding around his fingers and groaned. What a filthy thrill!

Mateo fucked himself with the dildo around Glen's fingers and grunted all the while. He squirmed his plump can around on the bed. He humped up and down and rode the rubber dick in a bucking frenzy. His lips massaged Glen's cockhead and his tongue dug into Glen's piss slit.

Glen was close to blowing and had to believe Mateo was working himself up to a similar climax with all that squirming around. But the skateboard punk had other plans. He abruptly rose off Glen's cock with a smacking slurp and reared back to crouch on his knees. Glen's fingers slid from their hot nest. He stood back on shaking thighs to await Mateo's next move.

It was bound to be surprising.

"I want to sit on one of my toys. While you watch. Give me the big plug with the ridges on it," Mateo said breathlessly. He grinned at Glen and licked his plump lips with a teasing slurp, then scooted around on the bed so that he was facing away from the blond.

Mateo sat on his thighs with his knees wide apart. His cute bubble-butt curved out from his slim waist. That ass was slick with lube and smooth as satin. Glen tore his eyes from that inviting sight to search down beside the bed for the box of toys Mateo had pulled out earlier.

There it was among a half dozen other lewd sex objects. A butt plug with a tapered point like a pyramid and succeeding rings of larger girth that led to a solid base. It was jet black. Glen scooped it up out of the box, surprised at how solid it felt. Could Mateo sit on all that rubber?

Mateo's amber orbs twinkled as he watched with his head craned around. "That's the one. My ass is lubed up good already, so go right ahead. Plant that monster on the bed between my legs and I'll sit on it."

"You got it," Glen murmured. He was already imagining the black toy filling Mateo's steamy hole.

Mateo leaned forward on his hands and lifted his ass. His balls hung down between his spread thighs. His stiff cock pulsed just below that in a twitching arc. He was obviously getting off on the scene. Just like Glen.

Glen placed the butt plug on the bed under Mateo's ivory-satin ass. He aimed the tip at the puckered maw he'd just been fingering, and Mateo squirmed around so that the rubber slid up between his well lubed asslips.

"Now watch while I sit on that fucker," Mateo promised. His buzzed scalp craned around and his bold gaze met Glen's.

Slowly Mateo squatted down over the black plug. The tip was slim and easily accommodated, but the first ridge took a moment longer and required a deep grunt to swallow. Mateo used his hand and pushed downwards and back on his own dick between his spread thighs. His balls mashed up against the big plug and his stiff dick pressed along it in a downward arrow.

While Mateo slowly sat on the dildo, he rubbed his own balls and cock along it. The first ridge stretched the skateboarder's asslips apart, disappeared, and then was followed by a wider ridge. Mateo moaned and squirmed. He was obviously loving it, but the little skank wanted even more.

"Give me another toy. I'll suck on it while you jerk off over my plugged ass!"

Glen had to laugh, even though it came out with more like a ragged snort. He rummaged in the box beside the bed and found a fat fake cock with a giant bulb of a head. He handed it to Mateo, who winked, then licked his lips with a filthy smirk before he began to lick the dildo head.

Glen got up on the bed and knelt behind Mateo. He ran one hand all over the plump, squirming can while he stroked his own cock with the other. Mateo's butt was coated in sweat and lube and slick as leather. The giant black plug slowly sank deeper up the skateboarder's asshole. Mateo both grunted and snorted as he smacked his lips over the dildo in his hand.

Groping Mateo's body with one hand, and jerking off with the other, Glen squatted behind the nasty sophomore and watched him toy fuck himself. The black plug disappeared between stretched buttlips, the heaving ass squirmed under Glen's stroking hand, and the dildo in Mateo's fist slid in and out of the sophomore's slurping mouth.

"God! Where did you learn all this nasty shit at only twenty?" Glen couldn't help asking. His heart pounded, and his cock was on fire as he pumped it faster and faster.

Mateo slid the dildo out of his mouth long enough to speak. With a wiggle of his sweat-soaked butt, he swallowed another ridge of the plug. "I've got a nasty imagination. And I practice a lot. Like now."

Glen tried to laugh, but couldn't catch his breath. He was so close! His hand flew up and down his own stiff cock. The head dribbled precum continually. His other hand roamed over Mateo's satin-ass. He fondled the rounded glutes, then slid his fingers into the crack to stroke the stretched lips as they struggled to accommodate yet another fat ridge of rubber plug.

Mateo gobbled up the dildo in his hand with filthy slurps just as he rose up off the plug and exposed several ridges of greased rubber. He arched his back and plunged back down to gulp up all he'd abandoned, and two more ridges at the same time.

Glen shoved forward with his jerking cock and thrust it against one slick cheek of Mateo's ass. He groaned from the heat of that jiggling muscle before he cried out and shot a stream of goo all over it.

Mateo plunged the dildo deep into his mouth, wriggled over the plug, and rubbed his own cock against it before he began to squirt too.

Cum spurted downwards over the base of the plug. Cum sprayed all over Mateo's writhing asscheek and crack.

They shot like dogs in heat. Glen humped Mateo's ass and Mateo humped the huge plug up his butt. It lasted and lasted before they toppled together over onto the unmade bed.

Mateo grinned and sighed as Glen slowly removed the plug from his snapping butthole. An evil smirk danced over his bowed lips. "There's still a few more toys we haven't tried out. Do you have another hour or two?"

Glen had work to finish, but with a jet-black butt plug in his hand and a slim and nasty sophomore under him, he couldn't have cared less about that.

"Sure. What's next?"

Unsurprisingly, Mateo proved himself inventive. The skate-boarder certainly loved his toys!

The Professor's Submission
David Holly

Gay bathhouses are not crowded on Sunday nights. Still, I was sitting in the hot tub watching the feast of sodomy being projected from a DVD player running in a farther room. The young performing artists upon the wall were enacting a scene from the ancient temple of Ur, their so-called sodomitic frenzies associated with the rising of Sirius. The action was hot enough to render me hard, but I was sitting alone in the hot, bubbling water.

The youthful, unrestrained fuck scene served to remind me of my age, thirty-five, just over the bulge of youth and the rest downhill; my profession, a college professor who would meet the fall quarter's students the next morning; and my knowledge, classical studies and literature. Who else would recognize the porn film's reference to the Enariae. Feeling a post-modern anguish, I rose from the pool, my tumescence still palpable, dried upon the gargantuan towel the bathhouse provided, and wrapped around my waist a truncated but vibrant red sarong, bold with yellow parrots.

As I wandered the nearly empty maze of cubicles, my nerves were jangling with a bodily urge to fill and be filled. I had counted thirty cars in the parking lot, but where were the men? The two fellows I passed would not meet my inquiring eyes, nor even sneak a peep at my cock jutting from my red and yellow sarong. After checking out the steam room, I went desperately seeking solace in the labyrinth of glory holes. Even anonymous sex would be better than none.

I saw three cocks projecting through the glory holes. Most nights there were far more, but of those three, one was nearly spectacular in its delectability. First, it was thick. I prefer thickness over length any day, though its length was nothing to quibble over. Second, it was firm. There was nothing wishy-washy about it; that cock was a diamond in its rigidity. Third, it was untrimmed, flaring out and upward and twisting slightly to its owner's left. Fourth, it still carried the pinkish flesh tone of youth. Its color spoke of health, vim, and the warmness of the blood.

When I touched my fingers to the cock's hood, a low howl of approval reverberated through the thin partition. That single ululation was all the encouragement I needed, so I moistened the cock with a bit of lubricant and stroked it. My heart thrilled as the thick cock filled my hand, and my own tightened harder. I could have jerked both, but jacking off could not satisfy my dry-mouthed lust. Crumpling to my knees, I pressed my burning lips to the hooded beauty.

As I kissed the naked flesh, the man flesh forbidden to men through so much of history, I rubbed my throbbing cock and let the tip of the mysterious dick pass over my lips. I had no idea what the secret owner of this bulky attachment may look like, but the part of him I could experience was wrapped in beauty. It even felt beautiful as it glided deeper into my mouth. As his foreskin skidded over my tongue, approaching toward my throat, my cock pulsed and released a thin stream, a harbinger of that glorious upsurge to come. My small release reminded me to take precautions, for though I had neither gum disease nor recent dental work, still I did not want to risk infection. Reluctantly I pulled back my head, fearing the fluids of another man, hesitance and desire wrapped into a single package and roofed with skin.

I untied my sarong and draped it over the top of the partition. Then naked, I sought the wrappers that promised safer sex. The ornate bowl of condoms contained none of the flavored ones I had used as former occasions demanded. However, the one I picked up was extra strength, which inspired another idea. I squirted a drop of lube on the inside tip of the condom and squeezed the tip as I unrolled the condom down to the base of his shaft. Through the wall, a voice squeaked in protest as I wrapped his cock, but he did not pull it away. Indeed, as I lubed his condom-covered cock for deep penetration, my mystery partner's squeak turned into a purr.

Lubricating my asshole was the work of a minute. Then I backed onto the cock. The horny party on the other side of the wall caught my intention immediately, thrusting his pelvis forward so that his dick jutted solidly. I let it slide between my rounded butt cheeks until my asshole touched the lubricated tip. Closing my eyes and drawing a deep breath, I pushed my asshole open while pressing my butt toward the wall. The cock slid into me easily, filling my dilating ass. Slowly I pushed back until my buttocks were compressed against the thin fiberboard.

I could not keep from jerking off while I fucked the dick with my ass. My own cock throbbed and leaked more of the sticky liquid. I rocked my hips back and forth, taking the anonymous cock while my hand busily flogged my dick.

"That's it, dude, take it, take it," keened a disembodied voice with a faint western twang from behind the wall. "Oh, man, you give good ass."

Inspired, I rode his cock harder, rode his cock faster, rode his cock until it swelled harder in my ass. Even as I tormented his cock with my asshole, I beat my own dick with a fierce fist, thumbing my dick's head with every stroke. By the time the besieged cock in my ass prepared to erupt, I was ready to shoot my load. I had been receiving a delicious prostate massage that interiorized my approaching orgasm. The pleasure did not even begin in my cock, but deeper. Then the tingles came, followed by waves of orgasmic pleasure that grew into the divine spasm. I was one with the Enariae I had seen earlier on the wall, part of the long human line of men who knew how to receive as well as to give. Then I was coming, and my asshole was throbbing, contracting, and dilating. The twang of my unknown partner reverberated through the thin board: "Oh, fuck, that's good. Oh, yeah, you're milking me off like a motherfucker."

After the luscious agony stilled, I pulled my ass away from the wall, emptying it of my benefactor's benevolence. As an act of love, I turned and pulled the condom off of the cock that had given me so much pleasure before its owner could retract it through the wall. After tossing the spent condom into the garbage receptacle, I wiped my hands on my towel, left my sarong lying across the top of the partition, and headed for the shower.

As I stood beneath the spray, shampoo running from my hair and blurring my vision, I sensed rather than saw a man enter the shower room. He stood beneath his own spray, but I could feel his eyes upon me. Somehow, I knew that he was my recent lover, and I wanted to say something to him, thank him, or arrange to meet him again, yet some shyness regarding our anonymous intimacy prevented me. I finished soaping my dick and thighs and in between my butt cheeks. As I rinsed, I heard the spray stop across from me. Suddenly, he was close, his lips nearly touching my soapy ear.

"Damn, you sure know how to take it up the ass, professor. You're one hot fuck."

Then he was gone, slipping away before I could see him, before I could clear the water and shampoo from my eyes. I rinsed my hair and face as best I could, even as premonitions of destruction beat upon me. "Professor," he had said. Was it a wild surmise, or did he recognize me from the college? From the photograph on my textbooks? Could he be a former student? The implications of that possibility washed over me, destroying any thought of further sexual glory. Fucking a student was the greatest crime in academia. Should some fink report that I had been anally receptive to a student, Dean Stout's reaction would be worse than a meteorite striking the earth, and J. Evans Shrubb, president of the college, would expire in his chair—immediately after ordering my execution. Crucifixion in the center of the quad would be the most lenient punishment I could expect.

Drying quickly, I hurried back to the glory hole maze. I found the empty hole where I had pleasured myself, but my sarong was no longer draped over the partition. I searched the maze without success and enquired at the desk when I turned in my locker key to retrieve my driver's license. No one had seen it, leaving only one terrible conclusion: my anonymous lover had stolen my sarong.

***

My first morning of the fall quarter was going along swimmingly until my specialty course on paganism in the arts. On the first day of each term, I explicate the course syllabus with my students before I call roll. The policy gives the latecomers, students who cannot find the classroom, a parking space, the campus, or their own dicks, a chance to find their seats before I call their names. Of course, I had noticed the striking male student sitting front row center, tall, shaggy blonde hair, stacked, and bulging in the right places. His face had an untamed expression that invited second looks. I did not hear his voice until I called roll. I was nearing the bottom of the alphabet before I reached his name.

"James Whitford."

"Here, professor," said he and those two words were enough. That twang in his voice was writ large upon my memory. I blanched and paused, but I had been teaching long enough to keep my head. I called the final name and dismissed the group.

After class several students lingered, some with questions, others with official forms for me to sign, and one for another purpose. My mind was a whirl, but I managed to answer most questions and sign my name on the correct lines. James Whitford slouched against the wall while I dealt with the other students. My heart was pounding as I answered the final student's question. I half hoped that James would give up, but another part of my mind kept focusing upon what I knew nestled concealed in his cowboy-style jeans. I had no idea what I would say to him.

The last coed left the classroom, and the door swung shut behind her. James fixed me with a knowing, even carnal, gaze. "Hey, professor," he said irreverently. "I'd like to pull down your pants, bend you over your desk, and fuck your hot, tight, grainy hole."

No, not crucifixion, I thought. Dean Stout will leave a loaded pistol on the table and lock me in.

"Excuse me?" I said, pretending that I had not heard aright.

James chuckled in a mocking and scornful manner, sort of the way I would imagine Dracula chortling over his dinner. Audacious and sneering, he reached into his backpack, extracted my stolen sarong, and dangled it accusingly.

"Perhaps this will refresh your memory, professor," hissed the student with a full measure of disrespect. James was relishing the power he knew he held over me. His visage was a mask of scorn, his every gesture a taunt. My face flushed as the physical memory of his cock sliding in and out of my ass aroused me, tightening my cock in my suit pants, and I seized the silky red sarong with the yellow parrots, stuffing it into my briefcase.

I could not allow his derision to continue. I was teacher; he was student. No matter who had fucked whom, I could not submit to his mockery. If I did, he would make me the butt of my own classroom. My beloved class would become a burlesque, a parody of learning, a travesty, a caricature of the pursuit of knowledge.

"We'll talk in my office," I ordered, grabbing up my briefcase, turning on my heel, striding toward the door.

"Talk?" he queried, forced to follow my lead. "Sure, we'll talk." He managed to inject a hint of raillery into his voice, but he had to scurry to keep up with me. I felt I was regaining the upper hand as we entered the Arts & Letters building with James two steps behind me. James managed to catch up as we passed the Tennessee Williams Performing Arts Theatre, but I forced him to double-step four flights of stairs, which left him winded when we reached my floor.

My cloakroom-sized office had a frosted glass in the door and one dusty window that looked upon the quad, though the shade was pulled down so the sun would not fade the spines of my books. Except for a double file cabinet underneath the window, bookshelves covered every bit of wall. Floor to ceiling, my office had space for two thousand volumes, though I had stuffed in closer to twenty-five hundred. Books piled upon books, piles of student papers and my own manuscripts overflowed from the file cabinets and rose high from every corner of the room.

I considered the psychological advantage of sitting behind my desk, putting thirty inches of old oak between James and I, but in the end I propped my left buttock on the corner of my desk and motioned him into the single student chair.

Insolently, James wiggled into the chair, his eyes locked on mine with a blunt, sexual stare. A smirk formed on his lips that I wanted to wipe off with a kiss, followed by an abrupt insertion of my dick. The closed door gave me a sense of security, however unwarranted. My office was my safe space. Here I was professor, master of my domain, and if James were lucky, I would let him lick my ass.

"I want to fuck you," he said.

"Maybe later," I said. "You're going to have to make me want that."

"How?"

"With your lips. With your mouth. With your tongue." Though my mouth gave the commands, I could scarcely believe myself. I was violating the greatest taboo in academia, worse than plagiarism even, yet something deep down rationalized that I had violated it already. The fates had already blown the whistle on me when I presented my anus to James's cock in the bathhouse wall. Thus, if I was doomed to crash, I might well enjoy the fall.

I unfastened my pants and threw them over my chair. My jacket, tie, and shirt followed. Then I was standing before my overwhelmed student, no longer so cocky he, and my dick was jutting the front of my sporty bikini underpants. "Kiss it, James," I ordered, and still sitting, he leaned forward, bringing his lips to the head of my cock.

"That's right, James," I whispered. "You're going to suck your professor's cock."

With a moan, James Whitford closed his lips around my dick. First, he grabbed the shaft with his fist, sucking the end as if it was a lollipop, wary of letting me in too far. But as his mouth grew familiar with my cock, he desired more of it and let it slide deeper until the underside of my dick was pressing down on the back of his tongue. Mine was not the first cock he had taken that far, for he knew how to swallow a dickhead. No gagging, but a hum of pleasure trilled up from his throat. His hand was slowly rubbing his cock through the tight denim of his jeans. As his excitement grew, he sucked me harder, bruising my dick head with his lips, caressing it with his tongue, kneading it with his throat.

"Hold onto my ass," I ordered, placing both of my hands behind his head and stoking his hair while he sucked me. "Hold onto my butt handles while you blow me."

He started sucking me harder as he felt the firm swell of my buttocks beneath his hands. I could not hold out against him. I felt my cock grow heavier as the tingles of approaching orgasm erupted in my dick's head. "I'm going to come in your mouth, James," I advised him, "and I expect you to swallow my whole load."

The tingles grew into an agony of need. James cupped my buttocks with both hands as he fed upon my cock. A thousand explosions of pleasure blasted conscious thought from my brain as waves of rapture rushed though my pelvis and my powerful muscles contracted again and again.

When I had finished and James was collapsed backward in his chair, I gave him an ironic smile. "You thought that the teacher would submit to the student because I took you anonymously last night. Now you know the truth. I submit to you only what I choose to submit. Today I have submitted my seed for your nourishment. Next time may be different, but it will be as I choose."

"Yes, professor," James said contritely. "I'm sorry I acted like a shit."

"Don't be sorry. Your lesson will continue following Wednesday's class. I expect to see you here at the same time."

"I'll be here," he agreed. "Will you let me... ?"

"I will submit only what I want to submit," I repeated. "If I allow you to penetrate me anally, it will be because I choose to take pleasure from your cock. Meanwhile, you will do your homework, write your papers, and take your tests. Those will determine your course grade. Whatever we may do sexually will have no effect on the way I evaluate your work."

"Uh, sure," James said shyly. Gone was the college kid who thought he could make his professor into his sex monkey. I gave him a condescending smile, while in my mind's eye I saw the opportunity and regarded it with wonder. I just might get away with it.

What I Learned from My Roommate
R. B. Snow

"So not cool, man." I breathed through my mouth so I wouldn't smell the vomit as I propped Ryan up against the tiles.

"I said I was sorry." Ryan opened his eyes and squinted at the bright lights of the bathroom. "Why are we in the shower?"

"Because you puked all over yourself and I'm not letting you in the room like this. Either you clean up or you're sleeping here tonight."

"Yeah, okay." He stepped forward to pull his shirt off and stumbled into me, pinning me against the wall. I could barely breathe, which was probably a good thing, since I could now feel the vomit on his chest soaking into my own shirt.

"Fuck! Get off me!" I pushed, but I couldn't move him. The ironic thing was that this was practically one of the fantasies I'd had about him: his gorgeous body pressed against me, his mouth on my neck, his hands gripping my shirt. It would have been perfect if he hadn't been completely shitfaced and covered in his own puke.

"Ryan."

"Mm."

"Ryan, you gotta get off me, man. Come on, move."

He let go of my shirt and put his hands on the wall on either side of my head. Then he looked up and smiled at me, all golden-boy perfection. "You're a good guy, Sev. I'm glad I got you as a roommate."

And like that, my annoyance was washed away by a wave of lust and affection. But then, Ryan had surprising me since the day I met him three weeks ago.

***

The good news from the housing office was that I'd gotten lucky in the dorm lottery and won a room in the mini-apartments.

The bad news was that my roommate was a jock from Oklahoma who'd gotten into university on a football scholarship. There was no way I could come out now; I'd get the shit beaten out of me every day, or he'd ask if I'd accepted Jesus Christ as my personal Lord and Savior, or worse, he'd request a room reassignment. No other straight guy would want to room with me and percentages were against me getting a gay roommate, so they'd probably just end up making *me* move, and there was no way I was losing that apartment. Oh, well. I'd been closeted since I was fourteen; another year wasn't going to make a big difference.

He looked almost exactly like I'd imagined: tall, blond, and tan, with broad shoulders and impossibly long legs. Typical, I told myself. Ordinary, common, straight, *boring*. Absolutely not gorgeous or fuckable in any way.

I suspect that I *wasn't* what he'd imagined. I saw his eyes go wide and his mouth drop open when he looked in the room, and I tried to picture what he was seeing: a white guy with raggedly cut black hair, eyeliner, three tiny hoops in one earlobe and one in the cartilage of the other ear, ripped black shirt, black pants. And he hadn't even seen the tongue stud or nipple ring yet. Okay, I didn't usually wear eyeliner, but that day I had definitely dressed for distress. I figured that if I couldn't come out, I could at least have some fun shocking him.

I stared at him, silently daring him to say something stupid, and got my first Ryan surprise. His lips curved up in a smile and he stepped forward, hand out. "Seven? I'm Ryan. It's really great to meet you." No hint of disgust or panic, but a genuine smile and a friendly gesture. The bastard had managed to shock *me,* and I shook his hand without thinking. It was warm and strong.

"Yeah. Good to meet you, too." Dammit. I'd meant to start early with the clever comments, the sarcastic remarks, but his smile turned into a grin, and I was lost.

He let go of my hand but didn't step back. Instead, he looked with open curiosity at my piercings. "Did they hurt?"

"A little."

"Wow." He shook his head. "I've never seen anything like that in Kansas."

"I thought you were from Oklahoma." I wanted to be angry at being stared at like a zoo animal, but he looked even better close up, especially when he grinned again.

"It was a joke. You know, 'we're not in Kansas anymore'?"

My mouth dropped open for a second, and then I laughed. I'd just been owned by an Oklahoma farm boy. And I'd liked it.

We spent a lot of time talking those first few days. He was incredibly grateful for the scholarship; he said that he never would have been able to go to university without it, and he was really looking forward to some new experiences. "I love my family, and the town's a great place to grow up, but... Do you ever feel like you don't fit in?"

I shot him a look and he laughed. "Okay, but at least you don't feel like you *have* to fit in. I mean, changing your name from Steven to Seven, that's cool. And all that stuff," he said, waving a hand at my piercings. "It's why I came here. I mean, I know I'm here for an education, but I'm also really happy about finally meeting different people and doing different stuff, you know?"

Fuck, yeah. If he wanted to do different stuff, I was so there. It would be really different for him to get a blowjob from a guy, to come with a finger up his ass. But all I said, and it was as close to the truth as I could get, was, "Well, let me know if I can help."

He smiled and went back to examining my iPod, while I tried to pretend that I wasn't examining him.

If only he'd been what I'd expected: a stupid, narrow-minded jock who'd have a group of equally stupid, narrow-minded friends. But he only spent time with his football buds during practice and hung out with me and our other apartment-mates when he wasn't in class or studying. He wasn't taking typical jock classes, either; we were in the same English class and he got through the books faster than I did. He was smart and fun to be around and I was utterly in lust with him.

The fantasies started three days after we'd moved in. I'd imagine him kissing me, or sucking me off in the back stacks of the library, or fucking me against the wall of the shower. It was kind of horrible, knowing that unless he turned into a jerk overnight, I'd have to suffer through the rest of the year with this wonderful, untouchable wet dream sleeping four feet from me. I started jerking off thinking about him after our first week of rooming together. I didn't *want* to find him attractive—such a stereotypically all-American boy—but my libido had other ideas.

And what was maybe the worst part was that I could have come out to him and he might have been okay with it *if I'd done it right away*. But now we'd been roommates for weeks, and no matter how open-minded he seemed, he'd probably freak out knowing that all this time he'd been getting dressed and sleeping in the same room as a queer. Plus, no matter how hot he was, he was also my friend, my first at university, and I didn't want him to hate me. So I kept my mouth shut.

Three weeks into the semester, a couple of girls from class who'd been practically salivating over Ryan had invited us to a party. I figured (very unselfishly, I might add) that at least one of us should be getting laid, so I took down the address while Ryan tried not to be too obvious about staring at the redhead's breasts.

"They can't be real," he said yet again, as we walked across campus to the party that night.

"Well, I'm sure you'll get to find out tonight," I muttered. I'd thought about just staying home, but Ryan had dragged me out. "Please. I'll look a lot cooler if you're with me." He didn't seem to realize he was a pussy magnet and that he didn't need me, but I agreed to go.

The place was packed by the time we got there. The red-head who'd invited us saw Ryan and shoved her way through the throng, bouncing and squealing, to get to him. I got a beer, and then parked myself near the stairs, trying not to notice that the girl was humping my non-boyfriend's leg while they danced. When Ryan caught my eye, looking a bit like a deer caught in the headlights, I pasted a fake smile on my face and lifted my beer to encourage him.

We'd been there awhile when someone bumped into me, spilling my beer onto my shirt.

"Sorry about that." I looked up and saw a guy with bleached-blond hair. He was wearing a wife-beater, jeans, and a smirk. "Can I get you a napkin?"

"Yeah, that would be—"

"Or maybe I could just lick it off you."

Ah. I wasn't really interested in him, but since I wouldn't be getting any from the guy I *was* interested in, I figured, what the hell. "It's soaked into my shirt. You'll probably have to suck it out."

He leaned in, putting his hands on my hips and whispering into my ear, "I'll suck whatever you want." Over his shoulder, I saw Ryan looking at me, his brows drawn together just a bit, and then his mouth flattened out into a tight line. Shit. The penny had dropped. I'd just have to have it out with him later. Bleach-boy headed up the stairs, looking back at me once. I waited about thirty seconds, then followed. I didn't have a ton of experience, and I wasn't sure how far he wanted to go, but I thought another guy might push Ryan out of my head for at least a few minutes.

He beckoned me into the bathroom and shut the door, then pushed me against it and started kissing me. It was okay. Just okay, which was weird, because kissing usually got me really hot. I didn't know if it was him, or the beer, or the look that had been on Ryan's face, but I wasn't turned on at all. He didn't seem to notice. After a few minutes, he pulled back and said, "God, I want to suck you so bad."

Whatever. "Go for it," I said.

He unzipped my pants and pulled my dick out, then got down on his knees and started sucking. Like the kissing, it was just okay. I leaned back against the door, shutting my eyes, and immediately fell into the library fantasy. I imagined that it was Ryan on his knees, sucking and licking my cock, and I got hard immediately. I grabbed onto hair that wasn't bleached, but golden-blond, and slid my dick in and out of Ryan's perfect mouth. I'd wanted this for weeks and it was finally happening, smooth and hot and perfect. He started sucking harder, and I was getting close to coming, and when he moaned and took me deeper, I shouted and shot down his throat. He moaned again around my dick, causing fantastic vibrations, and I kept thrusting as long as he kept sucking. Eventually my dick slipped out of his mouth, and I opened my eyes a little while later.

Bleach-boy was standing at the sink, cleaning himself up. He smiled at me in the mirror. "That was great."

"Yeah." I zipped up my pants and gave him the same fake smile I'd used on Ryan earlier that night.

"So who's Ryan? Your boyfriend?"

I couldn't keep from flinching a little. "What? No. He's...no one."

"No one, huh? You shouted his name when you came." He grinned, handed me a card, then kissed me. "Call me some-time," he said as he left the bathroom.

I went through the medicine cabinet and the cupboards un-til I found some mouthwash. I used it, took a piss, washed my hands, face, and neck, then went back downstairs.

I hadn't been gone for that long, but when I got back, Ryan was in bad shape. He was swaying and staggering, and the red-head was maneuvering him towards the door. As I got closer, I heard her saying, "I'm just around the corner, you can stay over." I was about to back off, when Ryan saw me. "Seven!"

"Hey, Ryan! Fun party, huh?" I knew I sounded like a jerk, but I felt guilty for having fantasized about him yet again. And I felt even guiltier for leaving him alone at our first party.

Ryan stumbled away from the girl and grabbed my shoulder for support. "You went upstairs with that guy."

"Yeah, he's in my History class," I lied.

Ryan stared at me, swaying a bit, then said, "I don't feel so good." Before I could say anything, his shoulders jerked, and a glob of vomit spilled out of his mouth and onto his shirt.

"Oh, shit. Come on." I pulled him towards the door, but it was too late. He heaved right onto the keg. People screamed and groaned in disgust. The guys manning the keg started swearing at him, and the redhead backed off fast, a look of revulsion on her face. Ryan wiped his mouth with his hand.

"Oh, no. I'm really sorry."

"MotherFUCKER! Get the FUCK out!" This came from a guy in a backwards baseball cap who started wiping off the keg with a rag.

I grabbed Ryan by the arm. "Come on, let's go," I said and pulled him out the door. He nearly fell down the steps, so I slung his arm over my shoulder for support. "Great. Now you're the guy who throws up at parties and I'm his friend. We'll never get invited anywhere, ever again."

"Are we going home?"

"Yeah."

It was a long walk home. Ryan was heavy, and I kept muttering about what a jerk he was the whole way back, trying to keep my anger built up. I was kind of hoping that drunken, vomit-drenched Ryan would be the image stuck in my head from now on so that I could stop obsessing over him. It might have worked, too, if he hadn't smiled at me in the shower and spoken those stupidly endearing words: "You're a good guy, Sev. I'm glad I got you as a roommate."

I sighed and pushed on his chest. "Yeah, fine, great. I should have left you lying in a pool of your own vomit."

"You didn't, though." He stepped back and pulled off his shirt. I took it from him, trying not to stare at his chest, and threw it in the corner of the shower. I went to get his washcloth, and when I came back, he was pulling off his jeans. They landed on top of the shirt. His boxers followed. I held out the washcloth without looking, but he didn't take it. "I got some on you," he said, reaching for the hem of my shirt.

"I can do it." My heart was pounding. I hesitated just for a moment, then pulled my shirt off and threw it on the pile of clothes. He turned on the water and rinsed his mouth out a few times, then he stood there under the spray, letting it hit him in the face. I couldn't look away. I knew it was wrong to stare, but he was too beautiful with the water running down his body and his arms lifting as he pushed his hair back. He ducked his head, and then opened his eyes, looking directly at me. Caught. I wet the washcloth and used it to wipe off my chest, then held it out to him.

He reached out, but his hand closed on my wrist instead of the washcloth, and he pulled me forward, into the water with him.

"Are you crazy?" I tried to step out, but he held on. With his other hand, he picked up the bar of soap and began to wash my chest. I froze. He moved the soap across his own chest and down his stomach. My eyes followed. He soaped his crotch, then pulled my hand down. "Touch me," he said, curling my fingers around his hardening dick.

An avalanche of thoughts crashed through my head. Screaming loudest were the Reasons To Not Do This. The Noble Reason: he's drunk, and it would be taking advantage. The Paranoid Reason: if the baseball game ended early, our apartment-mates would come home and find us. The Practical Reason: if we do something and he remembers in the morning, he'll kill me. He will fucking kill me.

And then there was the Reason *To* Do This, the one that was sounding better and better as he moved my hand up and down his soapy dick: I'll never get this chance again, and I should just do it and get him out of my system, and he'll probably be terrible anyway since he's both straight AND drunk, and if he does remember it tomorrow, I'll lie and tell him he must have dreamed it. I was putting together possible lies in my head when I felt his hand on my own dick. He'd managed to get my pants open while I was distracted with thoughts and reasons and lies, and his hand, slippery with soap, was moving up and down my already hard cock.

I leaned back against the cold tiles, feeling his hand working slowly and steadily, sliding down to rub my balls, then circling and coming back up, squeezing just the right amount. It was probably the best handjob I'd ever gotten. Why had I thought he'd suck at this? I started using the same movements on him, stroking and squeezing his dick, which was thick and heavy in my hand. I looked down in time to see his other hand come up and tug at my nipple ring. I gasped, and he rubbed his finger across my nipple, making me squirm, especially when I heard him mutter, almost to himself, "Been wanting to do that forever."

I began to move my hand faster, and when I looked up, his head was back, eyes shut, mouth open. Gorgeous. I leaned forward to suck on his neck, and he moaned. Then he tilted his head down and kissed me. His tongue pushed into my mouth and when it slid over my tongue stud, his dick pulsed in my hand, and he moaned into my mouth. His cum was warm on my chest and my hand, and he was panting when he pulled out of the kiss. Then he licked his lips and gave me a look I'd never seen on his face before, hot and predatory. His hand swirled over the head of my dick and I came, my spunk mixing with his on our chests and stomachs.

We stayed leaning against the wall for a while, but eventually he stepped away and helped me peel off my soaked pants.

We rinsed off, grabbed our towels, and got back to our room before our apartment mates got home. My last thought before falling asleep was that I hoped he'd forget what had just happened and that I'd remember it forever.

The next morning, I woke up when Ryan left the room, even though I could tell he was trying to be quiet. I nearly fell back asleep when I remembered that we'd left our clothes in the shower. I was wide awake in a heartbeat, working out my story. Yes, we went to the party, you got drunk and threw up on yourself and got some on me, we came back and took showers, *separately,* and left our clothes there so they wouldn't stink up the room. Okay, that sounded good. I lay on my side, facing the wall, waiting for him to come back. My heart was beating hard in my chest, but I hoped he wouldn't be able to tell.

He came back in a few minutes later, and I heard him sit on his bed. "Seven?" he asked quietly. "Are you awake?"

I made a show of sniffing and yawning, and turned over. "I am now." I tried not to react when I saw him, but he looked nervous. Scared, actually. Fuck. Fucking, fucking, fuck. "What's wrong?"

"I'm so sorry about last night."

Stay calm, stick to the story. "It's okay. Everyone drinks too much and gets sick sometime."

"That's not what I'm talking about. I mean, I'm sorry about that, too, but I'm talking about what happened in the shower after we got back."

Fuck! "The shower?"

"I know you remember. You weren't drunk."

"You fell into me and messed up my shirt, but it's okay, it'll wash out."

"Stop it!"

He looked so upset that I gave up. If it all fell apart, well, then we weren't meant to be friends. Or anything else. I sat up and cleared my throat. "Okay, I'm the one who's sorry. I shouldn't have done anything when you were so drunk, but—"

"I was practically raping you." I was speechless, so he went on, staring at the floor as he spoke. "In the back of my mind, I could tell you didn't want to do it, but I thought you might be gay, too, or at least bi, even though you've never said anything, but then you went off with that guy at the party and I was so pissed off that I got drunk. You're so hot, and I guess I used being drunk as an excuse. God." He squeezed his fists in his hair and scrunched up his face. "So I'm sorry. I wanted to tell you I was attracted to you, but if you weren't gay it would make it really uncomfortable to be roommates, and I couldn't let anyone find out, not until I've proved myself on the team because I can't afford to lose the scholarship, and even more than that, I don't want to lose our friendship because school would suck if we weren't friends anymore and—"

I shut up his babbling by shoving him onto his back and kissing him. He grabbed my ass as I settled between his legs and I could feel his dick twitch against mine when he licked my tongue stud. "That really does it for you, doesn't it?" I asked when we broke apart.

"You have no idea," he gasped. "And I had to go jerk off the first time I saw this," he said, flicking my nipple ring.

"Lots of guys have them," I said, grinding against him.

"They're not you," he replied, rolling us over so I was on my back.

I had to ask. "Do you really think I'm hot?"

"Yeah." He ran his hand across my chest. "I want to do everything with you." He suddenly looked nervous again. "But I haven't done any of this before. I couldn't, back in high school."

I stroked the hair that I'd been wanting to touch for weeks. "It's okay. I haven't done that much, either."

He smiled. "So we can learn together?"

"Absolutely."

His smile shifted into the predatory look I'd seen the night before, and he surprised me yet again by licking a stripe down my stomach and taking my dick in his mouth. I gasped and slid my fingers into his hair, feeling kind of bad for having misjudged him when we first met but happy as hell that I'd been so wrong. It looked like we were both going to be learning a lot more than we'd thought.

Bibliophile

Curtis C. Comer

My first year away from home and away from my church-going family was, I suppose like for most queer kids, a time of not only personal growth but also sexual experimentation. I was like the proverbial kid in the candy store, no longer under the watchful eye of my devoutly Christian parents, and I intended to make the most of this newfound freedom. Though my parents could only afford to send me to a small community college an hour away from our small town, the new faces I encountered that year were like a magical elixir for me. Never an outstanding student, I couldn't wait for the day to come that I would graduate from high school, though what I was to do after graduation was a mystery to me. My parents, pinning all of their hopes on my basic intelligence, if not my academic ability, suggested college. While the idea of four more years of school (not to mention the fact that I had no idea what I wanted to study) didn't appeal to me, the idea of personal freedom did. A loan was obtained from the bank, a Pell Grant was awarded based on economic hardship, and it was arranged for me to live in one of the dorms on campus. The dorms, lined up in a row at one end of the campus, resembled the sort of buildings that one might see in a Soviet bloc country, devoid of any ornamentation whatsoever, with gray facades and no balconies. This utilitarian ugliness didn't faze me though; to me these buildings were going to be my chance to grow, to find myself. Mom made a big show of saying goodbye, despite the fact that she would see me again the following weekend. I retrieved the last box from the backseat of my red '65 Mustang and placed it on the hood so that I could hug her one more time.

"You be sure and call if you need anything," she said, her eyes welling up again.

I promised her that I would, and my dad shoved a twenty-dollar bill in my hand, assuring me that I was going to "do al-right." As I watched them drive away in the family car I nearly sprinted to the dorm with my box, eager to do some exploring. Aside from some feeble attempts at making out with two or three girls in high school, I was an eighteen-year-old virgin who had known for quite some time that it wasn't girls that I was in-terested in. Reaching my room on the fifth floor, I was sur-prised by a lanky kid with bushy blond hair and blue eyes un-packing a box. He smiled as I walked in, offering his hand.

"You must be my new roommate," he said, his voice betray-ing a definite New Jersey accent. "My name's Charlie."

He explained that this was his second year at the college, though he was hoping to transfer to another school so that he could be closer to home. He suggested that I take the bed clos-est to the windows and he would take the one closer to the door, assuring me that I would have better light. I agreed but, as soon as winter arrived, realized that the gesture was less than altruistic. Winter, however, was the furthest thing from my mind that day; all I wanted to do was explore. Declining an of-fer from Charlie to head downtown to, as he put it, "scope for chicks," I stepped outside into a brilliant early fall afternoon. The grounds were teeming with other students, all scurrying around in the last bit of free time before the commencement of the semester. There were guys everywhere; jocks, frat dudes, nerds, Goths, rockers, rednecks, academics, and even foreign guys—a novelty for a small-town guy like me. I fantasized about them all, and marveled at the endless possibilities. I must have walked around the small campus for hours just for the opportunity to meet as many guys as I could. Finally, with the sunlight waning, I made my way back to the dorms. Find-ing my room empty, I jacked off on my bed, fantasizing about all of the hot guys I'd encountered on my walk around campus. By the time Charlie came in I was already in bed, my belong-ings unpacked and stowed away. I watched him as he undressed in the darkness, and noticed the large bulge in the front of his boxer briefs. Not wanting to get caught staring, I rolled over to face the windows.

"You awake?" he whispered in his sexy New Jersey accent.

I waited a moment before responding, deciding to act as though I had been asleep. I mumbled something about the time.

"Sorry it's late," he said. "I met this really hot babe named Amanda."

"Cool," I said, relieved that I hadn't made an ass of myself.

"Hey, dude," he whispered, sliding between his sheets. "You got a girl?"

"Yeah," I lied. "Back home."

Though the room was dark, save for the small bit of light coming from the window, I was afraid Charlie would see me blushing and know that I was lying.

"What's her name?" he persisted, sounding truly interested.

"Susan," I blurted, instantly mortified that of all the names I could pull out of my head, I had to choose my sister's name.

"Is she hot?" he asked, propping himself up on one arm.

I rolled over to face him, and noticed the moonlight playing on his pale features.

"Yeah," I said, wanting to end the conversation. "I don't really feel like talking about her, though."

He shrugged and reached down beneath the sheets, pulling off his briefs in one fluid motion, and tossing them at the foot of his bed.

"Goodnight," he said, yawning and turning over to face the wall.

"Goodnight," I replied, titillated at the thought of Charlie naked. I reached down and tugged off my own underwear, throwing them on the floor. The cool sheets felt good against my nakedness, and I went to sleep with a hard-on hoping that Charlie would climb in my bed.

I awoke the next morning, frustrated that Charlie hadn't visited me in my sleep, and still rock hard. I made my way down the hall to the communal shower/restroom, trying to conceal the pup tent in the front of my shorts. I walked into a stall and closed the door, eager to release my pent-up frustration. As I sat there jacking off, I discovered that, because of the layout of the room, I could see naked guys entering and leaving the shower stalls on the opposite side of the room by peering through a crack in the door. I sat there watching and stroking my meat for so long, coming at least four times, that I nearly forgot the time and was late for my first class. Vacating my hiding place, I hurriedly showered and dressed, running to my first class, French I, which was taught by a short, redheaded man, wearing ridiculously outdated horn-rimmed glasses. I did my best to make it through my classes that day, but the images of all of the naked guys I'd seen in the shower room that morning kept clouding my mind. When I finally made it back to the dorms at the end of the day I found Charlie on his bed, reading in his underwear.

"Hey," I said as I walked past his bed and dropped my book bag beside my desk opposite my bed.

"Hey," he echoed, snapping his book shut and jumping up. "I have to ask you a favor."

"Sure," I replied. "Anything."

"I want to bring Amanda back here tonight," he said, explaining that she wasn't allowed to have guys over to her sorority house. "Can you stay out until eleven or so?"

"Sure," I said, feeling slightly put out that, on my second day of freedom, I was being barred from my dorm room.

I had the notion to point out to Charlie that, technically, we weren't allowed to have girls here, either, but didn't want to come across as an asshole. After grabbing what passed for dinner at the campus cafeteria, I headed for the student union building in the middle of campus. I walked into the large main room, dark except for the light cast by giant-screen television blaring music videos. The place was nearly deserted, with a smattering of coed students seated randomly on the black leather sofas placed in a large concentric ring around the television. I chose an empty sofa, and was lost in thought, wondering if Charlie was in our room fucking Amanda, and what his stiff cock might look like when a Goth chick plopped down beside me.

Coming from a small town, I had only seen Goth kids on television but, given her black nails, hair, lipstick, clothing and a pierced nose, I was sure that my assumption was correct.

"Hi," she said, revealing a pierced tongue, visible even in the semi-darkness. "What's your name?"

"David," I replied, glad to have someone to talk to, but frustrated that she wasn't a Goth *dude*.

"My name's Donna," she said. "Isn't that a riot? I'm thinking of changing my name."

I laughed nervously, not sure if she was serious.

"Is this your first year here?" she asked, pulling a silver flask from an enormous red bag that I imagined might contain enough illegal contraband to get us both expelled. She glanced around the room then took a swig, offering me a drink as she coughed.

"No, thanks," I whispered, amused at her brazenness.

"You didn't answer me," she said, screwing the top back on the flask and depositing it in the bag. "First year?"

"Yeah," I replied, shifting in my seat uneasily.

"Well, don't worry about picking a bullshit major, no matter what they tell you," she said, fishing around in her bag again. "You'll only end up changing it five more times by the time you graduate."

She offered me a breath mint, which I accepted, not wanting to seem uptight.

"You have a girlfriend?" she asked, placing a hand on my thigh.

"No," I admitted, clearing my throat nervously.

"Are you gay?" she asked.

The nonchalance with which she asked the question took

me by surprise and I stared at the television screen, unable to speak.

"It's cool," she said, not missing a beat. "I think that you'll find college can be very liberating in that way."

I had the urge to ask her just how the hell she knew so much about the subject, but realized that I was really only feeling humiliated. Besides, there was something about Donna that actually calmed me. Finally able to speak, I turned to face her.

"How do I..." I faltered.

"Meet guys?" she asked, her voice low.

I nodded, my face hot.

"Well," she whispered, her tone conspiratorial, "I hear there's a lot of action in the library on the fourth floor."

"Why the fourth floor?" I asked, wondering if she was fucking with me.

"I don't know," she replied, sounding offended. "I've heard things, that's all."

We were both silent for a moment, the television the only sound in the room.

"I know a couple of straight dudes who got blow jobs there," she whispered.

I turned to face her, and she was smiling.

"It's either that," she continued, "or you can hang out in the art department."

I raised my eyebrows at this suggestion and Donna laughed.

"I'm serious," she said, rising from the sofa, the bag slung over her shoulder. "We're all freaks in the art department."

"I like your name," I called as she walked away, and she gave me a coquettish smile as she disappeared through the door.

I squinted at my watch, trying to make out the time in the darkness, and realized that the library was still open for another two hours. Hoping that Donna hadn't been fucking with me, I decided to follow her tip and see if there was any action on the fourth floor. I made my way out of the student union and across campus toward the library, a newer brick structure whose windows illuminated the dark night. I climbed the front steps, my heart pounding. As I hesitated at the door, a tall blond guy in khaki shorts passed me and walked through the revolving doors. He had the nicest legs I had ever seen, tan, hairy, and very muscular. Seeing him and those legs must have given me the courage to finally enter but, by the time I was in the building, he had disappeared behind the elevator doors.

"Hi," said a bookish looking girl behind the main counter. "Can I help you find anything?"

"No," I stammered. "I'm just looking around."

I walked over to a map of the library posted on a nearby wall and pretended to study it. Just then, as if by provenance, the elevator doors opened and I jumped in, breathlessly pressing the number four, which turned red.

As the car slowly ascended I got an erection, wondering what I would find when the doors opened. The only problem was knowing what to do once I got there, and I hoped that nature would take its course. When the door opened, however, there were only a few people seated here and there, and they actually seemed to be studying. Disappointed, I was about to turn back to the elevator when I was surprised to see the blond with the great legs sitting at a table at the end of one of the aisles. Deciding to try my luck, I swallowed hard and made my way down the aisle, wondering if I was totally out of my mind. He glanced in my direction to see who was there, causing me to stop in my tracks and grab the first book I laid my eyes on. This happened to be a thick, dusty tome on molecular biology, which I carried down the aisle, acting as if this was just the book I had been searching for.

I took a seat at the table opposite his, and positioned myself so that I was facing him. I opened my book, cursing myself for not having at least picked something with photos, but trying my best to look interested. I glanced at the blond dude's table, admiring the way his t-shirt hugged his pecs and arms. I was snapped out of my daydream when I realized that Mr.

Great Legs was staring back at me, and I quickly averted my eyes back to the dusty passages on the table in front of me. Trying to keep my head low, I glanced back at the neighboring table and felt my heart skip when he smiled at me. Totally humiliated at having been busted, I was again ready to run for the elevator when the tall blond cleared his throat. I looked up and saw that he had placed his right leg up on a chair beside his table, allowing his cock to hang out the bottom of his khakis. I looked up from the floppy piece of meat on the chair and our eyes met, but this time the look on his face was serious. Glancing back at the chair, I saw that his cock was stiffening, a very prominent vein running from the head and up the shaft. I felt my own cock stiffen, and I reached down to adjust myself, feeling like the seams on my shorts would burst if I didn't. The blond suddenly moved his leg from the chair and I felt my heart sink, but only momentarily, because he reached under his table and unzipped his fly. From my vantage point I was unable to see under the table but, based on the motions of his right arm, it was clear that he was jacking off. Our eyes met again and he motioned me to his table with a slight jerk of his head. My stomach on fire, I started to sit in the chair across the table from him that he had pushed back with his foot, but he shook his head, motioning for me to get under the table without saying a word. Glancing around at the nearly deserted room, I obeyed his wishes, climbing on my hands and knees toward the meaty boner that was pointing straight at me. Greedily, I took his stiff cock into my mouth and sucked with such vigor that I gagged each time I swallowed it. Savoring the taste of the swollen dick and the smell of his sweaty pubes, I pulled out my own stiff cock and began to slowly stroke it. I could hear him breathing heavily as I sucked his dick, and all sorts of thoughts passed through my head, mostly along the lines of getting caught and expelled on my first real day of college. I didn't care, though; being right there, between those beautiful legs and sucking that stiff cock was all that I cared about at that moment. Then, all too soon, I felt his muscular legs tense around me, his breath quicken and my mouth was filled with his creamy load. The taste caused me to shoot my own wad onto the carpet beneath me, my body convulsing with the effort. Before I could even climb from under the table, he was already stuffing his still-swollen dick back into the fly of his shorts. Ignoring the mess I'd left on the floor, I emerged from my hiding place, wanting to say something—anything —to assure that I could see him again. As I stood there, tongue-tied, I watched as he deposited his books in an orange backpack.

"I'm usually here on Thursday nights," he said, the first time he had spoken all night. He smiled, then turned and walked down the back stairs without saying another word.

I nearly floated back to the dorm, ecstatic at the realization that I'd had my first sexual encounter with a guy. Maybe I'd see the blond again, maybe not. It really didn't matter.

Besides, there was still the art department to check out.

Cultural Studies

Joel A. Nichols

In my senior year of college I was failing my Deconstructing Asian-American Identities class and went to see the instructor, a youthful graduate student who wore shiny brown shoes and chunky black glasses. His office was in Fisk Hall, which was famous for the basement cruising bathrooms I didn't have any time for that day. Those damn bathrooms had caused enough distraction: I often popped in for something quick in the middle of class and would miss twenty or thirty minutes of the lecture. I wanted to convince my professor to up my grade, so I wouldn't be cut from the team in my last semester.

The first thing he said was, "I'm not sure why you're in this class, Paul. You spend all your free time...wrestling, which you admit." He had a low, sonorous voice and as he spoke, he fidgeted with his short spiky hair and kept adjusting his glasses. He always wore a blue blazer and jeans in class, but that day in his office, he sat behind his desk in a white T-shirt. The sleeves hugged his dark brown biceps, and as he laced his fingers on the back of his neck and leaned back in his chair, I could see that his chest was worked out but that he had a belly: all push up and no crunch. "Paul, are you listening?" he said. "Why are you in this class?"

"I sort of like the readings, and—" I started to say.

"I know you haven't done the readings," he said, cutting me off and gesturing to the blue book in which I'd written the midterm. There was a D- circled in red on the cover. "On the midterm, you couldn't tell your Fae Ng from your Amy Tan, and don't try and sell me some bullshit."

"I have, some, sir. And I've caught up since then. But wrestling does take up a lot of my time, and I was wondering if there was something I could do, maybe redo the exam?"

"I can't let you do that."

"What about a paper? I could write it on the article of yours we read..." I trailed off, and he sat forward, and crossed his legs. I watched the bulge in his jeans, which I always found myself staring at in class.

"'Good Boy/Bad Boy, the Myth of Filipino Son?'"

"No, the other one: 'GayAsian Liberations.'" He shook his head no, but I could tell that he was impressed that I'd read it, since it was only on the recommended list and I had had to hunt it down in the library.

"Why should you have extra credit when you can't do the regular work?"

"I don't have a good reason, except that I promise I'll stay on track for the rest of the semester. I'll, I'll really do anything for this chance. I'm interested in your ideas about sexual liberation and its connections to the family." I was looking at the floor mostly, and glanced up a few times to see that he was listening. I'd skimmed through the first several paragraphs that morning. "I took your class because my mom pressured me to take Asian American studies, you know. She feels bad about divorcing my dad and raising me in Maine. But I love wrestling. I'm thinner than a lot of guys—I've got to put in extra time at the gym." I sat back in my chair. I was wearing a snug gray T-shirt with "College" in black letters. When I leaned back, my shirt rode up and showed an inch or two of my taut stomach. I have black fuzz running up to my belly button that stands out from my pale skin. I really had hoped that he'd let me write an extra credit paper, but I knew that sex might be my last resort.

"I don't know, Paul," he said, looking me up and down. I adjusted my cock and balls inside my baggy khakis and folded my arms across my chest. I smiled at him, and he said, "I think you're tall enough. Big enough..." he trailed off for a second, and then said, "I am working on a new project, and I could use someone to organize my research materials." He pointed across the dusty office, and I followed his finger with my head. There, tucked underneath a tall window where a spider plant hung, trailing paper-dry babies, was a work table piled with card-board boxes, file folders, and long yellow legal pads scrawled tight with blue handwriting. "It's kind of a mess."

"But I really appreciate this chance, professor. What do I do?" He stood up, pushing back his desk chair and hitched up his jeans by grasping his thick belt on either side of his zipper. I tried to look away. He said: "There are articles, my notes on articles, emails, and primary source documents. Everything's jumbled up. I'd like you to alphabetize everything and pack it into one of those filing cabinets. But separate out my notes and emails from the sources—those you can stack on my desk. Here's the hard part: I'll need you to make an index—just a list, really, that I can check and know which file drawer something is in."

I nodded. "When should I start? I could come in on Friday, maybe, before practice." He turned on his heel, and crossed his arms over his chest. The white sleeves inched up the swell of his bicep, and I noticed the curving green line of a tattoo hiding further up on his shoulder.

"No way, Paul. You've got to start right now. If you're serious about your grade, it's not something you can put off for later in the week... How many times have you promised that you'd do something before practice, like turn in a paper?"

I was still sitting in the chair on the other side of his desk, and I was craning my neck up. "OK, OK." I looked at my watch. I had told a buddy that I'd meet him at the campus center, but realized that I'd have to stand him up. "I'll start now. Absolutely."

He went back to his desk gathered up a stack of Interlibrary Loan Books, with their telltale blue wrappers. "I've got to run over to the library. If you have any questions, I'll be back in about twenty minutes." He struggled into a narrow blazer that was hanging on the back of his door, putting it on with the books hooked under one arm. I watched him leave, appreciating the round muscles in his dark jeans.

Over at the table, I started sorting through the photocopies, making a new pile of file folders. Some of the names I recognized from class; all the articles had overlong titles and all of them were about Asian or Asian-American identity. I skimmed through one called "Nisei in a Halfshell: Teenage Mutant Ninja Turtles and Japanese American Representations," because it had cartoon pictures I remembered from young Saturdays, and then started in on the boxes.

I went for one that had ten or twelve legal pad sheets floating on top, and unpacked them into a pile. There were meticulous notations at the top of each page with the date and the source. My stomach leaped when, underneath another stack of articles, I found a handful of glossy magazines.

The first one I pulled out had a skinny slip of a guy standing next to a pool in board shorts, with his brown arms in the air, as if he was waiting for someone to throw him a beach ball. I thumbed through and watched more mostly soft-core pictures slip past: almost all twinky Chinese guys shaved and waxed to look even twinkier. It wasn't a look that did anything for me. I wondered if he had remembered there was porn packed inside the cardboard box.

Underneath that one was a magazine called *Thai Me Up,* with the same kinds of twinks strapped up in leather or bent over a bench with their asses in front of a big white hand or paddle. One of the articles I'd skimmed for his class had mentioned this kind of fetish inside a fetish, and I wished I had paid more attention. I slid it into the magazine pile, and saw that the rest of the glossy stack was all issues of the same magazine, its title logo a California license plate: *AZN JCK.* The cover model was probably Korean, or a Korean mix, and he was ripped. He stood looking down at the camera, a tower of taut muscles that disappeared underneath a pair of white mesh shorts. He had a buzz cut and was wearing a thick sweatband on his left wrist with black basketball sneakers. I started flipping through, and found a gym scene: guys doing crunches and free weight reps with bulky but smooth spotters, then a progression of stills through to what looked like a really wet jockstrap blowjob. Next came four guys in a locker room, a shower and steam room circle jerk with four big uncut cocks. Here's where I started to get in trouble, and started to feel some of what I was seeing in my sweatpants. Those thick uncut cocks on boys that looked like me and who were lined up around the tiled drain…I reached down and pulled up my junk so it had room to grow, and flipped onto the next photo session. There it got worse: two stocky wrestlers in shiny, bulging singlets and fake-looking headgear faced off. A white guy stood off to the side, with a whistle hanging around his neck. I started reading the story in the captions and watching the two of them pose and grapple. As the picture series unfolded, they tore off their singlets and rubbed cock-to-cock. Eventually the white coach came over to the mats and started sucking one and jerking the other. And I couldn't help myself, I flopped my dick out the top of my boxers and started to pull myself off. This was his research! I thought about going down to the bathrooms to see if anybody was there, then decided I needed to take care of it right there, in the professor's office.

I went on to the next series and my balls got heavy. Then I heard the click of the door. My professor walked back into the office.

"Paul!" he said too loudly then, in a lower voice, "what are you doing?"

I stood there with my dick in my fist, and just looked at him. I felt about ready to come and didn't know what to do.

He crossed over to his desk and as he sat in his swivel chair, I saw that the front of his jeans was tenting. He looked over at me, then said, "Don't just stand there."

He planted his feet far apart from each other, and undid his belt. I straddled his legs, bringing myself slowly down onto him. His cock twitched, and I nestled it just under my balls and I slid my arms around the back of his neck and kissed him. He took my tongue and grabbed a hold of my hips, squeezing them with his strong fingers. I wiggled up and down on top of him, while he groped my cock. I went even more rigid in his hand, and, squeezing gently, slipped my balls through the boxers, too. It wasn't as tight as a cockring, but the pressure from my erection my made balls feel heavy. I ground against him more, and then slid off of him and pulled his jeans open, halfway down his thigh. His cock was bound up in tight black briefs, and I saw it was thick and had a slight bend.

He'd made a ring around the tip of my cock with his fist, and he bent down to keep a hold of me as I knelt in between his legs. I pumped my hips, jamming my cock into the palm of his hand and pulled the elastic band of his underwear away from his smooth brown waist. His cock rose up off his thigh, and I took it in my hands, rubbing the cockhead gently with one hand and reaching down into his black bush with the other. I cradled his balls as I licked the tip of his dick, and once it was wet, pulled it into my mouth. He moaned, and I started to squeeze his balls in rhythm to my tongue sliding around his cock ridge, and down and up his thick shaft. I pressed my knuckles up against his asscrack, and he moaned again.

Suddenly, he pushed me away and got up. He crossed the room, hobbling clumsily with his pants around his knees. He twisted the lock on his office door, and then turned around towards me again. His cock swayed in front of him, sticking almost straight out at me. I went to him, again, and he fell to his knees. I started fucking his mouth with long, even strokes. He looked up at me with his lips around my dick and I pulled out and jerked myself off slowly to hold off from coming. He closed his eyes with a sigh of pleasure.

I bent down and kissed him again, and he pulled me to the floor. I went for his cock again, groping underneath his balls to put my fingertips just inside his asscrack. He kept sucking me, taking me in all the way down to my balls. I thrust into his throat and took him in my mouth again. My mouth stretched around him, and I felt his ass relax and start to open to my fingers. I pressed my forefinger flat against his hole and he pressed back. He twisted again, rolling on top of me and letting my cock slide down the back of his throat. He reached down and fed his cock into my mouth backwards. I nibbled at it again, and then started to lick his balls. I took one into my mouth, then the other, then licked and nuzzled the base of his ball sac, then went onto the patch of smooth, sweaty skin that led to his ass.

I was getting close again, and reached down and took my cock out of his mouth. He licked my balls, and I pushed my forefinger into his hole. With my right hand, I slapped my heavy cock against the side of his face, trying to hold myself off, and sucked on one of his balls again. He bore down, thrusting his cock against my hard chest and started to moan again. My balls felt tight. Holding onto my cock at the base, I knocked it against his cheek a couple of more times, then aimed it towards his mouth again. I brought my hand back up as he swallowed me again, making my cock hot and wet. I had one finger in his ass, and I slid my other hand in between his dick and my chest, and let him slide in and out of my palm, which was slick from my precum and his spit. I felt his dick ooze and he started to pump harder. The palm of my hand and my chest were slick with his precum and sweat, and I felt his ass pulsating around my finger. I couldn't take it anymore, and I started to shoot with a grunt. He tasted it right away, and sprayed his load into my hand. He took me all the way in again, down to my balls, and as he swallowed another jolt of my cum, I felt certain I would pass his class.

Love in the Tunnels
David Mastromonica

The residential colleges at Yale sit atop a vast warren—a labyrinth, really—of steam tunnels. Laundry rooms with washers and dryers are housed down there, as well as storage rooms for student's boxes and workmen's supplies. Some of the tunnels are wide and almost spacious. Others of them are narrow, constrictive passageways just barely wide enough to allow a person to walk through them without turning sideways. But all of them are laced with steam pipes that lead either to or from the university's primary heat-producing facility and the colleges and other university buildings themselves.

A person could get lost in those tunnels for days if they weren't careful. Most students learn the way down to the laundry room fairly quickly during their freshman year and most never deviate from the path they learn. Carrying laundry baskets, stacked so high with clothes and detergent that you often can't see over the load in your arms, tempts you to leave a trail of quarters—like breadcrumbs—trickling out of the back pocket of your pair of jeans so that you can still find your way out again. Some hardy, intrepid souls go exploring after midnight on a Friday or Saturday night when beer or dope has reduced inhibitions and stupidity can be mistaken for courage. Most of these explorers make it back up to the surface by morning but, when asked, "Where exactly did you go down there?" no one can ever quite retrace their steps or remember where exactly they were.

I was a freshman, still new to the whole rhythm of college life even though it was almost Thanksgiving. Because it was my first semester, every couple of weeks was a whole new experience: orientation, choosing classes, midterms, Halloween, the post-midterm lull, and now the build-up to the holidays. So far,

Yale was everything—and more!—that I, a quiet nerd from the Pacific Northwest, had ever dreamed college life could be.

There was still one dream unfulfilled, however. Growing up in a semi-rural area of western Washington State in a broken family with limited resources, I had put my whole emotional and sexual life on "hold" during high school. I knew, in my heart of hearts, that I wanted to be with guys and to give and be given in exchange. But there was no easy way to get into the "big" cities where I might find men—grown versions of myself—who might be willing to tutor me in the ways of man-to-man sex. And I knew how my family would react if they found out. Not a scene I relished. And the taunting of my classmates—already jealous of my academic proclivities—would have been merciless. It was a big enough risk that I would occasionally peek at the handful of *Playgirl* magazines my sister had stashed under her bed. So I had held on, by my fingertips it seemed at times, until I got away to college and away from all the prying eyes and disapproving voices of my childhood.

I was sure there were more guys like me here at school—nervous, excited, and anxious to learn both in the bedroom as well as the classroom. But I had no idea of how to find these other guys like me.

I did know, though, that I could drool and dream in the meantime. There was a guy two floors below my dorm room that I would see on the stairs or around campus. Whether he ever noticed me, I had no idea. But he was swarthy and muscular, curly dark hair framing his clean-shaven face. I had heard that he was on the football team and came from Detroit or Chicago or somewhere in the Midwest like that. Rumor had it that there was a high school sweetheart waiting for Bruce (I was able to discover his name as well) back home, but it was impossible to know the veracity of that story. He was built, he was handsome, he was self-confident, he was popular. In short, he was a jock—everything that I wasn't! Everything I would probably never be.

Now it was the Friday before Thanksgiving and I was rushing to do my laundry tonight before going to New Jersey with a roommate to his family's holiday dinner. There was too much schoolwork to do in the next few days and so tonight—the libraries closed and everyone else out partying—was my chance to squeeze in a trip through the steam tunnels down below to the laundry room.

I took my overflowing basket of dirty clothes that included more cum-stained briefs than any one guy should be allowed to accumulate ("Damn! Why do I always wait so long between washes?!") down the dorm stairs and through the seemingly ancient wooden door onto the narrow spiral staircase that led down into the bowels of the labyrinth below. I was juggling the detergent atop the lopsided pile of clothes and trying to maintain my balance on the stairs beneath my feet which I couldn't see because of the mound of laundry in my arms. I reached the bottom of the stairs and turned right. Down this corridor, turn left, then right. I should be there in less than a moment or two. But, as I had done laundry so infrequently that the piles built up to abnormal proportions in my arms, I was also cockier of knowing my way through the tunnels than I should have been. I made my way down the corridor, turned left and then right. No laundry room. I peered around the laundry and detergent blocking my view. I was in a wider area of the tunnel that could have housed the half-dozen or so washing machines and dryers that I was looking for, but did not. I frowned a moment, and thought.

"I must have miscounted the turns," I decided. I backed up and turned down the passageway before this one. Was that the one I had just emerged from or had I missed it in my haste to get it on with my load of laundry? I plunged ahead.

The passageway became suffocatingly narrow almost immediately. "I don't remember this at all," I muttered myself, looking back over my shoulder to see if there was any clue that I had missed as to which way to go. Nope. No clue.

I inched forward, scraping my arms against the stone walls on either side of me. Steam hissed from the pipes above. Beads of sweat that had been hovering on my forehead began to drip into my eyes.

I began to get nervous. If I couldn't find the laundry, how could I get back to my starting point to try again? Or even just find my way out and then make the time tomorrow to come back and try again? I began to smell my own ripeness as my nerves and the steam heat began to take their tolls.

I edged around another corner. At least the passage widened, but still no laundry room. A burst of steam hissed loudly above me. I took a deep breath and tried to think. I had never had much of a sense of direction and had often gotten lost on the back roads back home. I closed my eyes a moment to shut out the distractions of the florescent lights, the thundering "hisssss" of the pipes, the pounding of my nerves....

"Hey." A voice caught me off guard. Someone was standing right in front of me. Someone with a deep, golden voice. Someone who sounded incredible. Someone I probably did not want knowing that I had gotten myself lost looking for the washing machines. I opened my eyes.

It was Bruce. He was standing right in front of me, close enough that his pecs could brush against the laundry that was overflowing my arms. How he'd gotten so close without my hearing him, I didn't know. I guess between the hiss of the steam and my efforts to block out distractions, he had walked right up to me and could have gone right past me and I would never have known. Like the proverbial ships in the night. His white T-shirt was drenched and couldn't have clung to his torso tighter even if he had entered one of the famous spring break "wet T-shirt contests." His sculpted pecs and perky nipples strained against the wet, white cloth. Although his muscular arms were fairly smooth, there were dark ringlets of dripping wet hair poking up from around his collar; these I had never noticed before. His gym shorts also seemed a bit tight, hugging his powerful ass muscles and a semi-erect pecker that was clearly outlined within the shorts as it strained to reach up and out, almost like a flower in time-lapse photography reaching for the sunlight. His dark, hairy legs reached down into his running shoes. He held a white towel in one hand, letting it hang down against his leg. His other hand ran through his hair. He smiled.

"H-hi," I stammered out. What a fool I must seem, I thought.

"You're Dave, right?" Bruce asked. "I think you live two floors above me." He reached out his free hand as if to shake mine. I adjusted the weight of the dirty clothes as best I could and reached out thee fingers to shake his. He chuckled amiably and then seemed embarrassed himself.

"Hey, I'm sorry. Let me help you with that." He reached out with both hands and took the laundry from my arms, setting it gently on the floor beside him. He looked back up into my face. "Looking for the washing machines?"

It was my turn to look embarrassed now. "Ah, yeah," I muttered. "I guess I should wash my clothes more often. Then I wouldn't have so many to carry. And I would remember how to get to the damn machines." I wanted the floor to open so I could crawl away before he said anything about how stupid it was to get lost looking for the washing machines.

"You're not far off." He pointed to his left. "They're actually just right down that way. I was just using the weight machines down that way." He pointed to his right. "It's not really an exercise room but there are some free weights and other machines there to use. It saves me a trip to the gym sometimes." He paused. "But sometimes I come down here anyway, just to have some time to myself. Y'know? No one bothers me down here."

I nodded. "He's being so friendly," I thought. I had never expected that he would be so easy to talk with. "I understand," I said out loud. "I like to get away from everything sometimes too."

He swung the towel up and tussled his hair with it and then draped the towel around his shoulders. The rich, natural scent of his body wafted into my lungs as he raised those thick arms of his. I licked my lips, trying not to seem too warm as we stood there under the hissing pipes, and not overcome with lust. The deep, dark forests of hair under those arms looked deep enough to dive into. But he seemed about to say something, but unsure of how to get it out.

"Sometimes down here, it seems like the only peaceful spot I have," he said. "No one to remind me of what I should be doing, or who I should be doing it with. Or what I should be preparing to do with my life." He looked up directly into my eyes, hoping for some kind of recognition.

I nodded. This chance to actually talk with Bruce was a wet dream come true! I would've said anything just to make the conversation last a moment longer now that I had gotten past feeling silly about getting lost. But, in this instance, what I said was perfectly true. "I know," I agreed. "Everyone back home keeps talking about what I should major in, what I should do with my life, how much money I can make if I study the right thing and make the right connections here." I looked around "I can see how this would be a good place to get away from all that." I smiled back at him, the butterflies in my stomach slowly fluttering away. I was finding it surprisingly easy to talk to him as well.

"Yeah?" he looked appreciatively at me, as if he had thought that he was the only one to face pressures like these. "I thought I would be able to start fresh here, be myself, not live up to other people's expectations here. But some things just won't seem to go away."

"Yeah, I know how that feels!" I laughed, and he—after a moment—laughed with me. "The one thing I most wanted to start fresh with, to start over with, seems just as unlikely here as it did back home." I looked into his dark eyes and wondered if he understood what I was hinting at.

He reached out and held my shoulder with one meaty paw. "I'm so glad to hear you say that," he said quietly. He leaned over into my face and kissed me.

Fireworks went off inside my head. Could this really be happening? The football jock, handsome and popular, muscular-hairy-sweaty was kissing me? I leaned forward and put my hand against the wall to steady myself. His tongue searched all the hidden corners of my mouth as it wrestled with my tongue; finally mine escaped to search his mouth as he was searching mine. After what seemed an eternity, I realized I had forgotten how to breathe and had to pull back to refill my lungs. I gasped.

I must have been looking at him as if he was crazy. He blushed. "I'm...I'm sorry," he said, pulling back. "Everyone back home would be so mortified if they knew what I had really wanted to do in the locker room all through high school. And here...here, I didn't know how to begin. I've seen you, though, and heard you came from out west—where all the loggers are. And I've heard stories about those logging men." He flashed a cautious smile at me. "I was hoping you might be feeling the same way." His gaze was curious. Hopeful. Knowing that he could crush and rape me if he wanted.

"I've been dreaming of doing this with a man, any man, for as long as I can remember," I said quietly, looking down at my feet. "But I've been dreaming of you in particular these last few weeks." I looked up into his face again.

"Mmmm, me too," he mumbled, leaning back into my face to resume our kissing. His hands caressed my body under my shirt and my hands found his as well. The pipes above hissed as our shirts each came up and over our heads. My pants and his shorts fell to the floor a moment later.

His chest and nipples were exquisitely sculpted islands, with the mountains of his dark nipples rising from the forest that surrounded them. All my life I had imagined sucking on nipples like these and now I could. I reached down and took a pec in my mouth, slurping and chugging on it. My tongue traced the outline of his pec up to his underarm and I buried my mouth there for a moment as well. He stretched his head down and around so that he could slurp on my chest as well, which was fairly flat and smooth with bright pink nipples. The opposite of his. But he didn't seem to mind. He was as delighted to explore my body as I was to explore his. After all those years of "Look, but don't touch" in the high school locker room, some part of my brain realized that this was as great a relief for him as it was for me.

I reached down and felt the great, strong spheres of his asscheeks which were a slightly paler hue than his torso. Smooth. Solid. He flexed them under my hands and reached around to hold mine with one as he kept his other up for me to continue licking his armpit as he continued to suck my nipple. He pulled our groins together so that both our cocks, by now as hard and straight as the big trees the loggers felled back home, were covered with darkness. There was no space for any of the bright, florescent light to come between us there.

I gasped for breath again and buried my face against the base of his neck, licking the wonderfully salty sweat that was pooling along his breast bone there. His tongue found the base of my neck as well and he began to gently lick his way up my sweaty throat.

"You know what I've been wanting more than anything else?" he asked me quietly, his teeth nibbling the edge of my ear. "I've been wanting to know what it feels like to have a big, stiff cock up my ass."

I could have fainted then and there if he hadn't been holding me. I guess I had just been making assumptions based on stereotypes—that a big strong jock like him would want to be the one who did the fucking. But here he was, saying that he wanted to be fucked. In the ass. He pulled his face back just far enough to look at my face. "Will you fuck my ass?"

I swallowed. Hard. I nodded. He grinned. "I've never done this. I'm not exactly sure how it works," I stammered, as he bent over in front of me. His ass was so round, so strong, so perfect. It hovered at just the height of my cock, which bobbed and swayed like a living thing, a hunter in pursuit of his prey.

"I've read about it." He laughed. "Not that porn ever has much to do with real life. But you can use your spit to make your dick slick and use your fingers to open my ass. I mean, I've never done this either. But I want to. Really, really want to."

I looked down at his ass and at my cock. There had to be some way to make this happen!

He reached around to his backside and pulled his asscheeks apart for me, revealing the hole between the cheeks. It was beautiful. I spat into my hands, using one handful to lubricate my cock, and with the other I reached out and tried to slip a finger into that hole. My thumb seemed to have difficulty going in, so I tried my index finger, which slid right in. I felt around, discovering—for the first time—what I now realize was his prostrate. He moaned.

"Is that a bad moan?" I asked, concerned I might be doing something wrong.

"Nah," he gasped. "That's a good one. Don't worry—you'll know when it's a bad one." He looked back over his shoulder at me and winked.

I tried to slip another finger in. It slowly eased its way about halfway into his ass, next to the other. I was surprised at how tight his hole felt around my fingers. I eased my fingers out and tried again with my thumb, which just didn't seem to be able to get in. Hmmm...if my thumb didn't fit, how would my cock?

"OK, OK," he said. "Enough with your fingers. Give me that hard cock. Now." His voice had a deep, animal undercurrent to it. A growl. That was more than just a request. I had just been given an order.

"OK." I applied more spit to my dick. "Here goes."

I pressed my dickhead up into his asscheeks and against his waiting hole. He pulled both as open as he could and pressed back against me. I pushed forward, bracing myself over his shoulders, putting my hands up against the wall in front of him.

My dick strained against his hole. Both seemed like granite boulders. Which would give way first? I grunted. He grunted and gasped. The head of my dick pushed against his hole. His muscular back arched and rippled before me. The matted curls of his head swayed from side to side.

And then it slid in. Was just engulfed, like a vacuum sucking up whatever is in its path. His asshole just slurped my dick into itself and we were fucking! We both gasped.

I just let the waves of delight wash over me for a minute. Then, as if acting by instinct, my body told me to pump and thrust, to hold his ass steady as I ground myself into him, deeper and deeper. He ground his ass back against my balls. It felt a little bit dry in there, as if some more spit was in order, but who wanted to pull out to apply more spit? Not me! And certainly Bruce would have been furious if I had pulled out at that moment. His squeals and grunts matched the gyrations of his ass. We were doing some kind of crazy tango, alternating whose movements "led" the other, every few seconds. It wasn't like anything I had ever imagined it would be like.

"I...I think...gonna come," I gasped between thrusts, recognizing the mounting pressure within my balls and dick from years of solo stimulation.

Suddenly we heard voices. Laughter. People walking through the steam tunnels on some exploratory escapade of their own. Had they heard us? Were they coming to the laundry room? Oh, God. Please don't let them come by here. Someone laughed again. We could hear their shoes slap against the stone floor but, given the echo-chamber quality of the tunnels, it was impossible to tell where exactly the sound was coming from or how far away they were. Or how many of them were coming.

Coming! Suddenly I just couldn't hold it back anymore and my cock exploded, pumping, and pumping, and pumping my cum up into Bruce's ass. It seemed to go on forever. Longer than it ever had by myself. There was so much I even felt some squirt back against my crotch from inside Bruce's ass. I collapsed onto his back, reaching around and grabbing onto his tits. He quietly purred, like a great African cat after an incredible feast.

I tried not to gasp too loudly. I think Bruce must have been jerking himself off with one hand and spurted onto the floor, judging by the gobs of cum there, but maybe it was all just mine dripping out his hole. I had been too preoccupied to notice what he was doing with one of his hands. I was finally able to regain enough strength to push myself up and off Bruce's back and stand semi-erect myself, leaning my dripping, sweaty body against the white stone around us. Should we grab our clothes? Were those people only steps away from turning a corner and discovering us?

Bruce slowly stood upright as well. I had been right—his delighted grin was so big that his eyes did look like a satisfied cat's, basking in the sunlight. The sweat ran down his torso in rivulets, then either slipping down his legs or off his balls. He tried to keep his deep, heaving breaths quiet as well, and we both grinned at each other. If I hadn't been so exhausted, I'm sure I would have burst out laughing at our predicament. The voices faded. The footsteps apparently followed another path, twisting away from us and the accumulation of sweat and cum which was pooling below us.

Bruce leaned over and kissed me again, lightly. "I think you need to do your laundry more often too, don't you?"

The Other Side
William Holden

"Sorry, I don't fuck on the first date." I watched the expression on the guy's face turn from temptress to shock-victim.

"Who said anything about a date?" He responded. "I just want to fuck."

"Sorry, it's not going to be with me."

"Well it's your loss. It would have been the best fuck of your life." He started to turn away.

"I doubt that." My voice rose so he could hear me over the music. I turned back around and leaned on the railing that overlooked the dance floor; which is what I had been doing before I was so rudely interrupted.

Gay life can be so ugly, especially in college. The football jocks can be the worst; wanting secret rendezvous to release their hidden desires, but never giving you the time of day in public. Sometimes I've wondered if the problem was me and not the other men, but I always come back to the same conclusion: I'm right and all the other gay men on campus are wrong. Perhaps I'm a bit jaded in my beliefs, why shouldn't I be? I've been dumped, cheated on, used, and abused more times than I can count—and for nothing more then ten minutes of supposed pleasure with someone's dick up my ass. No thanks. Not anymore. I have wasted the first three years of college sleeping with anyone and everyone who would give me a second look. I was getting ready to graduate and wanted something else. There had to be more to gay sex than all of that, and I was determined to find it or live a very solitary life.

I looked around at all the men in the club. Every type of college student was accounted for tonight. The scrawny freshmen twinks with their twenty-six-inch waist and hairless bodies; the sophomore and junior "pretty boys" who spend hours in front of the mirror, covering their face with products to "enhance" their features; and then of course the over-the-hill clubbers who frequent this bar looking for the young college boys. Yeap, they were all here tonight and just like I had done for many years, they were trying to be something they're not. I can't believe how stupid I was thinking that quick, nameless sex could get me through. Now all I wanted was a "real" man—a man with strong, masculine features, who leaves his body hair intact; a man who believes in being a man. Have they all been replaced in some evil plot to drive me crazy?

***

I glanced at my watch and saw it was only eight-thirty. I looked around at the crowd, trying to decide whether or not I should just pack it in for the night and head to the athletic department for a workout, when I noticed someone staring at me from across the bar. It was too dark to see him clearly, but he was obviously watching me. His long, thick hair fell down around what appeared to be broad shoulders. He wore a dark green T-shirt and blue jeans. I stared back mostly trying to get a better view of him, but it was no use. My view was being blocked by a group of "pretty boys." Giving up on the night, I dropped my bottle of water into a garbage can and headed for the door.

As I walked the badly lit street back to campus, I felt as if someone were following me. I looked over my shoulder, and in the distance I could see a darkened silhouette. He didn't seem to care that I noticed him, so I turned back around and headed across campus towards the gym.

The gym was deserted except for a few guys wandering the halls, heading for one room or another. I went for the lockers. The air was damp and smelled of sweat. A few gym bags littered the floor next to open lockers. Jock straps and sweat dampened T-shirts from the football team's practice early were scattered on the benches. In the distance, I could hear the sound of running water. I got to my locker and quickly changed into my shorts and tank top. On the way out I grabbed a towel from the table. They were still warm from their washing. I decided to skip the cardio room and headed straight for the weights to work off my sexual and social frustrations.

There were two varsity football players working out as I entered the room. They both stopped their routine as I entered and watched me walk the length of the room to the free weights. Even though I knew both of them intimately from my sophomore year, neither of them spoke to me. I stood and looked at myself in the mirror that stretched from wall to wall. I rubbed my arms and decided to start with the biceps. I placed the hundred and fifty pounds on the bar and positioned myself on the bench. I stared at my body and began the reps, breathing in as I curled the weights up, then slowly exhaling as they uncurled. I could already feel the muscles welcoming the workout. I was on my third set and beginning to break a sweat when I noticed someone in the mirror staring at me.

The green T-shirt and long wavy hair gave him away. He had replaced his jeans with a pair of loose fitting workout shorts. He saw me looking at him through the mirror and turned away casually to use the ab machine. As he brought his chest and knees together, his head remained motionless, locked into place watching me. His shoulders were wide. They set off his muscular biceps. His forearms were covered with a dark layer of hair. His chest stretched the material of his shirt; even from this distance and through the mirror, I could see the curves and shape of his abs. He looked vaguely familiar to me, but I couldn't place him.

I continued to watch him through the mirror as I began another rep. His chest expanded and contracted as he pushed himself to complete another set. He stood up and stretched, damp circles appeared under his underarm, coloring the green shirt even darker. He caught me staring at him and smiled as if he were pleased that I noticed him.

I sat there for a moment, half expecting him to make the

first move. After all, he was the one that followed me here. "I don't do that cat and mouse trick," I wanted to yell, but instead, I moved over to the bench press to continue my workout. I situated myself on the bench and grabbed the weights. By the sixth count, I was straining to get the weights up to their resting spot. My arms and body trembled. I became aware of how ridiculous I must look to him. Disregarding the pain and potential danger I was in, I continued to strain, pushing myself to complete the set. Suddenly the weights lifted with ease. I looked up. He stood over me smiling. His hands guided the weights back to their resting place. I took a deep breath to calm my overworked body. His musky scent surrounded me.

"It looked like you could use some help. Hope you don't mind." His baritone voice echoed through the now empty room.

"Not at all, I appreciate it." I lifted myself up and sat on the edge of the bench. He moved over in front of me and squatted down.

"I'm Kirk, by the way."

"Greg." I replied. I should have said more to ease the awkwardness that had fallen between us, even after all the pursuit. Words stick sometimes even when it's clear to both of you what's going on. Instead I kept quiet and let my eyes explore his body. His legs were large and beautifully sculpted with ripples of muscle and hair. The front of his shirt was stained with sweat. My eyes followed the stain leading downward. I wondered what he looked like underneath his clothes. I imagined that his chest was smooth, either naturally or by his own doing. The thought disappointed me. Men should have hair on their bodies. It's what makes a man a man. I tried to reassure myself that even with a smooth chest, he was hot. I tried to picture his skin glistening with sweat; as the smell of his body continued to invade my senses. His voice broke my concentration.

"It seems that neither of us is really in the mood to workout tonight. Care to join me in the steam room?"

I wasn't sure what to say. My mind told me to pass on the offer. "He's not looking for the same thing you are," I reasoned. But the more I looked at him, the more I wanted to take a chance that he may be different from the rest. I could feel the tension rising between us from my silence. I couldn't take it any more. From somewhere deep inside, I felt we understood each other and what we wanted. I stood up, without another thought, and grabbed my towel. We walked down the long corridor towards the locker room in silence.

His locker was in a different alcove than mine. As I undressed, I thought of Kirk undressing; anticipating seeing him without the mask of clothing. I heard a locker shut in the distance and quickly wrapped the towel around my waist. As I turned around, he was standing just a few feet away.

My eyes widened with excitement as I realized I was wrong about his smooth skin. His pecs were large, taut, and covered with a thick blanket of black hair. The hair ended briefly just below his chest, then started in a small trail down his stomach, dividing his rippled abs in half. A few long strands of hair fell over the edge of his towel. My cock lengthened underneath my own covering. Kirk's eyes glanced down at the movement. He smiled. He motioned towards the steam room with his head. My breathing became heavier with anticipation as we walked into the room together.

As we entered the steam room, he grabbed my hand and led me to the back wall. His grip was strong. His large hand made mine feel small and frail. He pushed a white button set into the white tile. The room echoed as the steam kicked in, surrounding us in a thick, damp fog. He leaned against the wall and pulled me into him; his arms crossed behind my waist. I could feel the rise and fall of his stomach with every breath he took. I looked down at our bodies. The hair on his chest clung to mine with sweat and steam. I could feel him rising behind his towel, pressing into me. Our eyes met and locked. Our heads moved towards each other. My heart pounded as I felt the thickness of his lips pressing into mine.

He pulled back and broke our kiss. His eyes examined my face. His finger ran down my cheek, and then traced the outline of my jaw. Our eyes met once again as his fingers moved down my chest. He traced the thin line of hair as it spread across my stomach, until he reached the edge of the towel. My body jumped as he ripped the towel away from my body and swung me around, pressing me against the wall. His force startled me.

A smile stretched across his lips as he removed his towel. I couldn't see what had been hidden behind it, but I could feel its thickness and length as he pressed himself into me. He hit the white button again. I felt the vibrations in the tile against my back as the steam exploded. The walls and ceiling dripped moisture. Kirk's body was blurred in the hot, thick air. I felt his body move against mine. His lips grazed my neck as he moved down. I leaned my head against the wall as he ran his tongue through the hair on my chest, licking the dampness from my skin.

His breathing became heavy. I could feel it beating against my cock. He moved in closer, pressing his face between my legs. He took a deep breath of my scent, and then exhaled. I could feel the heat of his breath surrounding my cock. I closed my eyes as his tongue made contact. Moisture from the steam covered my shaft. He licked it off. A soft moan floated up through the steam.

He wrapped his fingers around the base. His grip tightened. Slowly he moved my cock over his lips. He opened up and let me enter his mouth. My body trembled as he swallowed me inch by inch. My body was soaked with sweat and steam. I became lightheaded from the intense heat. My legs went weak. They buckled as he took more of me in. My body slid down the wall, his mouth never giving up what it held. He guided me down to the floor, his body pressed tightly between my legs. I could feel the muscles of his throat relax as he pushed me deeper into him. His mouth opened further to allow his tongue to make contact with my balls. He sucked them into his mouth as well. His hands caressed my skin as they moved up the length of my body.

The thickness of the air started to fade, allowing me to see his muscular body surrounding me. I watched the muscles in his back shift and tighten as he began to make short strokes up and down my cock and balls. His long hair, now matted with steam and sweat, bounced seductively against my stomach. I ran my hands up his arms; his muscles responded to my touch.

My body shook as he suddenly released me from his mouth. Slowly, he crawled his way towards me. I could feel the heat of his skin, feel his body next to mine, yet our bodies never touched. He leaned over me. His hair covered our faces in long thick strands. Our mouths connected, opening up to each others needs. I could taste my own excitement in his mouth.

"Let me feel you next to me." I whispered as he kissed my eyelids, nose and lips. My hands ran down his back as he lowered himself to me. His body was heavy against mine as he let his full weight come down on me. I ran my fingers through his hair as he lifted himself slightly to rub our cocks together. It was only then that I could see the thickness between his legs. My desire for him grew as I watched the silky, tender head of his cock move in and out of the thick folds of foreskin.

"You like what you see." His words echoed around us.

"Your cock is amazing, but I don't..."

"Don't worry, I know what you're looking for," he interrupted. He pushed himself up and straddled my shoulders. His cock dangled just above my lips. His hands grabbed the back of my head as he brought me closer to him.

Precum gathered in the folds of his skin. I watched in anticipation as it began to hang off his cock. The weight of it caused it to release itself from him. I watched as the thick liquid made its way to me. I opened my mouth. His flavors were sweet and pure. I knew I needed to have more. I moved my tongue into the folds of his skin, licking away what remained.

Suddenly his cock was out of reach. He stood up and held out his hand. I didn't want to move. I wanted more of his cock. He pulled me up with ease and pushed me back against the wall. His hand found the button and once again we became surrounded in the steam. He pressed his body into me as his lips caressed mine. Our tongues met again, exploring each other's mouths as if we might have missed something from our previous visits.

I felt his hand moving between my legs. He stroked my cock first before moving to his. The motion continued until he was stroking the both of us simultaneously. My breathing became heavy, my pulse raced through my body as I felt him sliding my cock into his thick foreskin. The head of our cocks butted up against one another.

He continued stroking us, gliding his hand down to the base of my cock, then moving up my shaft, over our enclosed heads and back down his cock. His grip tightened as his movements became faster. His tongue pushed deeper into my mouth. I could feel his hot breath pushing down my throat in long, heavy puffs. The pressure of his breathing changed to short bursts. His deep moans of pleasure vibrated into the depths of my body.

I needed to breathe as I felt myself reaching the final barrier of pleasure. I tried to moan to let him know I was close, but the force of his own breathing inside of me, was too much. I felt Kirk's body tremble against mine. His grip tightened more. The strokes became more pronounced.

Suddenly I felt Kirk's release. His warmth flooded our enclosed cocks. The pressure began to build stretching his foreskin to its limits. I could feel my own cock swimming in his cum. My knees weakened as I lost the control to hold out for more. I let go. My body shook unexpectedly causing Kirk's grip to loosen. As the first blast of my cum entered his foreskin the pressure was too great. Our cocks broke free showering our bodies with our cum. Kirk continued to stroke my cock as I spilled another load into his hand. He rubbed it over our chests then leaned into me.

He kissed me once more; then he looked at me. His face seemed gentle and at peace, and at that moment I knew I had finally found someone who I could be with. "I suppose we should clean up. Care to join me?" His answer was not what I had expected.

"No. Actually I wouldn't." He paused, "You don't remember me do you?" My silence was his answer. "I didn't think so." He wrapped his damp towel around his waist before explaining his early question. "Last year about this time, I saw you at the bar. You captured my heart that night."

"I don't understand."

"You know that twinge in the pit of your stomach and that warm fuzzy feeling you get in your heart when you first fall in love?" He didn't wait for my answer. "If there is such a thing as love at first sight, that night was it for me. I thought you were the one. I was willing to give you anything you wanted, just to be with me."

"Why didn't you say anything?" I couldn't believe this was happening. I tried to remember, but my mind kept coming up empty.

"I did. I went up to you and introduced myself. But you never gave me a chance. You never gave us a chance. You told me that names were not necessary, my cock up your ass was all that you needed from me."

"I..." the words didn't come out. My heart sunk as the memory came back.

"When I told you that there was more to me, then just fucking, you treated me like shit; acting as if I wasn't worth getting to know. You college kids are all the same. I haven't been able to step foot in that bar until tonight."

"So, what was all this? I thought you really liked being with me. I've changed. Tonight should prove that."

"Yes, I know you've changed. I was watching you at the bar

and saw you turning down those boys tonight. Seeing that gave me hope that perhaps I could hurt you the same way you hurt me last year. That perhaps, I could let you see what you missed out on. Let you know what you gave up for a quick fuck. Now you know."

Before I could say anything, he was gone. I sat there alone in the room with the scent of him lingering through the steam.

Jacking the Junior
Troy Storm

"What the hell is the matter with me, Danny? It must be my fucking hormones, right? I'm always fucking horny! I can't concentrate, man. I *can't* be horny. I'm too fucking perfect. Guys like me aren't allowed. The alumni dudes would have a fucking cow! A goddamn *herd!!*"

Jason sank into the crappy chair the university had provided for my "office" and plowed his fingers through his chestnut waves before burying his finely featured face in his hands. His wide shoulders rose and fell inside his expensive, not-too-tight polo shirt and his elbows sank into the thick muscles of his freshly pressed chino encased, widespread thighs.

Freshly pressed! My Donna Reed heart thrummed.

I pressed a damp palm hard into my crotch to re-shift the hot-poker of charging flesh inside my loose-fit jeans before easing from behind my small desk and leaning over to put a brotherly hand on the morose junior's slumped shoulder.

"Uh, Jason, I really appreciate your sharing this problem with me, but...."

"And you know what else?" His head shot up. I jerked back. "I beat off so damn much, I think I'm hurting my dick." His pleading eyes bore into me, staring me down. "I mean it doesn't, like, *hurt,* but I can hardly feel anything when I'm pounding away. You know what I mean? Just do it!" He gripped the wrist of his fisted arm and furiously pumped his muscular forearm—I gulped at the image. "And get it over with." He stared at his clenched fist, shaking his head morosely. "That's not natural, man." Then crumpled again.

"Uh, well, I guess it depends on who it is you're pounding away on...in."

His thick eyelashes flashed upwards as he gave a bitter snort. "Who? Look at me, Danny. I'm the fucking president of the junior class. I'm good-looking and my parents have money. What do you think? I can pump any good-looking piece of pussy on this campus I want."

"Oh."

"And the guys come on to me, too. Y'know, sometimes I think..."

Hope instantly flooded my midsection. "Yeah? Sometimes you think...?"

"You want to see it? It's like all...purple." He jumped up and unzipped his pants "And big! It keeps getting bigger. Man, it's *huge!*" My breath stopped.

He froze, his hand inside his pants. "What the fuck am I doing, pulling out my dick to show to another guy?"

"I am not 'another guy'." I indignantly pulled myself up. "I'm a Psych major specializing in societal problems in the young adult male...with an emphasis on sexual malfunctions. We're *frat brothers.* That's why you came to me. If you've got a problem with my being a *sophomore,* Mr. Hot Shot Junior Class Prez...." I firmly crossed my arms over my pounding chest. "Then keep your dick in your pants."

Psychologically speaking, it always amazes to me how you can make your mouth say one thing when your body obviously wants a totally whole other thing.

"No, man, no," he pleaded. "Fuck that sophomore/junior shit. We're buddies. If you hadn't bailed me out of that stupid Public Speaking assignment by giving me that speech about the penguins and North Pole warming—or was it the South Pole? —anyway, that was cool. Except I kept thinking about how it would be to boff on the *ice* with my bare butt turning six shade of *blue* and my jizz probably freezing into fucking icicles...."

He stopped, his despairing eyes on me.

"I'm freaking, right?"

I shrugged. "Let me see your freakin' meat, man. I've been wanting to check out your stuff ever since you did that Mr. Cool Dude Naked Collegeman Poster last fall...."

"Hey," he pulled out his dick, "that calendar was for charity. We made a bunch of bucks." His bone was semi-solid. Gripping it tightly, he stripped the thick cowl back. The bulbous purple head popped out, dribbling precum.

My jaw unhinged. My loose-fits almost split. "That's...an amazing...piece."

"It's too big, right? And it's so damn *hard*. Well, not right now, but...Danny, man, I am so stupid when it comes to, you know...doing it...hell, fucking. You'd think they'd have fucking given us some fucking little clue about fucking sex in high school. But I was such a 'gooood' boy." His snarl changed to a snicker. "You should have seen the look on this college chick's face when I pulled it out."

"Will you stop yapping about the chicks you fuck? Some of us have a different..."

"Hey, man, no, I didn't mean...you're way fine, and smart, and hot looking. You must get all...."

"...orientation! Different orientation. Some of us...Hot looking?"

Jason stopped talking...and stared. We both stopped...and stared, trying to compute all the words.

"Well...yeah. I guess maybe I figured...you might, look at things differently. That's why I," he gave a nervous snicker and punched me lightly on the arm, "came on to you."

"If this is the way you 'come on,'" I snapped, "no fucking wonder you're having a feeble sex life."

Still, he had pulled out the most beautiful dick I had ever seen. And, yes, it was huge. I went down on my knees to get a better look. My mouth went dry at the smooth, rosy poundage.

"What're you doing?" Jason death-gripped his throbbing dong, "Licking your lips?" The purple-headed pole turned rock under his clinched fingers.

And pointed at my mouth.

"I need something...wet...down my throat." I explained, hoarsely. My tongue swiped at the greasy tip. Jason jumped. I took a deep breath and made a professional suggestion. "How 'bout I give you a blow-job. That would put a load of lubricant into me and show you that getting off doesn't always have to be about pounding boring pussy. Maybe you need somebody who appreciates a big, hard, thick, gut-filling, drooling, purple-headed pole. I'm offering for research purposes, of course."

Jason's amber orbs widened. His hips pushed toward me ever so imperceptibly—as if his nuts were magnets. The slit of the mushroom-sculpted head gaped and the clear sweet muck I had gotten the merest taste of overflowed, stretching down in a thick gooey strand. I caught the honey load on my tongue. Pure sucrose.

"You're lapping up my...stuff. Isn't that...sick?" It was a fair question.

"No." I popped my lips over the purple knob, curling my tongue around the textured landscape.

"Oh, God." Jason gasped as my mouth pushed down the column of hard, hot, blue, vein-netted flesh encountering his clenched fist. I stretched my lips wider to lick at the digits. They loosened their grip and slid inside beside his half-ingested dick. "Soooo gooood," he moaned.

I nibbled on his fingers and worked over the first half of his meat, sliding my lips up and down the pulsing shaft, licking, chewing, and tugging at the throbbing skin with my teeth.

His breath hissed through his big teeth as he shoved his hips toward me. Teasingly, slowly, I took in his meat and deep throated the gut-stuffing sausage until my nose drilled into his sweat-drenched dick fur. He smelled...swell.

"I gotta...blow, man," he wailed, not making the slightest effort to extract his buried bone from the depths of my gulping throat. "So...fucking...beau-ti-ful...ungh!!"

I got my first gut full of Jason's sweet, thick milk as he fired blast after blast, grunting, trying not to yell.

The door to my "office" was open, adding to the utter insanity of the situation. But I was so low on the department's totem pole the little space they allotted me to interview my "clients" was so remote and buried in the depths of the main library that normally nobody but the guys who had made a definite interview appointment made it down my way.

Still, the open door provided a clear view from the corridor of me on my knees blowing hunky Jason's huge member. It made the situation even hotter.

The ecstatic dude finished coming. His jerking, jarring body eased. I nursed his massive meatstick, draining the last drops of his good stuff, dragging out the inevitable.

Situation: horny straight guy...first blow job by an equally horny homo who is willing to abase himself in the service of getting a full load of prime male liquid protein. Result: though the initiating experience might be near equal to bungee jumping off a mile-high canyon suspension bridge hanging by your ankles, the downside from the straight guy often proves to end in pain and suffering on the part of the queer.

I hoped Jason wouldn't revert to that kind of physical response.

He was taking his time allowing his finely-tuned musculature to return to his control—allowing me to continue to suckle on the thick leg of satisfied meat, tongue-buffing the round, meaty head, tenderizing the bumpy corona with my sucking cheek muscles.

Even if only for a few more seconds.

Usually it was the jocks who couldn't take the bliss they had just been handed—or mouthed...or assed, as the case might be—who afterwards would stuff their floppy well-serviced teeny peenies back into their droopy jock straps and climb up on their high and mighty I-just-needed-to-get-my-rocks-off-and-you-had-a-hungry-hole, ho. Thanks and so long, sucker.

More specifically, the jock soccer team. Even more bone-headedly specific: the fucking drop-dead gorgeous captain with the bowling-ball butt with its clinched tight asshole and his clinched tight mouth with the clinched tight luscious lips that didn't even have the fucking decency to say, "Thank you," sucker, for all the semester-long mouth action and ass fucks I had provided for his whining, "Could I have a quickie," sucker, "I'm feeling a little tense before the big game," and "You'd be doing the team a big favor" to help it's horny captain focus.

Fuck *focus!* Fuck the goddamn hard-hearted focus! Focus on...!

"Hey, Danny. You okay?"

Jason pulled up my chin. I was still sucking his dick. I blinked and melted into his gold-flecked ambers. Pure molasses. Through my watery vision I saw him grin slyly, his dimples firing a bout of energetic nursing on my part. He winced pleasurably. The side of his big, kissable mouth curled up. "I guess I owe you a big one, huh?"

My vision turned razor sharp, though my hearing must have been a little muddled.

He gave a quick tilt of his head sideways—just enough to make his chestnut waves glint with golden highlights from the one stinking florescent tube I was allowed in the overhead fixture. A curling tendril caressed his forehead. "Could we close the door? I'm not used to being so...exposed, especially when I get the best blow job of my life." I suckled like mad. "Oh yeah! Danny, man, you are the *best!*" His fingers threaded through my hair and stroked my sunken, slurping cheeks. "Man, I will never be able to match your awesome action." Another blinding grin. "I guess I'll just have to practice a lot, huh?"

Suddenly, a look of surprise flickered across Jason's handsome mug. "Uh, Dan, man, maybe you'd better...oh, shit, I hate to even say these words, that mouth is so unbelievable, but...I'm boned up again—jeez, it's harder than ever. Maybe you'd better pull off before I won't be able to...."

I gave a final strip of my o-ringed lips as I pulled up the length of his throbbing, fresh, hard meat pole and allowed the purple nose to pop out of my mouth accompanied by his silent gasp.

My jaw and my back took a little stretching to get back to fighting shape. I stood up and tugged at the collar of his polo shirt. He sat back on the edge of my desk, eyes wide at the closeness.

"You want to fuck me in the butt?" I growled. "You won't blow your wad so fast."

"But...?"

"Noooo," I returned his startled look—I love to shake up a straight man—with my own cutie-pie grin, as I leaned against his chest and pulled his hands around to caress my ass. My still sheathed hard dick mashed against his still unsheathed hard dick.

"You mean, '*butt*,'" I snickered. "Drive your big ole man-sized meat up my rear end. They tell me if that's even better than my A number one oral orifice workout."

He stared at my mouth, not inches from his. "Not possible." It was a raspy whisper. He wrenched his eyes up to mine. "You don't have to...." It was hard for him to finish, my offer was too tempting.

I shrugged and leaned in to kiss him. "So...you'll owe me two." I spiked my tongue down his throat. After an initial frozen moment, he grabbed my slathering spear with his lips and sucked hard and rough like I had done with his dick. Wow! I went from a redwood boring into his crotch to a sequoia.

Suddenly Jason pulled away. "Fuck this," he snarled and stalked the two steps it took to get him to the door. Slamming it shut, he threw the bolt from the inside. He whipped my shirt off and went for my pants. In about two seconds he had me naked.

"Jeez," he eyed me smugly. "Welcome to the club."

"That meat has been known to strike fear in the hearts of trembling freshmen," I proudly noted, pumping my big fella to its most impressive. "But, given time and inclination, it has drilled its share of happiness into willing holes." I remembered the soccer dude. He couldn't get enough of throwing his heels over his head and begging me to split his ass open. Until another member of the team found out he was being "flexible" in his sex needs and took over reaming him out. Damn seniors.

I started to undress Jason. He shook his head. "I'll do it." Then carefully stripped, neatly folding his clothes—leaving his socks on. Cool. He looked down at his throbbing meat. "I, uh, don't have...."

I quickly pulled a handful of pre-lubed, super strongs out of the drawer of the desk.

"It gets lonely down here," I explained, somewhat sheepishly stroking the pile of male porn I had tucked away in the drawer." Clearing the desktop, I flopped my ass down, spreading my legs wide, ready for Jason to jam his juice-filled cannon up my rump and blow my mind.

"Gee, it feels awfully tight."

Gee? My tender-hearted, virgin rump-buster tentatively poked the head of his rock-and-ready hole-puncher at my anal entrance.

No fingers? No tongue? I figured it was time for me to take the initiative again.

"Okay. Assume the position. I'll show you how to loosen up a butthole."

"Uh. You're going to loosen *me* up?"

"Sure. Take notes. Then you'll know how to drive your big daddy up my ass." I rolled on a condom to its full length, snapping the tight ring three-quarters of the way down my dick. "That's what you want, right?"

"Uh...well, yeah...."

I felt a little sad about what I had in mind, but, hell, if a junior can't handle a devious sophomore, then he needs some quick instruction. Said soon-to-be senior's gonna be out in the big ole cold in a couple of years. He needs to get a little sex cred. Besides, I intended to make it up to him for whatever "discomfort" the learning process might entail. No pain...

Jason eased himself onto the desk, watching me warily. I

grabbed his asscheeks and yanked his tense buns wide as I suctioned my mouth onto his hole. He yelled and gripped the desktop. I rammed my tongue inside, stabbing through his stunned sphincter and thrumming against the wrinkled flesh until it began to give.

My hands gripped his balls and bone, yanked, and milked. He yelled louder and began to beat the desktop with a fist. His ass was open. I shoved a couple of fingers inside and fingerfucked alongside my swabbing, piercing tongue as I beat him off. Suddenly I felt his thrashing body tense and his nuts pull up. "Gaaa." He gasped and let loose a load as I stripped my fingers down his dumping dong and caught a handful of hot cum.

I slapped it into his gaping asshole, hitched my butt up and drove my love pole pubic hair deep. Jason howled and began to pound both fists. I pulled out and pushed back in steadily, determinedly. He knew I wasn't gonna stop. His insides were still jerking from popping his wad. The grinding grip on my ripping manpole was awesome. Jason's virgin butt was a winner. I was gonna keep it.

It didn't take long before he relaxed and let me have my way with cramming and creaming his colon. By the second time I came he had figured out he could jack himself off at the same time and add another earth-shattering sensation to his repertoire. The third time he turned into a total sex whore and snarled, "Again. Fuck me again, man. Ram it in!"

I did.

Jason decided he needed "therapy" every afternoon in my office, and sometimes he'd stop by my dorm room at night and we'd do it under a bush or behind an alumni statue. The broads didn't get him anymore. I got all of him.

His concentration cleared. He went on to win senior class president, and stayed on for his Masters and to help me with my "research." I get my M.A. next year. My dissertation on the sexual appetite of initially deprived young adult males is going to be a doozy.

Spin Cycle
Hank Edwards

The air of the laundry room is damp and heavy with the spent perfume of years of various detergents. I breathe it in then let out my breath with a sigh. The room is empty, the fluorescent bulbs buzzing quietly above the only witnesses to my holiday weekend domesticity. I set down my overflowing laundry basket with a grunt then sort my clothes into three separate machines. After pushing quarters in with plungers coated with old detergent and God knows what else, the water begins to fill the washer tubs and I stretch out across the sorting table.

Idly squeezing the steadily firming bulge of my crotch with one hand, I slide the other up the loose leg of my sweat shorts to fondle my freshly shaved balls then finger the smooth, damp pucker of my anus. The hot, sensitive muscle twitches at my touch and I moan. This is the best part about staying in the dorms over a holiday weekend, other than having the laundry room to myself: the chance to jerk off in any part of the mostly empty building. I am, I have discovered, an exhibitionist at heart.

The machines grind into action one after the other, and I close my eyes, losing myself in the rhythm of the agitators as I slip my right hand beneath the loosely tied waist of my shorts to take hold of my thick, rigid meat. I grab it hard and squeeze as I pump my fist several times along its full length. I look down at the pearls of thick, clear precum that ooze out into the hair of my treasure trail, and I rub my index finger along the wide, mushroom head of my dick, pressing the tip into the piss slit to collect a sample. Raising the finger to my mouth, I suck the stuff off.

Reaching down, I unbutton my flannel shirt and spread it open then ease my shorts down over my hard cock and kick them off. With my left hand I take hold of my smooth balls and tug hard as I begin to jack the tight, solid length of my dick with serious intent. I want to shoot a heavy, thick load all over my chest, feel the hot splash of cum as my nuts pump their jizz up through my cock and out onto my torso. The memory of a football player who fucked me in high school pounds into my head. I recall the sense of invasion as he drove his thick cock into me for months after school my senior year. The smell of his hard, hairy body comes back to me, the clean, masculine scent of him as he grunted above me and I groan.

The machine containing my jeans begins to rattle and thump, unbalanced, and my fantasy dissolves with the distraction. I roll my head back and forth across the chipped surface of the sorting table in frustration, still trying to finish myself off, but it's no use.

"Fuck!" I snap and release my painfully hard cock as the machine emits a warbling buzz to alert me that it has shut down. "All fucking right already, shut your pie hole." I observe the "Unbalanced Load" light on the control panel and sympathize with the machine as I lift the lid: You and me both, buddy. I lean over the machine, the white metal cold against the skin of my chest and the flannel shirt pulling up to expose my bare ass as I reach into the cold depths of the laundry water. I adjust the heavy, soaking denim, standing on my toes as I even out the weight of the load.

A *snap* sounds behind me and the lights go out, plunging the room into total darkness.

I freeze and turn my head, my arms immersed in the machine as I listen to the darkness surrounding me, very aware of my nudity. "Hello? Is anyone there?" I say and feel simultaneously stupid and terrified: I am suddenly a special guest star in a Wes Craven movie. Around me the other two washing machines are agitating the dirt from my clothes, masking any sound an intruder might make. My eyes have not adjusted to the dark in the small, windowless room, and I pull my hands from the cold water to lean on the machine, standing still to listen, my back to the room as I come up with all sorts of reasons for the lights to be out: blown fuse; power failure; psycho killer.

I hear a quiet, stealthy shuffle to my left, and my heart jumps, but I am too afraid to move. Every horror movie I have ever seen comes back to haunt me, and I imagine numerous ways for me to die, all of them hideously awful. My stomach clenches, and my bladder nearly lets go as my erection wilts, and my balls pull up against my body.

"Who-who's there?" I whisper, hating the sound of fear I hear in my voice. "I know someone's in here. Who is it?"

A hand touches the small of my back and I let out a quiet yelp and start to turn to defend myself. But the phantom intruder's other hand presses firmly against my shoulder to hold me in place with my bare ass exposed to him. The washers around us fall quiet as they pause between cycles and in the sudden silence I can hear deep, heavy breathing behind me, and realize I can feel my visitor's breath on the back of my neck. It is hot and damp, and the heat from his palms burns into the small of my back and my shoulder as he keeps me pressed against the washer.

"What do you want?" I ask quietly. "I don't have any money on me. Just quarters for the machines."

The hand at the small of my back slides down to caress my bare ass, fingers gripping my cheeks hard. I start to turn my head and say something but his other hand plants itself on the back of my head, stopping me. The protest, mild anyway, dies in my throat. I am scared and completely turned on.

"Shhh," he whispers and kneels behind me.

"Wh-what are you doing?" I say. As I wonder who the hell this guy is, he moves my legs apart, and I feel his palms on each of my asscheeks as he kneads the twin swells of my buttocks then spreads them wide open. I gasp and lean forward over the gaping mouth of the washing machine, groaning down into the cold darkness of the water filled tub. I feel the warm brush of his breath just before the tip of his tongue flicks across the sensitive creases of my anus.

"Oh, fuck," I gasp and close my eyes.

Stubble from his cheek scrapes against the shaved skin in the crack of my ass and along the twitching pucker of my hole as his tongue slides deep into me. His thumbs press down on either side of my asshole and it pops open to admit an amazing length of his tongue which he pokes into me over and over, licking and slurping at my damp, horny hole.

"Oh, yeah," I moan.

He licks and sucks at my asshole, running his tongue all around its wrinkled edges with slow, firm strokes then burrowing it deep into me. My cock is hard again, pressed up against the front of the washer and leaving a smear of pre-cum on the white enamel surface.

A hand, strong and rough, reaches up between my legs and pulls on my shaved nuts. I let out a groan as his fingers tighten around my sack, tugging on it as his tongue moves down over my perineum. He maneuvers his head between my legs, sticking his face between my thighs as he takes my balls into his mouth and sucks them greedily. As he slurps down my nuts he slides a finger up the slick trail of spit left on my perineum and slips it into my hole.

"Oh, fuck yeah," I sigh. "Get that fuckin' finger up my ass. Fuck that hole."

He crooks his finger and twists it inside me, sweeping it back and forth within my rectum. He pulls it out then slides it back in, picking up speed until he is finger fucking my hole.

"Another one," I gasp. "Get another one in there. Fill me up."

He slides a second then a third finger into me, plugging away as he sucks my nuts. He must sense I am close to coming because he suddenly stops and stands up to take me by the shoulders and turn me around for a hard kiss. His hot tongue tastes of my ass and sweaty nuts as it bursts into my mouth. I kiss him back and press my hard-on against the bulge in his sweats. I cup a palm over the firm package of his cock and balls and squeeze; he moans into my mouth and grinds his hips forward against my hand. His dick is big, bigger than my own, and my asshole puckers at the thought of taking the thick, hard length of him to the hilt.

I jump slightly as the mysterious man reaches past me and closes the lid of the washing machine. The agitator begins to spin once again and the thrum of the mechanics tingles into my back and ass. I untie his sweats and push them down, releasing his cock so that it brushes up against mine. I take both our dicks in my fist and pump them as we kiss and he reaches up to unbutton his own flannel shirt. His chest is smooth and firm, and I run my free hand over his hard pecs and the ripples of his flat belly. His nipples are large, swollen into points that I twist hard, which makes him moan into my mouth.

He takes me under the armpits and lifts me up to sit on top of the washing machine, kissing me a little longer before he moves down to suck at my nipples as I press my hands against the back of his head. His hair is long, shaggy, but I still have not been able to recognize him, and I start to wonder if it really matters. His tongue swirls around my navel a few times before he slides his soft lips along the shaft of my dick and then I gasp as the head of my cock is enveloped by the wet heat of his mouth. His tongue slides around the slick head, slurping up the pre-cum before he takes me completely into his throat.

"Oh, fuck!" I gasp at the sudden intensity of his sucking. My cock is buried in his throat and I feel the heat of his breath as his nose presses into my pubes. "Oh, God."

He sucks me a little longer then slowly raises my legs, easing me back against the operating panel of the washing machine. I slide my hips forward so my ass is just over the edge of the machine and feel the scruff of his beard as he once more presses his face into the crack of my ass. He eats me slow and deep, the spinning clothes beneath me vibrating against my spine.

Raising his head, he suddenly pushes my legs up higher and crawls on top of the machine with me. I feel the singe of the hot, wide head of his cock brush against my thigh, and then it pokes at my wet, waiting asshole as he adjusts himself.

"Oh, yeah," I say. "Slide that big dick up my ass. Fuck me good."

The machine beneath me goes silent, pausing between cycles, and I hear him spit down into his palm to grease up his cock. He takes hold of my ankle then feels for my hole with his finger, directing his dick toward it. The pressure of his penetration makes my mouth drop open, and I groan as the fat head of his cock pushes into my anus. The machine beneath me begins to spin once again and the sensation tingles up into my body as the man between my legs presses himself completely into my ass. I focus my energy on relaxing my rectal muscles to accept the thick, hot dick as it parts them and burrows deeper into me.

A moment later, he has fully invaded my hole and leans forward to kiss me before pulling his hips back so the ridge of the head of his cock catches on the edge of my sphincter. He plows forward again, hard and deep, and I let out a loud grunt. The machine dances beneath us as he pounds my ass, fucking me with long, deep strokes of his fat cock. His fingers grip my ankles tight, holding my legs in the air as he grunts between them.

I take hold of my throbbing dick and stroke it in time with the thrust of his hips, jacking my dick as his cock pumps into me. He takes both my ankles in one big, strong hand and pulls my dick from my hand to take over, jerking me off in his large, warm fist. I am bent nearly double, staring up at the dim outline of his hand pulling on my cock straight above my face. I groan in encouragement and start to pinch my own nipples.

Moments later I feel the rush of orgasm and gasp out a quick warning before my own semen blasts down onto my face. I open my mouth and catch as much of it as possible in the dark as his hand milks my cock dry. The muscles in my asshole tighten around the length of him as I come, and he grunts at the feeling. I work those muscles, squeezing his cock like a hot, wet fist, and he gasps, spreading my legs open wide. The spin cycle ends beneath me as he grunts out a single word, "Yeah," just before he shoots his load inside my ass. His cock is buried deep inside me, his pubic hair brushing up against my balls as his fingers tighten on my ankles.

"Oh, fuck," I say with a sigh. "That was fucking amazing."

He slowly pulls out of me and climbs down, then leans over to give my gaping hole a kiss. He helps me down and we kiss again then he licks the drying cum off my face. I dress awkwardly in the dark, stopping with one leg in my shorts as I realize I am once again alone in the laundry room.

"Hello?" I say but I can tell he is gone. My mystery fuck has come and gone, literally. I pull my shorts the rest of the way on and button my shirt over my sweaty chest, then make my way to the door of the laundry room where I flip the light switch. The overhead fluorescents buzz into life, and I blink in the sudden glare as I look around the empty room.

The washers have finished their duty and are silent behind me as I step into the hallway and look across the empty basement. There is no sign of anyone having been in the basement and, if not for the warm feeling of cum oozing from my stretched and tingling hole to trickle down my thigh, I would think I had imagined the encounter.

I transfer my clothes to the dryers and lie back across the table, hoping for a repeat encounter. As I wait I try to think of the men who remain in the dorm this holiday weekend and decide to spend a little more time in the community showers this evening in case my mystery man decides to come back for an encore.

About the Contributors

Shane Allison has published four chapbooks of poetry. His fifth book *I Want to Fuck a Redneck,* is forthcoming from Scintillating Publications. His stories and poems have graced the pages of *Mississippi Review, Windy City Times, Outsider Ink, Suspect Thoughts, Velvet Mafia, Van Gogh's Ear, zafusy, Mc Sweeney's, Cowboys: Gay Erotic Tales, Hustlers, Best Black Gay Erotica, Sexiest Soles, Ultimate Gay Erotica 2006* and *Best Gay Erotica 2007.* He is the editor of *Hot Cops: Gay Erotic Tales.*

Armand works full-time and spends much of his free time writing erotic stories, poetry, and fiction. He is currently working hard to publish his first novel and lives by himself in Ohio.

A native Californian, **Bearmuffin** lives in San Diego with two leatherbears in a stimulating ménage a trois. He writes erotica for *Honcho* and *Torso.* His work is featured in *Alyson's Friction, Ultimate Gay Erotica, Hustlers* anthologies, and in the *Truckers and Cowboys* anthologies from Cleis Press.

Lew Bull lives in Johannesburg, South Africa. Currrent publications which include published writing are *Ultimate Undies, Secret Slaves* and *Travelrotica.* Upcoming publications include *Ultimate Gay Erotica 2007* (Alyson) and *Superheroes* (STARbooks).

R. K. Bussel authors smut of all kinds. She also serves as senior editor at *Penthouse Variations,* writes the "Lusty Lady" column for the *Village Voice,* and hosts *In the Flesh* erotic reading series. Her erotica anthologies include *Ultimate Undies, Sexiest Soles, Secret Slaves: Erotic Stories of Bondage, Naughty Spanking Stories from A to Z 1 and 2, Up All Night, First-Timers, Glamour Girls: Femme/Femme Erotica,* and *Caught Looking: Erotic Tales of Voyeurs* *and Exhibitionists,* with more on the way. When she's not writing porn, she can be found blogging about cupcakes at cup cakestakcthecake.blogspot.com. Find out more at www.rachel kramerbussel.com

Curtis C. Comer is a frequent contributor to Alyson's anthologies, and lives in St. Louis with his partner Tim, their cat Magda, and lovebird, Raoul.

Hank Edwards has published over thirty stories of erotica for Alyson, Haworth, Cleis, STARbooks Press, as well as for many magazines.

Jeff Funk is a big ole tramp who skulks the leather bars and dance clubs of Fort Wayne, Indiana looking for his next trick. He kisses and tells. In his spare time, he's managed to write a bunch of choral music published by Warner Bros. Publications, more than 1.7 million copies in print. His fiction appears in *Asylum 3* and the forthcoming *Distant Horizons*. He lives in Auburn, Indiana (he's in the phonebook). Visit www.jefffunk.com if you wanna, you know, hook up or somethin'.

T. Hitman is the nom-de-porn for a full-time professional writer who has published numerous short stories and novels. Always writing his first drafts using trusty Sheaffer fountain pens (some of them 24-years-old), he lives with his awesome partner Bruce and their two cats in a very small bungalow on a very large plot of land among the pines of New Hampshire.

William Holden lives in Atlanta with his partner of nine years. He works full time as a librarian on LGBT issues. He has sixteen other published short stories and one unpublished novel. He welcomes any comments and can be contacted at Srholdbill@aol.com

David Holly is the nom-de-plume of an academic who knows what can happen in a college teacher's office after class. David's stories appeared in a variety of gay erotic publications through the 1990s, including *Guys, First Hand, Manscape,* and *Hot Shots.* Under his given name, he is the author of works of both fiction and non-fiction. David's gay erotic science fiction, fantasy, and horror stories appear regularly online at Tommyhawk's Fantasy World.

Marcus James is the author of *Blackmoore,* which author Blair Cameron called "*a heart-wrenching, adventurous supernatural suspense in the tradition of television's* Dark Shadows *and Anne Rice's* Lives of the Mayfair Witches..." He has been featured in *Ultimate Undies: Erotic Stories About Underwear and Lingerie, Best Gay Love Stories: NYC Edition,* and *Ultimate Gay Erotica: 2007.* He lives in El Paso Texas and is twenty-two-years old.

L. J. Longo is an aspiring writer with several awards for academic and fiction writing, as well as a literature student who probably spends more time than she should reading and writing homosexual erotica. She founded the underground gay porn magazine at her college and finds herself more than qualified to write about randy college boys.

David Mastromonica, a Washington state native and Ivy League grad, is a third-generation Italian-American whose grandmother came from a village near Rome to the logging territory of the Pacific Northwest for an arranged marriage with an Irishman. His "day job" involves social services for the disabled, and he often writes about his experiences—both professional and sexual—for a variety of publications.

Joel A. Nichols was born and raised in Vermont. His stories have appeared in *Ultimate Undies, Sexiest Soles, Full Body Contact,* and *Just the Sex,* and will appear in *Tales from the Den* and *Love in a Lock Up.* An excerpt from his novel in progress won second place in the Brown Foundation Short Fiction Prize 2005. In 2002, he was a Fulbright Fellow in Berlin. Joel studied German at Wesleyan University and has a Creative Writing M.A. from Temple University. He lives in Philadelphia with his boyfriend, works at an internet video company, and teaches English. For more information, go to joelanichols.blogspot.com

Stephen Osborne is a former improvisational comedian, now working in the fascinating world of retail management. He lives in Indianapolis with two cats and Jadzia the Wonder Dog. He's been published in Jesse Grant's anthology, *Hustlers.* He's still single. What's up with that???

Tony Pike lives in London, England, when not traveling in Spain and France. His erotic fiction has previously appeared in *Zipper* and *Vulcan* magazines in the UK.

After his appearance in the first *Dorm Porn,* **Michael Roberts** had a story featured on the website www.cruisingforsex.com. His work (if indulging in sexual fantasies can be called work) is scheduled for the Alyson anthology *Ultimate Gay Sex 2007.* Under various pseudonyms, he has also been published in several national gay magazines.

Lawrence Schimel is an award-winning author and anthologist, who has published more than seventy books in a wide variety of genres, including fiction, cooking, gender studies, sports, poetry, and more. His short stories, poem, and essays have appeared in more than 190 anthologies. He divides his time between New York and Spain.

Simon Sheppard hasn't been in college for many years, but has been in college boys much more recently. He's the author of the books *In Deep: Erotic Stories, Hotter Than Hell and Other Stories, Kinkorama: Dispatches from the Front Lines of Perversion, Sex Parties 101,* and is the editor of the forthcoming *Homosex: 60 Years of Gay Erotica.* His work has also appeared in more than 200 books, including many editions of *Best Gay Erotica* and *The Best American Erotica,* and he writes the syndicated column "Sex Talk." He lives in San Francisco and loiters shamelessly at www.simonsheppard.com.

John Simpson is the author of *Murder Most Gay,* a full length E-book carried by Renaissance E-books, and currently looking for a print publisher for the book, *The Virgin Marine,* published in the *My First Time,* series volume four, by Alyson Books. John just finished writing another short story called, *The Smell of Leathern* which will be shown to publishers shortly. Additionally, he has written numerous articles for various gay and straight magazines, and a full-length non-fiction novel.

What I Learned from My Roommate is the first published work from **R. B. Snow**, who lives in the Atlanta area and thinks that one hot guy is a good thing, but two hot guys together is even better.

From Vancouver, BC, **Jay Starre** has written for gay men's magazines including *Men, Honcho, Torso,* and *American Bear.* Jay has also written for more than thirty gay anthologies including the *Friction* series for Alyson, *Hard Drive, Bad Boys, Just the Sex, Ultimate Gay Erotic, Bear Lust,* and *Full Body Contact.*

Troy Storm has had more than two hundred erotic gay, bi, and straight short stories published in various magazines and anthologies, including several Alyson collections. His dorm days are long past, but the memories (and fantasies) linger on vividly.

Although originally from west Tennessee, **Shannon L. Yarbrough** now calls St. Louis, Missouri home. He lives with his partner, John, and thcir two cats and two dogs. Shannon is the author of the book, *The Other Side of What,* published in 2003; and an autobiographical book of poetry entitled *A Monkey Sonnet* which was published in early 2006 through lulu.com. His short stories have also been featured on amazon.com as part of the "Amazon Shorts" program, and in the *Gay Love Stories NYC* anthology published by Alyson Books. Besides writing, Shannon enjoys watching movies, painting, reading, surfing the web, and traveling. He is currently at work on a second novel. Email Shannon at misteryarbs@msn.com.